LONDON NOIR

LONDON NOIR

EDITED BY CATHI UNSWORTH

AKASHIC BOOKS
NEW YORK

Series concept by Tim McLoughlin and Johnny Temple
London map by Sohrab Habibion

Published by Akashic Books
©2006 Akashic Books

ISBN-13: 978-1-888451-98-6
ISBN-10: 1-888451-98-X
Library of Congress Control Number: 2005934828

First printing
Printed in Canada

Akashic Books
PO Box 1456
New York, NY 10009
Akashic7@aol.com
www.akashicbooks.com

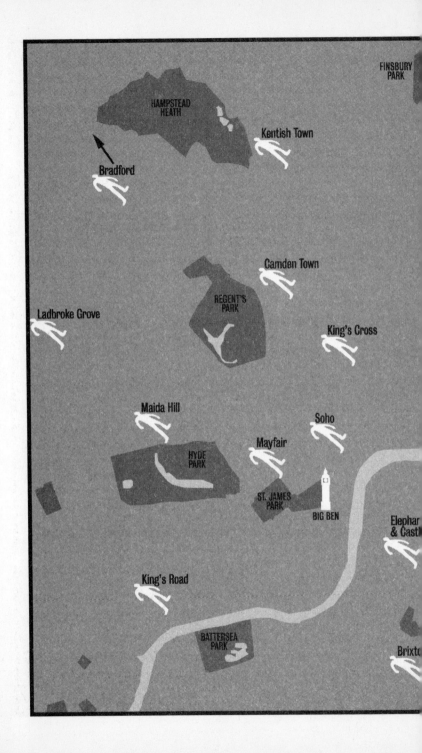

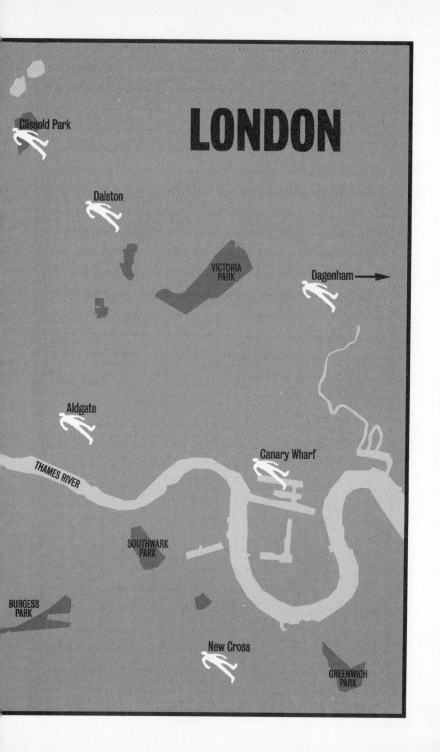

TABLE OF CONTENTS

13   *Introduction*

PART I: POLICE & THIEVES

21   **DESMOND BARRY**   Soho
        Backgammon

36   **KEN BRUEN**   Brixton
        Loaded

44   **STEWART HOME**   Ladbroke Grove
        Rigor Mortis

54   **BARRY ADAMSON**   Maida Hill
        Maida Hell

PART II: I FOUGHT THE LAW

79   **MICHAEL WARD**   Mayfair
        I Fought the Lawyer

99   **SYLVIE SIMMONS**   Kentish Town
        I Hate His Fingers

115   **DAN BENNETT**   Clissold Park
        Park Rites

124   **CATHI UNSWORTH**   King's Cross
        Trouble Is a Lonesome Town

142   **MAX DÉCHARNÉ**   King's Road
        Chelsea Three, Scotland Yard Nil

PART III: GUNS ON THE ROOF

157   **MARTYN WAITES**   Dagenham
       Love

176   **JOOLZ DENBY**   Bradford
       Sic Transit Gloria Mundi

186   **JOHN WILLIAMS**   New Cross
       New Rose

200   **JERRY SYKES**   Camden Town
       Penguin Island

PART IV: LONDON CALLING

225   **MARK PILKINGTON**   Dalston
       She'll Ride a White Horse

234   **JOE MCNALLY**   Elephant & Castle
       South

242   **PATRICK MCCABE**   Aldgate
       Who Do You Know in Heaven?

261   **KEN HOLLINGS**   Canary Wharf
       Betamax

281   **Acknowledgments**

282   **About the Contributors**

Sic gorgiamus illos subiectatos

INTRODUCTION
CRIME AND ESTABLISHMENT

W hat you have in your hands is not a collection of crime stories set in London. This is rather a collection of crime stories that *are* London. The things that happen within these pages would not be unfamiliar to those who have come before to render the city's psyche in words, art, music, theater, or magic. It's not that this *was* the city of William Blake, Charles Dickens, Dr. Johnson, Samuel Pepys, Daniel Dafoe, Oscar Wilde, George Orwell, Dylan Thomas, Francis Bacon, Joe Strummer, or Johnny Rotten. It's that it still very much *is*.

London needs illumination from its own darkness, from its perpetual cycle of crimes. This is also the city of Newgate Prison, Bedlam, Amen Corner, Tyburn Cross, the London Monster, Spring-heeled Jack, Jack the Ripper, Jack the Hat, the Blind Beggar, the Baltic Exchange, and 10 Rillington Place. The most famous detective in the world, Sherlock Holmes, stepped out of the smog of a London night, shouted, "The game's afoot!" and conspired to send his creator Arthur Conan Doyle, along with every actor who tried to make him flesh, mad.

London always extracts its price.

The keys to the city are contained in a line you'll find in Patrick McCabe's story "Who Do You Know in Heaven?" "Consciousness," his know-it-all café-owner spouts, "prompts you to hypothesize that the story you're creating from a given set of memories is a *consistent history*, justified by a consistent narrative voice . . ."

London's stories seep out of its walls, rise up from the foundations laid by the Romans two thousand years ago, up through its sewers, buried rivers, and tube tunnels, and out through the pavements. They wind their way through twisting alleyways that formed themselves so long ago, before the order of the grid system could be placed upon them. They whisper their secrets through the marketplaces where every language on earth is and has been spoken; every measure of trade haggled over, from fruit and veg to children's lives. They drift up at night from the currents of Old Father Thames, through the temples of commerce that form the Square Mile, across the halls of Parliament, the Cathedrals laid by Norman kings, the tunnels dug by Victorian engineers.

Listen to London for long enough and the city will impart in you your own notion; your own form of navigation through the maps laid down over centuries; your own heart's topography of the metropolis. Your soul blends with the walls and pavements, the tunnels and spires, the street markets and the stock exchanges. But is that notion really your own, or has the suggestion been planted, the story already written long ago?

The stories in this collection form maps of the city you will not find in the A-Z. Already, the city has exerted its collective subconscious over this creation without the authors being aware of it, so that the bohemian West, the iconic East, the melancholy North, and the wild South are linked. By lines of songs from the same jukebox; angles in the heads of priests, coppers, witchdoctors, lawyers, pornographers, psychopaths, con men, and terrorists; even the trajectory of a skein of wild geese.

Every kind of crime has been committed here; most of them never solved. London is responsible for all of them. London confuses the mind: Pat McCabe's IRA man comes to the mainland on a mission and gets seduced by a black-and-white photo of a London only felt in his blood, of a haunted '40s dancehall. Jerry Sykes's lonely pensioner dreams of '50s Camden Town even as he is mugged by its twenty-first-century offspring. Sylvie Simmons's psychiatrist talks to a ventriloquist's doll. Joe McNally sees London's ectoplasm form into grotesque, mythological shapes as he traverses the labyrinth of Elephant & Castle.

Some can see through the veils more clearly than others. For Joolz Denby, the Great Wen is an even Greater Con, a gray eternity without a soul, beckoning you into its clip-joint belly for more addictions you can never beat, more itches you can never scratch. For Barry Adamson's Father Donaghue, the Maida Hill community of losers and bruisers he serves are all souls worth fighting for, so that he may even redeem his own. But for Stewart Home's dead-eyed policeman, the souls of the neighboring parish of Ladbroke Grove are mere commodities, investments for his pension scheme.

London favors the entrepreneur. London thrives on the violence it incites. London built its Parliament on a bramble-riddled mire known as Thorney Island a thousand years ago. It is policed by villains, ministered to by the damned, carved up by Masonic market traders.

London's perennial themes rise to the surface in relentless waves. Martyn Waites stirs up the mob mentality in the mean estates of Dagenham, the traditional dumping ground of the city's poor, manipulated and united by self-destructive hatred. Daniel Bennett places a Ripper in Hackney's Clissold Park, just slightly north of his old stomping grounds. The city's most infamous bogeyman takes on a new shape here, no longer an eminent Victorian surgeon or the wayward off-spring of the Queen but a disturbed adolescent, pulsing with the red rage of the city's demented heat. Mark Pilkington gets down among the traders of lost souls to record human trafficking and child sacrifice in Dalston, where John Dee reincarnates himself as a Nigerian *sangoma*, in the opposite end of the city from where he started in the reign of Elizabeth I. Michael Ward reminds us of the Establishment, those bewigged members of the Temple, and the closet of the Cabinet: They Who Are Really Pulling the Strings, and always have been.

London's Burning, London Calling, Waterloo Sunset, the Guns of Brixton. London pulses to the music of the world, each district retelling its own folk legends through bhangra, reggae, ska, blues, jazz, fado, flamenco, electronica, hip hop, punk—pick your own soundtrack. John Williams's ageing punk rocker finds the man he could have been, lying wasted and dribbling at a gig in a New Cross bar. Like the lines from a song, the past comes back to haunt Desmond Barry's would-be filmmaker, through a wormhole in time and out in the middle of Soho.

London is a siren, calling you to the rocks of your own destruction, taunting and teasing and offering you a flash of its flesh as you teeter drunkenly in the doorway. Ken Bruen's gangster finds her on a Brixton dancefloor. My own creation, private eye Dougie, tries to spirit her out of the city through the portal of King's Cross.

That London has survived so long comes down to its foundation in the root of all evil. The river, as the Romans knew, meant the riches of the world could be shipped directly to its ravenous mouth. London has controlled the world for many of the years of its existence. London is the Grand Wizard. It's no coincidence that Ken Hollings writes a future projection for the city from the gleaming towers of Canary Wharf, the monument to capitalism laid down on the ashes of the working class East End by the Wicked Witch of Westminster, Margaret Thatcher.

So again, this is not really a collection of crime stories. This is a compass for the reader to chart their own path through the dark streets of London, to take whatever part chimes most closely with their soul and use it as a talisman.

London is shadows and fog. London is haunted. London is the definitive noir.

Cathi Unsworth
May 2006
London

PART I

POLICE & THIEVES

BACKGAMMON

BY DESMOND BARRY

Soho

At three o'clock, on Thursday, September 5, I was supposed to be at Soho House on Greek Street to meet with Jon Powell, the film director. Jon was interested in a script I'd written called *Rough House* about nasty goings-on in Soho in the late '70s. He'd had a top-ten box office success with his last film, *Anxiety*—a horror flick with reality TV overtones—so sitting on the tube train from Kilburn down to Piccadilly Circus, I don't mind admitting that I was well gassed up and a bit nervous because I really wanted it all to go well. The thing is, I had to eat something fast, both to silence the juices gurgling away in my stomach and to deal with the lack of blood sugar making me more nervous and edgy by the second. I was lucky. I still had an hour and a half to kill before the meeting, and the Ristorante Il Pollo, which serves the best lasagne in Soho, was close to the corner of Greek Street where the meeting would take place. The Pollo was definitely going to be my first stop.

I jostled up the packed escalator of the tube station, pushed my way up the stairs, and I was out onto the Dilly— Eros, lights, action. I dodged a couple of taxis and ducked up Great Windmill Street. It could have been a scene from the film script: beautiful girls on the doors of the strip joints, all with flashes of cleavage, coy smiles, or lewd words to tempt me inside. But I wasn't biting, was I? I had work to do. I turned right onto Brewer Street and then jagged right and left onto Old Compton Street, where I got the eye from the pretty boys sitting at the tables of the cafés and leaning in the doorways of the hip gay boutiques. Everybody wants something in Soho. I wanted lasagne.

I pushed through the glass door into Ristorante Il Pollo and breathed in the rich meat and tomato smells oozing out of the kitchen and the whiff of coffee from the Gaggia machine that roared behind the counter. The Pollo had been selling the same lasagne in steel dishes for at least thirty years and probably longer, and I was really counting on that béchamel and meat sauce and a nice glass of wine to sort me out before the meeting with Jon. The waitress seated me at a little table in the front.

That's why I didn't see Magsy at first. Not until after I'd dug my way through the crusty cheese and into the soft green pasta and scraped the brown and crispy bits off the edge of the steel dish. It was a shock to see the old bastard come walking down between the booths from the back of the café. Twenty-six years ago. How did he happen to be in here right at this moment when I hadn't seen him in twenty-six years? We had a bit of a history, me and Magsy, I got to admit. I pushed the steel dish back and smiled at him, but my shoulder muscles got tight and my knee started bouncing as if somewhere inside me I was all ready to run for it. Like a lot of people who'd gone bald these days, Magsy had shaved his head.

But then there was that old Mickey-taking smirk on Magsy's face when he saw me. He wasn't a tall bloke, about 5'8", still five inches taller than me though. He looked well enough off in his cord jacket, checked shirt, and jeans. I'd heard he'd gone to live in Spain after he'd come out of prison.

Twenty-two years back that must have been. But he didn't look at all tanned. He'd been through some real damage, I reckoned: the tiredness around the eyes, the deep wrinkles, the grayness of the skin of a longtime smoker.

"What are *you* doing here?" he said.

I got up from the table and I even gave him a hug. It was a bit stiff to tell the truth, but he still had that pleased-to-see-me grin on his face when we stepped back.

"I got a meeting," I said. "Business thing in about . . ." I jerked my sleeve so the watch showed on my wrist, "ten minutes."

"What business you in then?"

"I'll tell you about it later, if you like, if you gonna be around."

"Half past 4 in Steiner's," he said.

"Right," I said.

Steiner's, yeah. One of our old haunts.

We came out of the Pollo and into the sunshine on Old Compton Street, walked the few yards to Greek Street in the glare, and then crossed the road to the shady opposite corner.

"You working down here again?" I said.

I hoped he wasn't.

"Nah, I live in Bridgwater now."

"Bridgwater?" I said. "What you doing in Soho then?"

"Meeting Richie when he gets off his shift."

Richie was one of Magsy's oldest mates, though I didn't know him that well myself.

"He still work here?" I said.

"Yeah. Manager of about four Harmony shops."

"Corporate porno."

"Fully licensed and legit," Magsy said. "New Labour, son. As long as it makes money, it's all right. Liberal attitude, innit?"

"Fair play," I said.

"So I *will* catch you in Steiner's?" Magsy asked.

"Yeah, right," I said.

He just walked off then. I watched him as he headed west. Weird that I ran into him in the Pollo after all those years. It gave me the wobblies a bit. But I checked my watch. I was bang on time for the meeting. I had to get Magsy out of my head for now. I rang the bell on the door of the club and then went up the stairs to meet Jon Powell.

On the roof of Soho House, in the bright sunshine, over a couple of bottles of sparkling mineral water, the meeting went okay. Not great, but okay. It would appear that trying to get a film made is a process that requires a lot of patience. I told Jon that I wasn't sure how the producers who'd got the soft money for me to write the script planned on coming up with the hard cash to get this thing into production but they did have some serious coproduction interest. That's filmspeak for a lot of hot air that might one day float a balloon. Jon said that he really liked the script and promised he would pass it on to someone he knew with Pierce Brosnan's company who might well be interested in the project, and that Jon would do that as soon as he came back from the Toronto Film Festival and a trip to L.A. This was all very positive. But no one had, as yet, signed on the line, or was eating a bacon sandwich on the set of the first shoot. This was either a great way to make a living, or I was chasing a total mirage. Still, I'd been paid for the script and I'd get more money if the film got made, and the sun was shining. It was not a bad way to make a living. I swallowed the last of the mineral water and we went down about five flights of stairs to the street. Mineral water? Christ, I'm losing my identity. I can't even drink much coffee these days.

I shook hands with Jon and he set off north toward Soho Square while I went west along Old Compton Street toward Steiner's. I *was* going to meet Magsy—if he was there. Me and Magsy had been mates together in the mid-'70s and I'd spent long hours back then in his flat, just lying around and listening to music. He'd lived there with his girlfriend, Penelope. I was in their flat in Camden so often that I practically lived there. I *did* live there when the lease ran out on my own little gaff in Chalk Farm. Then, after I'd crashed there for six months, him and his girlfriend found a place for me in Dalston, "through a mate of Penelope's," they said.

So they didn't have to officially throw me out. We had some times, me and Magsy. Incredible times. Like . . . just before I was due to move into the new gaff on a hot July afternoon in 1975 . . . me and Magsy decided we'd celebrate my last night in the flat. We bought a 100-gram bag of salt and half a dozen lemons from a corner shop, and three bottles of tequila from the offy on Camden High Street. Then we picked up Penelope from her job at the Royal Free Hospital. She was standing outside the gate with this petite longhaired girl, Angela. We hadn't expected this at all—we *had* just planned on going back to the flat and getting blasted on the tequila—but Angela invited us all to dinner at her place on Cornwall Gardens, just off the Gloucester Road. Cornwall Gardens—now that is a class-A address, mate. And it was a bright and lovely summer's day, and we had the salt and lemons and tequila to donate to the proceedings, so I felt okay. We drove down Haverstock Hill and through the West End and into Kensington in Angela's car, and Angela said that her boyfriend, Ted, owned the flat that I was just about to move into in Dalston.

Ah, I thought, the flat connection.

So we turned onto Cornwall Gardens. Angela had a permit to park on the street and she opened this big Georgian door for us and took us up in a lift to a lovely three-bedroom flat with all these Persian carpets in the lounge. It was gorgeous. And the balcony overlooked the fenced-in private gardens.

Angela started cooking a vegetarian dinner in the open-plan kitchen. She said she always ate macrobiotic food, but she kept having a break from the kitchen every now and then so she could smoke a cigarette, which didn't seem somehow kosher to me, her being macrobiotic and that. Ted arrived home about half an hour after she'd begun preparing the dinner. He wasn't that big, a bit skinny with wire-rimmed glasses and a ponytail. A bit of an old-time hippy. He'd been out doing business, according to Angela. What with the sunshine and the shooters and the fresh taste of the lemons, by this time we'd already finished the first bottle of tequila: at least, me and Magsy had; the girls had been chatting most of the time in the kitchen.

So then we all sat down around a tablecloth that Angela spread over the Persian carpet in the lounge and we polished off the brown rice, pickles, and veggies. I was feeling really healthy after that meal. We slumped back against the giant cushions and started on more shooters of tequila, and Ted brought out this lovely pearl-inlaid backgammon board. We all tried to concentrate on the game. That was when Ted produced a large mirror and laid out five enormous lines of white powder that he said was Colombian cocaine. Ted vacuumed up a line of powder and took the tails off the other lines and handed the rolled-up note to Magsy. Magsy dug into it and then Penelope had a line. I had a sense of relief when Angela said she didn't want any. It made me feel a little less like a dork when I said, "Thanks, but I'll stick with the tequila." I'm not a prude—but I get these terrible asthma attacks if I breath hostile flower pollen, let alone cocaine, and I didn't want to risk anything at all, given the state I was already in. The black and red and white triangles on the backgammon board already had a glow all their own after we'd finished the second bottle.

So we threw the dice and moved a few counters and then Ted laid out another set of lines of the Colombian coke and I downed another three shots of tequila and I felt a lot less nervous about the heavy drugs the boys on my right kept snorting and we threw the dice some more and we finished the third bottle of tequila and I was feeling all sunny even though it was dark and time to go home and I stood up and my knees didn't seem to work so good and I thought, well, it's all right because I'm going to go home now, and I really hadn't realized just how good I was at backgammon. I thought, I really wouldn't mind meeting Ted again, even if he *is* a bit of cokehead. I really wanted to play another game with him.

But you know what? I never did get to go back to that flat . . . not ever again, did I? I'd been there by chance, really, I suppose. I mean, it was Magsy and his girlfriend who Angela had meant to invite and I'd just happened to be along with Magsy after we bought the tequila. So I had no real business being there, did I?

Just as we were about to leave, Ted grabbed Magsy by the arm, all friendly.

"Hey, Magsy," he said. "Think you can shift some coke for me?"

Magsy's face lit right up. A business opportunity . . . Magsy liked that . . . and no doubt he really had enjoyed all that marching powder, and Ted liked him so much that, right there and then, he laid a couple of ounces on Magsy and told him to pay it back in a week. Even with all that liquor in me, I knew that this was probably a bad idea, but Magsy was dead thrilled. Fair play, I know for a fact he paid Ted back on the fronted coke two days before the week was up.

Ted, of course, was now my landlord. That made me feel a bit uncomfortable, but after a month or so a lovely woman of thirty-one by the name of Sheri moved in with me and I was glad I had my own gaff. Sheri was a real cockney. I met her when I got a job as a shipping clerk in Mile End. I had to pay the rent somehow. I took her round to see Magsy. He was still my mate, wasn't he? By now he was doing a brisk trade. What I felt though . . . when we were around there . . . was that Magsy seemed a lot happier to see his clients than he did to see us. I thought, well, he's my mate. I'll confront him, like.

"What's going on?" I said. "You know, really going on?"

He knew what I was talking about, when you're mates, you do; but he just said, "I'm doing fine, son. Doing well. Just the sniffles, like. It's just like having a cold, really. No bother at all."

The sniffles? What the . . . ? I wanted to push him on it, but right then Ted walked in. He had this bloke with him called Danny. Danny had a very good haircut, a very expensive suit, a black crewneck cotton pullover, and a camel's-hair coat. He was not an old-time hippy at all. He was very definitely an old-time villain—even if he was only about twenty-eight or so. Danny oozed charm.

"Magsy," he said, "how would you like to make a very sound investment, my son?"

"What's that?" Magsy replied.

"How would you like to take out a lease on a small pornography outlet on Dean Street? Reckon it might be the perfect front for your proper business."

Magsy's proper business was now, very definitely, hard-core narcotics.

"Yeah," Magsy said, big smile on his face. "I could get into that—a finger in every pie, innit? Sex and drugs and rock and roll."

I laughed along with him. He was charmed. I was charmed. But I still didn't know if this investment was a good idea at all. I didn't know the financial details, of course. But who was I to know, anyway? At that time I had a shit job in a shipping office on the Mile End Road while Magsy was about to move up to the West End with all the villains. And he did. After he opened up the porn shop, I used to go up to Soho every Friday night to have a drink with him after work.

To tell the truth, I enjoyed meeting all those strippers and hookers and pimps and hustlers—who all seemed to be his mates—especially after I'd just spent the previous five days filing bills of lading. I felt like I was a very well-connected desperado . . . Well, not exactly . . . just a sort of desperado by proxy, really, wasn't I? Magsy moved with the big fish like Ted and Danny, and, more and more often, the time came when we were out for a drink and he'd say, "Sorry, Dex, I got to push off. There's a party at Ted's flat."

I used to go home to Sheri then.

"He's leaving you behind, love," Sheri would say. "He don't give a damn about you, does he?"

"No, he's just busy with all that business," I'd respond. "Ted probably don't want him bringing his mates around there, does he? Got to keep a low profile and that."

But it hurt, I tell you that.

I still met Magsy every now and then for a drink. I still liked it when he'd spin all those yarns about all the gangster stuff.

So this one Friday night we were on the cognac in Steiner's and Magsy said, "Hey, Dex, remember that flat on Gloucester Road?"

"Yeah," I said.

"Me and Penny are moving in next week."

"Get away," I said.

"Ted got tipped off, didn't he? The Old Bill are looking for a major bust, so him and Angela got to leave the country in a hurry. He asked me and Penelope to house-sit for him."

"Ace," I said.

The weird thing was . . . Magsy never—ever—invited me round to the flat in Cornwall Gardens . . . not once.

"Why d'you keep meeting up with that bastard?" Sheri said. Meaning Magsy.

"Well, a mate's a mate, innit?" I said. "He'll come round . . ."

But I didn't see him for about three months after he moved into Cornwall Gardens. Then I met him on Old Compton Street one weekend.

"What happened to you?" I said.

Magsy's face was swollen on both sides. And the skin was all swirls of green and yellow and purple.

"Let's have a drink," he said.

He had his jaw wired shut so he spoke through clenched teeth. We went into Steiner's.

"Ted sent me this blotter acid from the States," Magsy sort of hissed and gurgled. I think he was all coked up so he kept on talking. "Mr. Natural tabs. Pure acid. One drawing of

Mr. Natural perforated into four parts. Ted fronted it all, didn't he? Told me to sell it on for a pound a go and he'd collect when he came home. A few months later, Ted did come home—very sudden. And when he came home, he came to collect. Fair enough, I thought. But he went berserk. Claimed I was giving him only a quarter of the money I was supposed to. I said that he told me to sell the Mr. Naturals for a quid apiece. Ted said I should have sold them for a quid per perforated square."

I wondered if Magsy was bullshitting me. How much was this a genuine misunderstanding with Ted and how much of the money might have gone up his nose?

"So he did you over?" I said. I found that hard to believe. Ted didn't look that hard.

"Not just Ted. His family and all . . ."

"Ah," I said.

"They're all old-time villains—just like Danny. So I had to leave the flat, didn't I? Under some duress . . . with the aid of all of Ted's brothers and father and uncles and Danny, who, when they were finished with the duress, like, threw me down the stairs, didn't they?"

He hissed a bit as he laughed. I was glad he could laugh about it.

"How's Penny?" I asked.

"They didn't touch her. She's with some mates of hers out near Epping."

"Where you staying?" I asked.

"Sleeping on the floor of the shop."

"Come back to my flat."

I thought, well, those bastards have done him over, maybe he'll drop all the gangster crap and get back to normal. He shook his head.

"Nah, gotta stay in Soho," he said.

We arranged to meet the following Sunday at Steiner's, and in those few days the swelling on his face had gone down a bit, though the bruises had started to take on some very spectacular greens and blues. I got us in a couple of pints of Stella Artois.

"I gotta meet someone here," he said.

Ah shit, I thought.

This curly-haired bloke with a squashed nose and a lot of gold chains came through the door. He went down to the gents and Magsy followed him. Then they came back out and Curly left.

"Got to pay off the debts to Ted," Magsy said. "Had to borrow some money."

Ah no, I thought.

Magsy was practically bouncing all of a sudden—his fingers drumming on the bar, the shift of his shoulders. And he was probably low on coke, which gave him a sort of added drive. Magsy necked his lager in three large swallows.

"Sorry, Dex," he said to me. "Gotta score. Adios, amigo."

So off went Magsy to buy a load of coke and I went home to Sheri.

And, truth to tell, that was the last I saw of Magsy. Not that I didn't think about him. The police must have been watching him for ages and they decided to pay a visit to his Dean Street porno shop very early the next morning. They found about an ounce of coke and a weight of grass. Magsy got four years in Brixton. I never went near him in there.

Twenty-six years later and I bump into him at Ristorante Il Pollo in the heart of Soho and we were going to meet in Steiner's, the last place we'd seen each other before he went down. I took a breath and pushed through the door into the saloon bar. There was Magsy, standing at the bar with Richie Stiles, an old mate of his, who was as tall as ever but plump now, with a receding hairline and fuller cheeks. He *was* in an Armani suit though.

"Dexie!" Magsy said. "Good to see you, son."

He and Richie were already three sheets to the wind on the shots of tequila and Corona beers that were lined up on the bar. I couldn't resist it. Blame it on old time's sake, or maybe because I was a bit nervous, but I had a lick of salt, a shot of tequila, bit on the lemon, and then soothed the burn in my throat with a cool slug of the Corona.

"Richie!" I said. "Corporate bigwig now, son."

"Still a party," Richie said. "But government-licensed now, innit? Make more money being legit these days. No police raids or nothing."

"So what are *you* doing with yourself?" Magsy said.

If I said I was a writer, it would have had this stink of me being a bit of a braggart—which I am, really.

"I'm a writer."

"A writer?" Magsy said. "You make money at that?"

"I got to hustle to make a living," I said. "But it's okay. Better than any other job I've had . . . and I've had a lot since working in the shipping trade: laboring on building sites, bookkeeping, library assistant, then I decided to get a real life."

I could see that I'd stung him a bit with that. I hadn't meant to. What was he doing? Bookies' clerk? On the dole? I knew he wasn't dealing.

"God, how long has it been since I seen you?" Magsy said.

I was sure he knew well enough.

"Twenty-six years," I said.

I was buzzed but not drunk.

"Yeah . . . right . . . since just before the trial," he said.

I nodded. "Yeah, right."

What he meant was: *You didn't come to see me in prison, you gutless shit.*

And I didn't, it was true, because when Magsy was sent down—call it total paranoia if you like—I was thoroughly convinced that if I *had* gone to see Magsy, I would be on a police list of known consorters with convicted drug traffick-ers and that within a very short time I would receive a simi-lar dawn visit from the police just as Magsy had. And if the police needed to make up their arrest rate and decided that a consorter with known traffickers was worth fitting up, then I would be on the inside with him—with a criminal record and fighting off anal rapists. I just couldn't face even the remotest possibility of it.

Now he wanted me to feel guilty for it, which he had def-initely succeeded in doing, and that made me really mad. What he was doing, you see—what he was really doing—was trying to return me to that position I'd been in back then: him as Jack the Lad and me as the shipping-firm employee dogsbody. Knock me back to square one. He'd always thought of me as a bit of a wimp for not having the balls to do what he'd done: ducking and diving right into the thick of the coke dealing and the porn business. But he'd had his life and I'd had mine, and I wasn't sorry at all with the way mine had gone. I wasn't any shipping clerk anymore, was I? And what was he? What was he? Tell me that.

And then it dawned on me . . . a slow creeping-up kind of dawn. I'd never forgiven him for treating me the way he did when he was all coked up with the Soho dope dealers and porn traders, had I? He'd been in the middle of the trade, and I was just a nobody, and our being mates hadn't counted for a thing in his eyes back then. And all that shame and rage I felt over being dissed by Magsy, of being dissed by someone I thought was a mate, and, yes . . . all right . . . the guilt of my not visiting him in prison . . . it was that which had driven me to use the story of Magsy's rise and fall in Soho for the script of *Rough House*. I hoped he'd like what he'd see when his life story would be all up there on the big screen in glorious Technicolor. If we got the money it would be me who put him there. Magsy on the big screen. *Now* who was the hot shot? What was he doing—in Bridgwater of all places—while I was on the roof of Soho House drinking expensive gassy water? Well, I thought. Well, the truth is . . . really, the truth is . . . it really didn't matter what *he* was doing—or what *I* was doing—because we were both here in Steiner's breathing the same air and drinking the same tequila, and sucking the same fucking lemons, and nothing was ever going to put the clock back to the time before he went to prison, before his trial, before the cops, before the loan shark, before the coke, before Ted, and before that fucking game of backgammon in Cornwall Gardens. And the truth is . . . the truth is . . . I was sorry. I really fucking was.

LOADED

BY KEN BRUEN

Brixton

Blame the Irish.
I always do.
The fuckers don't care, they're used to it, all that
Catholic guilt they inherit, blame is like, habitual. Too, all
that rain they get? Makes them amenable to bad shit. I've
known my share of micks—you grow up in Brixton, they're
part of the landscape. Not necessarily a good part but they
have their spot. Worked with a few when I was starting out,
getting my act together. I didn't know as much as I thought I
knew, so sure, I had them in my early crew.

Give them one thing, they're fearless, will go that extra
reckless yard, laugh on the trip, and true, they've got your
back, won't let you get ambushed. But it's after, at the pub,
they get stuck in it, and hell, they get to talking, talking loose.
Near got my collar felt cos of that. So I don't use them anymore. One guy, named, of course, Paddy, said to me: "Not
that long ago, the B'n'Bs . . . they had signs proclaiming, *No
coloreds, no dogs, no Irish.*"

He was smiling when he told me and that's when you
most got to worry, the fucks are smiling, you're in for the high
jump. Paddy got eight years over a botched post office gig,
he'd torn off his mask halfway through the deal, as it itched.
I'd driven to The Scrubs, see if he needed anything, and he
shook his head, said, "Don't visit anymore."

I was a little miffed and he explained, "Nothing personal but you're a Brit."

Like that made any sense, he was in a *Brit nick*. Logic and the Irish never jell, but he must have clocked my confusion, added, "In here, I'm with my countrymen. They see a Brit visiting, I'm fucked."

Let him stew.

Life was shaping up nice for me. Took some time but I'd put it together real slow. Doing some merchandise, a little meth, some heroin, and, of course, the coke. Didn't handle any of the shit my own self, had it all through channels, lots of dumb bastards out there will take the weight. I arranged the supply, got it to the public, and stayed real anonymous, had me a share in a pub, karaoke four nights a week, the slots, and on Sunday, a tasty afternoon of lap dancing. The cops got their share and everyone was, if not happy, reasonably prosperous. None of us getting rich but it paid for a few extras. Bought into a car park and, no kidding, serious change in that.

Best of all, I'd a fine gaff on Electric Avenue, owned the lease, and from outside, looked like a squat, which keeps the burglars away. Inside, got me Heal's furniture, clean and open-plan living room, lots of wicker furniture. I like it, real laid-back vibe. No woman, I like my freedom. Sure, on a Friday night I pick up some fox, bring her back, but she's out of there by 3 in the morning. I don't need no permanent company. Move some babe in and that's the end of my hard-bought independence.

Under the floorboards is my stash: coke, fifteen large, and a Glock. The baseball bat I keep by my bed.

Then I met Kelly.

I'd been to The Fridge to see a very bad hip hop outfit

who were supposed to be the next big thing. Jeez, they were atrocious, no one told them the whole gangsta scene was, like . . . dead. I went down to the pub after, needed to get the taste out of my mouth. I ordered a pint of bitter and heard, "To match your mood."

A woman in her late twenties, dressed in late Goth style, lots of black makeup, clothes, attitude. I've nothing against them, they're harmless, and if they think the Cure are still relevant, well, it takes all kinds . . . better than listening to Dido. Her face wasn't pretty, not even close, but it had an energy, a vitality that made it noticeable. I gave her my best London look with lots of Brixton overshadow, the look that says, *Fuck off . . . now.*

She felt an explanation was due, said, "Bitter, for the bitterness in your face."

I did the American bit, asked, "I know you?"

She laughed, said, "Not yet."

I grabbed my pint, moved away. She was surrounded by other Goths but she was the center, the flame they danced around. I'd noticed her eyes had an odd green fleck, made you want to stare at them. I shook myself, muttered, "Cop on."

On my second pint, I chanced a glance at her and she was looking right at me, winked. I was enraged, the fuck was that about? Had a JD for the road—I'm not a big drinker, that shit becomes a habit and I've plans, being a booze hound isn't among them. Knocked it back and headed for the door, she caught up with me, asked, "Buy me a kebab?"

Now I could hear the Irish lilt, almost like she was singing the words. I stopped, asked, "What the hell is the matter with you?"

She was smiling, went, "I'm hungry and I don't want to eat alone."

I indicated the pub. "What about your fan club, won't they eat with you?"

She almost sneered. It curled her lip and I'd a compulsion to kiss her, a roaring in my head, *What is happening to me?*

"Adoration is so, like, tiresome, you fink?"

The little bit of London—*fink*—to what? To make me comfortable? "I wouldn't know, it's not a concept I'm familiar with."

She laughed out loud, and her laugh made you want to join in. She said, "Oh don't we talk posh, what's a *concept* then? Is it like a condom?"

I'm still not sure why, but I decided to buy her the bloody kebab—to get rid of her, to see what more outrageous banter she'd produce? She suggested we eat them in the park and I asked, "Are you out of your mind? It's a war zone."

She blew that off with: "I'll mind *you.*"

The way she said it, as if she meant it, as if . . . fuck, I dunno, as if she was looking for someone to mind. So I said my place was round the corner and she chirped, "Whoo . . . fast worker. My mammie warned me about men like you."

I'd just taken a bite of the kebab, it was about what you'd expect, tasteless with a hint of acid. I had to ask. "What kind of man is that, a stranger?"

She flung her kebab into the air. "No, English." Then she watched the kebab splatter on the road, sang, "Feed the birds."

Bringing her back to my place, the first mistake—and if it were the only one, well, even now, I don't know what was going on with me, like I was mesmerized.

She looked round at my flat, and yeah, I was pretty damn proud, it looked good.

"Who lives here, some control freak, an anal retentive?"

Man, I was pissed, tried: "You have some problem with tidiness, with a place being clean?"

Fuck, you get defensive, you've already lost.

She was delighted, moved to me, got her tongue way down my throat, and in jig time we were going at it like demented things. Passion is not something I've had huge experience with—sure, I mean, I get my share, but never like that.

Later, lying on the floor, me grabbing for air, she asked, "What do you want?"

She was smoking. I didn't think it was the time to mention my place was smoke-free, so I let it slide, not easily, bit down. I leaned on one elbow, said, "I think I just had what I want."

She flicked the butt in the direction of the sink; I had to deliberately avert my eyes, not thinking where it landed. She said, "Sex, sex is no big deal. I mean in life, the . . . what do they call it . . . the *bigger picture?*"

I wanted to be comfortable, not go to jail, keep things focused. I said, "Nice set of wheels, have my eye on—"

She cut me off, went: "Bollocks, fecking cars, what is it with guys and motors? Is it like some phallic symbol? *Got me a mean engine.*"

Her tone, dripping with bile. Before I could get my mouth going, she continued, "I want to be loaded, serious wedge, you know what I'm saying?"

I nearly let slip about my stash, held back and asked, "So, you get loaded, then what?"

She was pulling on her clothes, looked at me like I was dense. "Then it's *fuck you, world.*"

She was heading for the door, I asked, "You're leaving?"

That's what I always wanted, get them out as soon as possible. Now, though . . .

Her hand was on her hip and she raised an eyebrow. "What, you think you're up for another round? I think you shot your load, need a week to get you hot again, or am I wrong?"

That stung, I'd never had complaints before, should have told her to bang the door behind her, near whimpered, "Will I see you?"

Her smile, smirk in neon, said, "I'll call you."

And was gone.

She didn't . . . call.

I went back to the pub, no sign of her. Okay, I went back a few times, asked the barman. I knew him a long time, we had, as they say, history, not all of it bad. He was surprised, said, "The Irish babe, yeah?"

I nodded miserably, hated to reveal a need, especially to a frigging barman, cos they talk to you, you can be sure they talk to others, and I didn't want the word out that I was, like . . . bloody needy, or worse, vulnerable. That story goes out, you are dead, the predators coming out of the flaming wood-work. He stared at me. "Matt, you surprise me, hadn't figured you for a wally."

Bad, real fucking bad.

I should have slapped him on the side of the head, get the status established, but I wanted the information. I got some edge into my voice, snapped, "What's that mean?"

He was doing bar stuff, taking his own sweet time, stashing glasses, polishing the counter, and I suppressed my impatience. Finally he straightened, touched his nose, said, "Word to the wise, mate, stay clear, she hangs with that black guy, Neville, you don't want to mess with that dude."

Neville, story was he offed some dealer, did major trade in crystal, and was serious bad news. I moved to leave, said: "I knew that."

He didn't scoff but it was in the neighborhood. "Yeah, right."

Fuck fuck fuck.

The bitch, playing with me, I resolved to put her out of my head, get on with my business. Plus, I had to get a new carpet, the cigarette had burned a hole right where you'd notice.

A week later, I was in the pub where we had the karaoke nights, nice little earner, punters get a few on, they want to sing, did brisk sales those nights. I was at the back, discussing some plans with the manager, when I heard a voice go, "I'd like to sing 'Howling at Midnight.'"

It was her, Kelly, with the Lucinda Williams song, one of my favorites, she no doubt saw the CD in my gaff. I looked quickly round, no sign of Neville, the pub hushed as she launched. Her voice was startling, pure, innocent, and yet, had a hint of danger that made you pay attention. When she finished, the applause was deafening. The manager, his mouth open, whispered, "Christ, she's good."

Then she hopped off the stage, headed in my direction, small smile in place. I resolved to stay cool but to my horror whined, "You never called."

Even the manager gave me an odd look.

"What happened to *hello, how have you been?*" she asked.

I moved her away, touching her arm lightly, and just that small gesture had me panting. She said: "Yes, thank you, I would like a drink."

I ordered two large vodkas, no ice, and tonics. She took the glass. "I'd have liked a Bushmills, but shit, I just can't resist the alpha male."

The touch of mockery, her eyes shining, that fleck of green dancing in there. I was dizzy, decided to get it out in the open, asked, "What do you want?"

She licked the rim of the glass, said, "I want you inside me, now."

Never finished my drink, never got to mention the black

guy either. We were in my place, me tearing off my shirt, her standing, the smile on her lips, I heard: "White dude is hung."

She'd left the door ajar. Neville standing there, a car iron held loosely in his hand. I looked at her, she shrugged, moved to my left. Neville sauntered over, almost lazily took a swipe at my knee. I was on the floor.

"Cat goes down easy."

Kelly came over, licked his ear. "Let's get the stuff, get the fuck out of here."

He wanted to play, I could see it in his eyes. He drawled, "How about it, Leroy, you want to give us that famous stash you got, or you wanna go tough, make me beat the fucking crap outta you? Either is, like, cool with me. Yo, babe, this mother got any, like, beverages?"

I said I'd get the stash, and he laughed.

"Well get to it, bro, shit ain't come les you go get it."

I crawled along the carpet, pulled it back, plied the floor-board loose, Kelly was shouting, "Nev, you want Heineken or Becks?"

I shot him in the balls, let him bleed out. Kelly had two bottles in her hands, let them slide to the floor, I said, "You're fucking up my carpet again, what's with you?"

I shot her in the gut, they say it's the most agonizing, she certainly seemed to prove that. I bent down, whispered, "Loaded enough for you, or you want some more? I got plenty left."

Getting my shirt tucked into my pants, I made sure it was neat, hate when it's not straight, ruins the sit of the material. I looked round, complained: "Now I'm going to have to redo the whole room."

RIGOR MORTIS

BY STEWART HOME

Ladbroke Grove

I've been in the Mets all my adult life and I've spent most of that time pounding the mean streets of West London. After the war the area around Ladbroke Grove was known as the *Dustbowl*. This was where smart property developers came to make their mint. Back in the '50s and '60s, during those thirteen glorious years of Tory rule, anyone who wanted to could make a bomb from the slums. Houses changed hands over and over again, with their values being inflated on each sale. Before the introduction of ridiculously strict controls on building societies at the start of the '60s, it was common for property speculators to off-load houses to both tenants and other parties with one hundred percent mortgages which the seller had prearranged. Despite the prices paid under such arrangements being above market value, ownership still proved cheaper than renting. Unfortunately, it was all too common for the new owners to take in lodgers to cover the costs of their mortgage, rather than working to earn their crust like a free-born Saxon. The resultant overcrowding bred crime and this law-breaking stretched police resources to the limit.

The investigation I've just completed took me back nearly twenty years to the early '60s. I knew Jilly O'Sullivan was dead before I arrived at 104 Cambridge Gardens, and in many ways I considered it a miracle she'd succeeded in reaching the age of thirty-five. I'd first come across Jilly in 1962 when she was a naïve young teenager and I was a fresh-faced police constable. I'm still a PC because rather than striving to rise through the ranks, I long ago opted to take horizontal promotion by becoming a coroner's officer. This job brings with it substantial unofficial perks, and I'm not the only cop who's avoided vertical advancement since that makes you more visible and therefore less able to accept the backhanders you deserve.

Returning to O'Sullivan, when she arrived in Notting Hill she rented an upstairs flat on Bassett Road for five years before moving to nearby Elgin Crescent in 1966. The bed in which Jilly died was but a few minutes walk from her Notting Hill homes of the '60s. I'd first called on her at Bassett Road after the force was informed that one of her brothers was hiding out there. My colleagues and I knew parts of the O'Sullivan clan like the backs of our own hands. The family was involved in both burglary and protection. Jilly and her brother had grown up in Greenock, but headed for the Smoke as teenagers. Jilly was doing well back in the early '60s, making good money in a high-class Soho clip joint, and at that time she even had a pimp with a plumy accent and public school education. Jilly's brother was eventually nicked alongside a couple of his cousins while they were doing over a jeweler's shop and that's how I learned he'd actually been hiding out with his gangster uncle in Victoria. After he'd served his time in a civil prison for burglary, Jilly's brother was sent to a military jail for being absent without leave from the army. By the mid-'60s, when her brother was finally let out of the nick, Jilly was the black sheep of the family. It wasn't prostitution but an involvement with beatniks, hippies, and drugs that alienated O'Sullivan from her kith and kin.

If Jilly had been smart she'd have married one of her rich johns and faded into quiet respectability. She worked with a number of girls who had the good sense to do just that. Jilly was a good looker, or rather she'd been a good looker back in the day—anyone seeing her corpse would think she was in her late forties. That said, right up to her death O'Sullivan's eyes remained as blue as a five-pound note. When Jilly was a teenager, these baby blues had men falling all over her petite and innocent-seeming self. O'Sullivan's eyes looked like pools of water that were deep enough to drown in, and naturally enough, she made sure her carefully applied makeup accentuated this effect. O'Sullivan lost her looks through hard living, and since I knew the story of her life, I didn't need to take many details about her from the woman who'd found the body.

I didn't even bother to ask Marianne May how she'd got into Jilly's flat; I'd already heard from Garrett that he'd left the door to the basement bedsit open after finding O'Sullivan dead in bed and making a hasty exit. Being a dealer and a pimp, Garrett considered it wiser to disappear than inform the authorities of his girlfriend's death. Even if he wasn't fitted up for his Jilly's murder, Garrett figured he'd get busted for something else if he stuck around. After I'd got the call to go to the back basement flat at 104 Cambridge Gardens to investigate a death, I'd headed first for Observatory Gardens, where I found Garrett nodding out with Scotch Alex. Garrett lived with Jilly, and since only one death had been reported, I'd figured that either one or both of them would be in "hiding" at Observatory Gardens. Before I got to Scotch Alex's pad I hadn't known who'd died, and I'd entertained the possibility it might have been one of their heroin buddies.

Garrett told me what he knew, which wasn't that much. He'd gone home after cutting some drug deals and found Jilly dead in bed, so he'd left again immediately. Garrett was inclined to think O'Sullivan had accidentally overdosed, although he considered it possible she'd been murdered by some gangsters, who'd threatened to kill her after she ripped them off during the course of a drug deal. I told Garrett not to worry about a court appearance, since I wasn't about to drag him into my investigation if he was cooperative. He got the idea and handed me a wad of notes, which he pulled from his right trouser pocket. I patted down the left pocket of Garrett's jeans and he realized his game was at least partially up. He removed another wad of notes from the second pocket and gave them to me. After I'd prodded his abdomen he stood up and took more bills from a money belt that was tied around his waist. I then made Garrett take his shoes and socks off, but he didn't have any cash secreted down there.

Satisfied with my takings, I told O'Sullivan's pimp that in my report I'd state that Jilly was living alone at the time of her death. I didn't tell him that I'd have done this even if I hadn't succeeded in shaking him down, since recording that O'Sullivan lived with a heroin dealer would make matters unnecessarily complicated for me. Although Garrett was scum he wasn't stupid, so I didn't need to tell him it would be a good idea if he found a new place to live. Likewise, I had absolute faith in his ability to find some fool to rip-off in order to provide PC Lever with his cut from the drug money I'd purloined and cover various other debts he simply couldn't avoid meeting if he wished to remain alive and in reasonable health. While I was in Observatory Gardens I also took the opportunity to touch Garrett's junkie host and co-dealer, Scotch Alex, for a few quid.

Marianne May, the woman who'd called the authorities to report Jilly's death, was middle-class and respectable. What Marianne had in common with Jilly were some bizarre New Age religious interests. Aside from this she was the ideal person to have found the body since she created the impression that O'Sullivan's friends at the time of her death were middle-class professionals. In all likelihood, prior to Marianne's arrival, a stream of junkies had called at the flat hoping to score, and having found the door open and Jilly dead in bed, departed without telling the authorities there was a corpse stinking up the bedsit. Garrett wouldn't have left his drug stash in the pad, and there probably wasn't anything else worth stealing. If there had been it would have disappeared long before my arrival.

There wasn't much I needed to ask May, but for the sake of appearance I had to make it look like I was doing my job properly. I told her to wait upstairs with Jilly's neighbors while I made some further investigations. I was able to go through the flat and remove used needles and various other signs of drug use before the medics arrived. I then examined Jilly's body. As you'd expect it was cold to touch. O'Sullivan was lying on her side, naked on the bed.

After the corpse had been loaded into an ambulance I went upstairs and told May she could go home, saying I'd contact her if there was anything further I needed to ask. I had no intention of troubling Marianne again, but since she was a middle-class professional, I had to make it look like I was doing everything by the book. May had fine manners and excellent verbal skills, so there was an outside chance that if she was moved to make a complaint about my investigation, what she had to say would be taken seriously.

Because Jilly certainly had traces of heroin in her body, it was important I arranged things so that any need for toxicological analysis was avoided. That said, since I knew O'Sullivan was an intravenous drug user, there was nothing to worry about in terms of a purely visual inspection of the body. Indeed, even in instances of suicide brought about by the ingestion of pills, evidence of a drug overdose is only visually detectable in fifty percent of such cases. Likewise, there is necessarily a good deal of mutual understanding between all those involved in the investigation of a death, one which is sometimes greased by the circulation of used fivers. I have many good reasons to request a particular result from a pathologist, and the croaks I work alongside know this without my having to spell it out. Aside from anything else, I don't have time to properly investigate the circumstances surrounding every death that occurs on my beat. It would waste a considerable amount of taxpayers' money and my time if the circumstances in which every miserable junkie overdosed were fully investigated. Every pathologist understands, regardless of whether or not a fistful of fivers are being pressed into their greasy palms, that the police know what's for the best.

Given that I wished to avoid an inquest into Jilly O'Sullivan's death, it wasn't much to ask of medical science that it should back up my false contention that she'd died from natural causes. Something will invariably be found in the lungs after death, so bronchopneumonia would provide a suitable explanation of Jilly's passing, as it had in so many other instances where I found it imperative to avoid a full-scale investigation. Death, of course, is always the result of the failure of one of the major organs, and according to the legal rule book, what matters is the chain of events leading up to such a failure. In practice, the letter of the law can be safely ignored in favor of its spirit. Only the elderly and homeless die from bronchopneumonia in truly unsuspicious circumstances. Bronchopneumonia is often brought on by a drug overdose, but my colleagues and I will nonetheless routinely treat it as a natural cause of death in a young addict. We see no point in arriving at an accurate conclusion that will only upset and confuse the family of some wastrel who didn't deserve the loving home she grew up in. Grieving is a difficult process and I've done countless decent parents a huge favor by making it possible for them to avoid facing up to the fact that their child was a good-for-nothing junkie degenerate.

To shift the focus once again to the particular, there wasn't much in O'Sullivan's basement flat. Jilly and her pimp Garrett had only lived there for a few weeks. They'd occupied an equally spartan Bayswater bedsit over the autumn. Junkies mainly use possessions as a form of collateral, they rarely hang onto stuff, personal items tend to be stolen and sold as required. However, Jilly's diary was in the flat and the final entry was dedicated to Garrett:

COMPUTER IN PURSUIT OF A DREAM

You lie there, legs straddled, an easy lay
Like some "gloomy fucker" (your words)
For hours you have put me through mental torture
Because I desired you
Sure I wanted love anyway I could
But you denied me both fuck & fix
And then dropping a Tuinal, like an over-the-hill whore
You became an easy lay

I knew this nonsense was merely one of many pieces of proof that Jilly's drug use had been ongoing. That meant jack shit to me because my considered professional opinion was that O'Sullivan's death was entirely unsuspicious and solely due to natural causes. Any police officer worth his or her salt knows that to lie effectively one must stick reasonably closely to the truth. Therefore, in my official report I wouldn't gloss over the fact that Jilly had been a long-term drug addict. Aside from anything else, the pathologist couldn't ignore the track marks on her arms. All I needed to do was claim that her addiction was well in the past.

After acquiring some cash from Jilly's landlord in return for overlooking the fact that drug dealing was taking place in his gaff, I phoned my chum Paul Lever to acquire suitable evidence to back up the fictional content of the report I was in the process of compiling. PC Lever had a thick file on Jilly and this included several of the fraudulent job applications he'd directed her to make. Back in the mid-'70s Paul had wanted to know exactly what was going on in various local drug charities, so he'd sent Jilly into them as a spy. He provided me with a copy of a successful application she'd made for a job as a social worker at the Westbourne Project. In this Jilly claimed to have a degree and postgraduate qualifications in philosophy from UCL, despite the fact that she'd left school at sixteen and had never attended a university. Something else that made the document Lever handed me fraudulent was Jilly's claim that although she'd been a smack addict, she'd cleaned up in 1972. While I knew this was untrue, it placed her long-term drug addiction seven years in the past, which was good enough for my purposes.

Since the general public is blissfully ignorant of the problems police officers face, people are often surprised to learn of my working methods, should I choose to speak openly about them. What needs to be stressed in relation to this is that since it is impossible for the police to completely suppress the West London drug scene, the next best thing for us to do is control it. Only dealers we approve of are allowed to carry on their business, and cuts from their profits serve to top up our inadequate pay. Likewise, Paul Lever and various other police officers, including me, had been getting our jollies with Jilly during the early '70s.

Lever had the evidence, both real and fabricated, to get O'Sullivan banged up for a very long time. To avoid jail, Jilly had made a deal with him. O'Sullivan had to sell drugs on Paul's behalf and provide him with information about anyone who set themselves up as a dealer without his approval. She also agreed to see us once a week at the police station where we had a regular line-up with her. Jilly wasn't the only junkie Paul had providing us with sexual favors, all of which might give the impression he's a hard man. Certainly this is the appearance he cultivates, but actually he's somewhat sensitive about his macho self-image. Back in 1972, Jilly had the singular misfortune to be around just after a colleague made a crack about Lever always taking last place in our gang-bangs.

Paul, like any virile male, enjoys slapping whores around while he's screwing them, and on this particular occasion he was determined to prove through sheer ultra-violence that he didn't harbor any unnatural sexual desires. As I gave Jilly a poke, Lever grabbed her right arm and broke it over his knee. O'Sullivan was in agony, but Paul took great pleasure in amusing himself by making the bitch indulge him with an extended sex session before allowing her to go to the hospital. On the surface this might sound somewhat sick, but Paul is basically a good bloke, and he genuinely believes that being a bit psycho is the most rational way to deal with whores and crims. After all, the only thing these reprobates respect and understand is brute force. Indeed, what other way is there to deal with someone like O'Sullivan? In the early '60s she had offers of marriage from more than one of her upper-class johns, but she turned them down and became a junkie instead.

It was Jilly's decision to live the low-life and what she got from us was no more than she had coming for choosing to subsist, as her extended Irish family have done since before the days of Cromwell, beyond the pale. Jilly wasn't just a junkie and a prostitute, she was also a pickpocket, a thief, and she engaged in checkbook and other frauds. Any reasonable person will agree that without laws and police officers prepared to carry out a dirty job vigilantly, society would collapse into pure jungle savagery. That said, there are still too many do-gooders who love besmirching the name of the Metropolitan Police, and an inquest into Jilly's life and death would in all likelihood bring to light the type of facts that fuel the enmity these bleeding hearts feel toward us.

Police officers like me deserve whatever perks we can pick up, providing this doesn't impinge upon the rights of law-abiding citizens. Bending the rules goes with the territory of upholding the law; if I stuck to official procedures my hands would be tied with red tape. Punks and whores really don't count as far as I'm concerned, nor do the pinkos who bleat on about police oppression. In a sane society criminals wouldn't have rights, and the police wouldn't have to break the law to protect decent folk.

MAIDA HELL

BY BARRY ADAMSON

Maida Hill

Above the sound of sirens, my view is as always: stark, sullen, and eldritch. I'm prone to believe that it's a vile and disgusting world below.

Where I stand, the Harrow Road Police Station is to my right, and Our Lady of Lourdes and St. Vincent de Paul Catholic Church is to my left.

Crime and redemption carved into each set of knuckles.

I catch myself on the turnaround—reflected in stained glass. I am at once as black as night and yet somehow as white as a sheet.

Moiety me!

I hang my head and lean on a knee that sways gently. The smell of tumble dryers and fried food pique my hunger for something more than the reminders of a not so comfortable existence.

Beneath me: the Harrow Road. This is the main artery that divides (at this juncture) Notting Hill and Maida Vale into an area uncommonly known as Maida Hill.

More commonly known as Maida Hell.

If it were a pen it would be broken. The scribe's grasp sullied by an unthinkable, irremovable liquid; marking him forever as the guilty one.

If it were a book it would be stolen. Pushed into a dark alley; fingers around its throat; gasping and bleating for its very existence to be ratified before being hauled over the coals and the very life beaten out of it.

Sucked in.

Chewed up.

Spat out.

Stepped on.

MAIDA HELL.

I spy with my little eye; the red, white, and blue blood vessels that jam their way through this darkened gray conduit we'll refer to as the "Harrowing Road." The number 18 bus domineeringly crawls the entire length of it like a fat, hideous tapeworm; its red and shining sixty-foot body bulging with sweating parasites. This *Dipylidium caninum* heads as far west as one can imagine, taking in "Murder Mile" Harlesden, where you could very well be "starin' down de barrel of a 'matic," as though you were merely being greeted by an old friend. Then forever you'll sit on your backside next to some undesirable with few manners, as the nauseating carrier snakes its way through Wem-ber-ley and finally sets in Sudbury. Which is as far west as one can imagine.

Or: it heads northeast, over Ballard's Concrete Island; ceremoniously known as the Paddington Basin (which, in my opinion, is as good a place as any to let go of the contents of a now infested stomach!). Scolex features, then slithers up the Marylebone Road, and finally breaks itself down by Euston Railway Station to complete its lifecycle and let everybody get the hell out to the rest of the country. Which is precisely what I intend to do when all this is over.

Not a hundred yards from where I stoop, the Great Western Road jumps over the lazy Harrow Road and becomes Elgin Avenue. This is also the sector where

Fernhead Road comes to an end, along with Walterton Road, creating a psychic wasteland of sorts. This circumambience consists to my mind of five corners. (Traditionally four. Nineteenth-century ordinance survey maps will forever testify that Walterton and Fernhead came much later. However, bananas to all that.) These *five* corners shall become evinced and bring into our very consciousness the indurate domain of:

THE SPACE BETWEEN.

I'll take you there.

On one corner: the bank.

Always full and with few tellers, most of who are off shopping in Somerfield and grabbing all the reduced-priced stock before it goes out of date later that day. Outside of the bank, they'll flirt with the locals they looked down upon not a moment earlier. (Don't kiss her, she's a teller!) Then stroll lazily back to the jam-packed treasury, where one guy is now screaming the place down.

"YOU KNOW ME! *NIG NOG.* WHERE DID HE GO?"

The toothless, yellow-eyed man with the pee stains on his coat then begins to cry, and shamefully leaves.

"Tosser. Jennifer, will you buzz me in?"

The teller then shirks in to stuff her face with tuck and gossip, before slipping into a dream of tonight's date with the new business manager, Clive. Twenty-two. Looks a bit like Ronaldo without the skills.

He'll part my lips with first and third and slip in the second. He'll stare into me. Through me . . .

Cream oozes from the doughnut she scoffs and lands on her skirt, which she wipes off with her hand. The rest of us? Well, we just lose another day silently practicing the art of queuing; bemoaning a self-confidence we just don't seem to have been born with.

On the other corner: the mobile phone shop.

"Mobile phone, please?"

A skinny girl in a tight sweater hands out flyers, which nobody takes, except this one bizarre-looking guy who lurks ominously, scratches his crotch, and then approaches her with a greasy smile.

"Oh, this is the new Ericsson, right?"

"Yes. Please. To take. My boss . . ."

"It's the flattop, isn't it?"

"Please, just take."

"Yeah. It's got those buttons that really stick out. You could play with them all night. What are you, love? Polish? Latvian?"

"Please, I don't . . ."

He gives her the killer's stare.

"Mark my words, love. You fucking do. And you fucking will. All right?"

He holds her gaze before leaning away and into the distance. Feeling exposed by the coruscating sunlight, she pulls her coat together, mumbles an idea of faith while thinking about her mother and the friends she left behind, and moves onto the next.

"Mobile phone, please?"

On the other corner: the public toilets.

Usual setup. Standard, heading underground. Disabled, at floor level. Toilet of choice for drug addicts.

"The animals went in two by two, hurrah, hurrah."

"Fuck off. Give me the gear."

"You make me feel like dancin', gonna dance the night away."

Lucy takes the first boot. The back of her knees fold and immediately she's scratching like a monkey.

"Gimme that."

Sandra, not singing for the first time since these two scored, squirts Lucy's blood into the sink and then rinses the syringe in the toilet bowl before drawing up the heroin, tying up, shooting up, tying off, and time ending and trouble saying goodbye. She looks to Lucy who now slides down the wall like a lifeless doll, smashing her head on the toilet bowl in the process.

"Get up, you stupid bitch."

Nothing.

Sandra gets the hell out of there. She makes a fuss to an oncoming guy who's wheelchair bound.

"They're broke, love. You should try downstairs."

The guy looks at her. "Un-fucking-believable." Finally she notices the wheelchair; scratches her face in slow . . . motion.

"Sorry, love. You must have done all right though, eh? Couldn't lend me a fiver, could you?"

On the other corner: Costcutter. *The* most expensive twenty-four-hour supermarket in the world.

What the fuck are they on about? Nine pounds sixty for a couple of newspapers, some fags, and a drink?

"Nine pounds sixty."

Someone bursts through the door.

"Give me a single, you get me?"

The shopkeeper (*There're six of them. Remember the time some posh kid walked in followed by fucking Crackula himself, wielding a crook-lock and swinging at the poor cunt, whose only crime was to point out that the Count could take a piss in the bogs instead of in the road?)* responds with, "No more singles. Out. Get out."

A couple of stray Australians, believing themselves to be in the warmer reaches of Notting Hill, wander in. Seeing a chance to exercise an act of old-country benevolence, the Aussie guy pulls out a smoke and gives it to this arsehole. Now this idiot's all over him.

"Nice one, bruv. SEEEN. Let me carry you shit for you."

"I'm good, thanks."

"I WASN'T TALKING TO YOU. I WAS TALKING TO THE LADY."

"It's cool, buddy, just er . . ."

"Just what?"

He stares hard into the Aussie guy's eyes and presses his head against him, the poor sod now reeling; purblind; red in the face and his girlfriend is starting to really get the shits.

"Tell him to go fuck himself, Dobbo."

Dobbo decides to wade in, kakking himself.

The shopkeepers surround the scene and the guy walks, lighting the smoke; grinning and staring between the Aussie girl's legs as she puts some breakfast stuff, eggs and the like, on the counter.

"Nice nice nice nice nice."

"Rack off, numb-nuts."

"Lay down, gal, let me push it up, push it up."

"Look, mate, just fuckin' . . ."

"Leave it."

"Twenty-four pounds thirty-eight."

"What?"

* * *

On the final corner: the pub.

Well. I wouldn't know about that anymore, would I? Be the last place I could afford to be seen in. I mean, what if they decide to reopen the case? Then what?

When Mary tells me that it's "the best craic in town," I undoubtedly always agree with her that it just might be, and change the topic as fast as I can, save that she might see me faltering.

The ways of W9 lives are reflected in the otherwise preposterous comparisons with the South Bronx.

The five corners.

The five boroughs?

Preposterous.

Henceforth, the tradition of tolerance for the rights of ordinary fucked-up people, a communal tradition that was fought for in the '70s right on this spot by the one and only Joe Strummer and company, intertwines and combines to make up the disfigured landscape.

Truth is, there's no shrugging off the fact that these folk are forever condemned to scrape around like lunatics, sucking for dear life on yesterday's rotten air, cast over hill and vale.

Hanging over W9, Mr. Goldfinger's Trellick Tower watches as the nuclear sun sets down. This architectural abomination stands creaking, turning a blind eye to Japanese photographers, while at its roots, skulls are caved in and crack rocks are sold to whoever the hell wants, by dealers who freewheel the nearby Grand Union Canal on stolen bicycles.

Meanwhile Gardens is also apparent as it skirts both canal and tower and is the divider and last breathing space before visitors to this hellhole say goodbye to common logic. Forever.

On the canal itself, most are as oblivious to the Canada goose; Gray heron; Mallard; Kestrel; Coot; Moorhen; Black-headed gull; Wren; Robin; Song thrush; White throat; Chiffchaff; Willow warbler; Starling; Greenfinch; Goldfinch; Woodpigeon; Gray wagtail; Dunnock; and Blackbird, as the birds are to them.

Best keep it that way.

Meanwhile.

Gardens.

The underdeveloped.

The youth.

The hood rats and the squeaks.

Hood rats (mainly black), who like any young voluble yet asinine revolutionary, guise themselves and any sign of vulnerability in a uniform of oversize sports clothes; hoods pulled down low over cap even lower, with one hand always down the trouser front. *Listen listen listen listen. I do what the fuck I want. Don't arsk. A gun is a gun and I DO have one. Next to my blade. Live at my mum's, innit. My sister's got three kids and she's younger than me, innit. My dad? Don't know, mate. Don't fuckin' know. Three guys, right. Chase me in my car and I get mashed, innit. Don't want no fuckin' hospital though, innit.*

Squeaks (mainly white), who like any terrified young revolutionary, guise any sign of vulnerability by wearing a uniform of tight-fitting sportswear which also doubles as a mask for the lack of a soul. Obsessive about their appearance to the point of perfection, their goal is to have you believe that the projection of superiority is indeed true. *Nice trainers. Gleaming. I do the right thing by me mum. If you (dirty filthy fucking animal) do anything to hurt any one of my family or their kids, I'll fuckin' kill you. I'll clump you with a fuckin' hammer. I'll cut your fuckin' heart out (after I've cleaned the house for me mum and taken me gran up to the hospital). All right? Have you been fuckin' smokin'?*

A community of chagrins and fighters set against a world of cheap booze and even cheaper promises.

Fighters against a war they started.

Fighters for peace.

Secondhand peace.

A community of losers and bruisers.

A community nonetheless.

Life made difficult is practical by default, with little room for the spiritual.

Even less room for the likes of me.

My mobile rings.

"Hello?"

"Johnny."

"Yes. This is . . ."

"I fuckin' know all about you, you cunt. You won't get away with it this time."

Then the line goes dead.

I look at the last caller to find the number withheld and flick a somewhat tentative snarl into the eye of my fear.

Loud pangs begin in my temples. My throat tightens, and remembering to breathe, I look around to see where I might fall if I were to pass out. The world begins to swim around me and the deafening sound of an ambulance threatens to pop my right ear. As though a six-foot tuning fork has been struck at the core of my very being, I vibrate from the inside out. Then I stumble to a chair and clench my eyes as a million pinpricks pepper my forehead, squeezing out tiny beads of alternating hot and cold sweat. I don't know if I will ever see again as I open my eyes and hear a high-pitched wail that accompanies the darkness. A backward scream travels into my chest, and as though a light has just exploded, I begin to make out solarized shapes in front of me. I can also hear my heartbeat and I know I'm back. After a few deep breaths, I manage to look out of the window from behind drawn curtains. Fade up to a rat and a squeak and a Mazda. Music so, so loud.

Back from the dead
Back from the dead
To put a fucking hole in your motherfucking head.

Their own heads bop up and down together, as though choreographed like two ornamental dogs that people used to place in the back window of their cars in days gone by.

Arseholes.

Easy now.

Remember the foundations of morality and grace.

Hovering on Johnny's lowest periphery, Colleen O'Neill staggers along Harrow Road toward Our Lady and curses those red-nose buggers in Alcoholics Anonymous.

Her bright red hair ambuscades the crowd; the stench of sperm keeps them at bay. She is literally dying for another drink. She now sweeps aside her blazing locks to reveal a face that resembles a weather-torn cliffside, as she sniffs an air not quite good enough for her and surveys the space with a condemnation reserved for the damned. Her goal is to head out of the space for Westbourne Park Road, where she just might get lucky with a punter, preferably three.

Since the age of eleven, Colleen has been fucked into one bad situation after another. At the age of twelve, when she realized she could get paid for getting laid, there was no looking back. There were also no trips to the seaside. No hopscotch. No crushes on boys. No *Bunty* or *Judy* magazines with cutout dresses and little tabs attached to place on figures that you could also cut out and keep. No bedroom where she and her friends could practice kissing on their arms. No "what's for tea today, ma'am?" Just no one. When the boxer said he'd take care of her, he kept his promise: beating her to a pulp, using her as an ashtray, and raping her daily. The drink became her only means of protection from a world that offered ineffectual amounts of faith, and little by little the price of that protection got higher and higher and higher.

I walk around my own little "space between" and straighten everything, catching parallel lines and matching them up to other lines, like the edge of the carpet with the sideboard, the table with the edge of the carpet and the sideboard. Crouch down. Oops! That's got to be out by two millimeters. I dust and vac just to make sure and straighten the cushions. Then I wash all the dishes. Well, they need it and you never know, do you? I dry them and put them away and wipe down the sink. Polish it? Go on, then. Wow. What a smell. The guy who makes CIF or JIF or whatever they're calling it now is a genius. *Removes even the most stubborn of dirt.* That's the truest statement I've heard today. I breathe in synthetic alpine drives and here I am.

Back from the dead.

Kelly Mews.

Kelly's eye. Number one.

Ready?

As I'll ever be.

I wash my hands and face several times so I can only smell the soap and brush my teeth again. Then I decide on a shower, where I'm tempted into an act of turpitude, but no. Come on. We all know that the devil makes work for idle hands. Cleanliness is next to Godliness. Next to! Alongside!! The very next thing in line!!! I towel down and look at my lean body. Not an ounce of fat. I iron five shirts and lay out several tracksuit tops and stand before them.

Days off always did throw me into a spin.

How to blend in? Achieve total stasis?

No. Freedom. Freedom of choice. That's the key.

I pick my clothes for the evening and after several changes of mind (real freedom) I agree on smart but casual and decide I will roam into the open before catching up on some paperwork at the office.

Into the open.

Into the space.

I double-lock the door and then unlock both locks and reenter to straighten out a couple of the cushions that seem to be slightly sagging at their corners. I then stand still. Quite still. I can't see or hear any dust and breathe yet another sigh of relief. I double-lock the door and bounce down the stairs but the smell and the din of human life begin to take ahold of me, sending my guts into a whirl.

Here comes Manny. I know him but I don't know him so neither of us trades any goodwill.

Best keep it that way.

In fact, I quickly decipher that he thinks I am not me! That, for all intents and purposes, I am somebody else. He gives me a *You're not who you say you are, are you?* kind of a look, and since, truth be told, I *am* in all earnest pretending to be somebody other that who I really am, I have no argument with the man. At all.

I turn onto Harrow Road, past the "bus stop of doom." Twenty people on mobile phones, waiting for a number 18, piled on the pavement and not moving as I approach. The signal of an oncoming bus sends everyone into a frenzy and I just get past before possibly ending up a victim of a human stampede.

I cross the corner of Woodfield Place and Harrow Road and a 4x4 speeds up to get around the one-way system; it could have all ended right there. Luckily I glanced down to where his indicators are and, seeing no light flickering and knowing that the art of indication has been lost forever, guessed he was going to turn right. I jumped back as the deafening sound of throbbing bass covered the sound of my own aorta. He missed me by an inch. I imagine his face behind the blacked-out glass panel and give him the stare. He stops the car dead in the middle of the road with a screech.

Suddenly I'm the people's choice, Mr. Fiduciary!

I continue to stare at the blacked-out window, letting him know that if someone has to die, let it be me. The door is about to open and I raise the stakes as I spread my arms in a gesture of fearlessness.

Time stops.

The light goes on.

He pulls away with another screech and I cross the road next to an old West Indian gent, in a *très chic* outfit from Terry's Menswear. He sees an old flame on the other side of the street; her stockings falling own by her ankles; her stained pinafore billowing in what he perceives to be a *lucky gust*.

He calls out, "Old stick a fire don't tek long to ketch back up!"

She laughs out loud. "Tiger no fraid fe bull darg!"

He takes his time crossing.

Nobody minds. Except for a Prammie (*Eighteen and born pregnant, with a hand extended to the council. Hair scraped back, causing a do-it-yourself, council-house face-lift meant to reverse the ageing process. Cigarette extending from an expensive mani-cure. Two kids and another on the way. Shell-shocked and suicidal seventeen-year-old boyfriend carrying a maxi pack o' nappies*), who pushes out in front of the old guy and kisses her teeth in disdain.

I hit the five corners.

Situated here, circus performer and audience participation reach their mutual understanding.

Crossing at the lights, I see seven drunken Bajans cussing and laughing outside the bookies. They pass the bottle from plastic cup to plastic cup. Close your eyes and you might think you were listening to a bunch of Dorset farmers discussing the price of beef and Mrs. Mottle's lumbago.

I see a drunken redheaded woman and walk into the beginnings of a bad dream.

Sancta Maria, Mater Deu, ora pro nobis peccatoribus, nunc, et in hora mortis nostrae. Amen.

A performer runs out into Harrow Road, just in front of where I'm positioned. He cajoles his potential crowd.

"You tink me nah got money?" Everybody turns and laughs.

Within a moment.

A lean *yoot*, one jeans leg rolled up to the knee but not the other, chews on a matchstick and stares into the eyes of potential protagonists.

A woman in her sixties—jeans emblazoned with the

words *Foxy Lady* across the buttocks, swinging her hips vera-
ciously—blows a bubble from too much gum and bursts it
loudly, laughing and adjusting her bra.

A man in track pants, too short, no socks, beaten-in shoes,
and unshaven forever, stands rooted to the spot and dribbling.

A guy selling scratch cards and methadone is able to pick
someone's pocket as she turns to see what the fuss is about.

Someone asks for change.

Someone asks for a cigarette.

Two crackheads: "See my fucking solicitor?"

"See my fucking selector?"

Somebody screams.

The performer stops the traffic dead.

A couple of hood rats, left hands disappearing down
tracksuit bottoms as though hiding some obscene disfigure-
ment, steel themselves.

"If yuh no ketch me a moonshine, yuh nah ketch me a
dark night."

Someone's mobile pipes up with an unrecognizable series
of beeps meant to be the popular tune of the day.

The guys outside the bookies carry on arguing about irri-
gation, feigning oblivion to *dis stupidness*.

A Fiat Punto's tires screech as the driver just misses the
performer, who is now hitting himself on the head and throwing tens and fives into the air. He then sets about grabbing an
aluminum chair from outside of Jenny's bad food restaurant
and throws it at the window.

Loud smash.

Applause.

I enter the chemists opposite the commotion and feel a
slight nausea as I automatically smile at the dirty-blond trans-
vestite who works at the sales counter. She knows I know she

knows, and I enjoy watching her hoodwinking the locals, our secret tryst sending me into a childish bout of rubescence.

The chemists is like Doctor Who's Tardis, as from where I came in; I now stand in a huge space filled with the cheapest goods possible. A queue forms in front of the pharmacist, who's stationed in the top left corner. Mr. Pill for every ill. He's got the purple rinses and the overweight hooked into his whole world and is dazzling in his diagnoses.

I stare at Mishca's hands, and catching me (as she's telling some old bat with a mole that's sprouting more hair than is on my head), she seemingly mocks us both: "Yes. It will work on you every time."

She quickly rubs the crotch of her jeans to guide my eye toward her. I over-stare and feign arousal before looking at the various '70s shaving foams and after-shaves that I remember seeing in Mike's bathroom at the home.

My knees begin to knock and I want to fight somebody.

I approach the counter, not sure what I'm to say.

"Pack of Wrigley's, please."

"What flavor?"

Everything grinds to a halt. Freezes, and the natural sound fades out.

What flavor? How about fucking . . . COQ AU VIN, eh, Johnny? Be there at 6; bring the van round the back or I'll fucking kill your sister, all right?

"Er. Spearmint . . . ? No freshmint."

The chemists now seems small. Dirty. That pharmacy guy should be shot.

So much for providence.

Mishca licks her lips. "Anytime, sugar."

She then turns and reaches up to the shelf for the gum and I'm taking myself out of this place fast.

I move quickly so that she imagines me to have been merely an apparition.

I'll deal with her later.

I walk back toward Kelly Mews.

Looking skyward and seeing red, I remember it all.

Red sky at night, Shepherd's cottage on fire.

Cops are clearing the place out, as that idiot who threw the chair is being pushed, shirtless, into the back of a van. One slimy copper is talking to a girl of about fifteen and asking her where she lives, with a grin.

I'll deal with him later.

The redhead is talking to some old woman and nodding her head as though she was a kid being told where bad girls go, and catching a ray of hope reflected in my eye, looks to me like the ghost I might have just become. She makes toward me but the woman holds her arm, pulling her back.

"Just listen to me, Colleen, and you might learn something."

I dip my head and keep moving. Someone bumps into me, he's about seventeen and I can just make out his eyes beneath that hood. I think twice as I know he is armed. He recognizes me. His face widens as I get in first.

"How's your mum?"

"Yeah. She's good."

I'll have to deal with him later.

I cross the road by the bank, or at least try to. The lights are on red but the cars just keep coming, afraid that if they were to stop, someone would drag the driver out and beat him to death. I walk out anyway, knowing I've got the law on my side. Hit me and I'll sue you for everything you're worth, after I've dragged you from your vehicle and beaten the life out of you, of course!

Haven't been in a gym for a while, but you never lose it. Right cross. Uppercut. Jab. Pow. Pip. Pow. Super-middleweight titleholder from '74 to '77. Mike said he'd never seen a lad like me. Said I had the "killer's gaze."

I get to the other side. Away from the din. I cross again and dip between east and west, keeping an eye on Woodfield Place in case the 4x4 has found his stomach and decided to come back and face me.

No one.

I'm on the home stretch thinking about later, now I've made my decision.

A drunk is relieving himself against the bins outside the futuristic Science Photo Library next door to mine. A *trustafarian*, some spill from the Hill seeking a cheap thrill, opens the door from one of the flats upstairs, and seeing what the drunk's up to, pretends, *It's all good in da hood, bro.*

"Don't mind me."

The guy spits, "I fucking won't, cunt."

After dumping his rubbish, *I'll fucking dump him in a minute*, he shuffles off back to where he came from, counting out his father's money, no doubt, in his ironic "chav" Burberry pajamas and fluffy slippers.

He glances, the guy still peeing, and he gives me a limp smile before hopping back indoors.

Life on the edge of a very plush cushion.

Indeed.

Something in the air catches me and sends me spiralling back through time.

Bernadette: Diorella.

Eileen: Diorissimo.

Margaret: Chanel N°5.

In the distance, a crackhead screams for all she's worth,

maybe for all *we're* worth.

"THE WHORE OF BABYLON! THE WHORE OF BABYLON!"

Blood songs coagulate in the black currents of a cold cold night.

The need to believe.

Credo in unum Deum, Patrem omnipotentem.

Ready?

Ready as I'll ever be.

I approach the mews and should I go in and change or just get on with it? I decide to perform the latter and go to the office. I skip around the back of the building and turn the key, walk in, and head for my desk. Mary approaches me with a smile.

"Father Donaghue?"

"Yes, Mary?" I toss my keys onto my desk. "What is it?"

"Well, Father, I know you're very busy, but I was wondering if you might be able to add a few prayers tomorrow for my sister. A remembrance, if you would."

"How long has it been now?"

"It's been five years, Father. Five years since he took her away from us." She begins to cry.

I put an arm round her and remind her that the Lord is with us. And to call me by my first name, which is Johnny.

She begins to feel a little uncomfortable, questioning my grasp ever so slightly with her eyes, and so I let her go and then offer her a drop, which she accepts.

"Father. I didn't know."

I stare at my glass.

"Neither did I, Mary. Neither did I."

Mary takes a sip as I put my glass down onto the desk and pick up my crucifix.

We both laugh now and chat about the bargains to be found at Iceland and Somerfield and how the new pound shop is really quite amazing. Mary lowers her now empty glass back onto the tray by the whiskey decanter.

"Thank you, Father, I feel so much better now. Yourself? Settling in? Getting used to our little neighborhood? I know it seems a bit on the rough side, but . . ."

"Oh, I've seen worse, Mary, believe me. Now. I've plenty to do, as you can understand?"

"Oh, forgive me, Father, for taking up your time."

"Not at all, Mary. And I'll be sure to mention . . ."

"Molly."

"Molly. Yes. I won't forget."

"Goodbye, Father."

I sit and wait. For an hour. I fill my glass as tears begin to well up in my eyes and roll down my face.

Poor me. Poor me. Pour me a drink.

Believing in Him. Not believing in Him.

Deus Meus, ex toto corde poenitet me omnium meorum peccatorum, eaque detestor, quia peccando, non solum poenas a Te iuste statutas promeritus sum, sed praesertim quia offendi Te summum bonum ac dignum qui super omnia diligaris. Ideo firmiter propono, aduvante gratia Tua, de cetero me non-peccaturum peccandique occasiones proximas fugiturum . . .

The phone rings and the glass smashes in my hand, just as I bring it to my lips.

"Johnny. You know I will have to kill you."

A smile widens across my face. "How can you kill what's already dead?"

Twelve Canadians were the first to welcome the next day as

they took off from the Grand Union on their way to the much gentler climate of Kew. Their wings making a terrific, terrifying noise. Pete, the cleaner of the Grand Union pub, was mopping up the beer garden; lost in the fight with his wife, who'd said before he left at 5 in the morning, "Panic, stupidity, and withdrawal. That's all you've got to fucking offer."

"Fuck away from me."

When he first heard the noise, he almost dropped dead believing, *This is it*, expecting Osama himself in a Harrier jet, with eleven henchmen in tow.

Pint and eleven white wines for the ladies?

Pete was mysteriously taken by the magnificence of those beasts and marveled in slow motion when they, first down low and then rising up under the Halfpenny Step Bridge, yelled out as they made their ascent, "What a beautiful sight!"

He looked around to see if Carmel was about.

"Carmel, you should see this. Come here."

Carmel shook her head from inside the pub, and thinking about her eldest daughter's latest abortion, snapped, "What is it now? Don't you fucking play games with me, because I'm in no mood."

Carmel threw a rag down and turned again to see Pete standing there like a frozen statue. She laughed to herself and walked out toward him. "What's got you all fucking excited?"

Pete was still motionless, as though aliens had taken his soul. He was now white as a sheet. "Jesus."

"Oh yeah? And I suppose the fucking holy Virgin Mother of Mary, too . . ." Carmel's voice trailed off, as *now* she understood.

Tied by the wrists to the railing under the bridge.

Black tights pulled tight around her white neck.
Eyes, nose, ears, fingers, and lips removed.
Half-submerged in the canal.
Dead as a fucking doornail.
Legs severed at the thighs.
Red hair ablaze.
Senseless.
Legless.

Beneath the sound of sirens, my view is as always: stark, sullen, and eldritch. I'm prone to believe that it's a vile and disgusting world above.

Where I'll die, the Harrow Road Police Station, now a hive of cordoned-off activity—choppers and coppers setting the landscape on fire—is to my right. Our Lady of Lourdes and St. Vincent de Paul, where in less than half an hour I will asseverate Mass before a shaken community, is to my left.

A community brought together by God only knows whom.

A community of chargrins and fighters.
A community no less.
Fighters for peace.
Secondhand peace.
Crime Time West Nine.
Meanwhile.
Gardens.
Animals.
Birds.
Amen.

PART II

I Fought the Law

I FOUGHT THE LAWYER

BY MICHAEL WARD

Mayfair

I pressed PLAY and the screen on the dinky digital cam-corder came to life. Vanya's face the only thing in view, gurning and sticking her tongue out as a kind of visual "*testing, testing . . .*" before disappearing.

Good girl.

From where the camera was positioned on top of the wardrobe, it takes in about half the room. In the far right-hand corner is a bed with a large mirror next to it, to the left a small chest of drawers, and in between, against the far wall, a coat stand with a French maid's outfit, a leather basque, and a nurse's uniform with a white cap; a pair of black thigh-length boots are slumped in front.

Two seconds later Vanya reappears into view, carrying the chair she'd just used to reach the top of the wardrobe, and placing it in its usual position next to the chest of drawers. She looks in the mirror, makes a cursory adjustment to her hair, and smoothes her hands down her slip before exiting the frame stage left to the door that leads to the sitting room.

Ten seconds of stillness, then back to moving pictures as he enters the room. Four slow, graceful strides bring him to the mirror, where he stops to take in his reflection. A tall, slim, handsome man in his early fifties wearing a tastefully expensive dark gray suit offset by a weighty flop of silver hair. The epitome of conservative English style. He runs an index finger over each arched eyebrow, taming any rogue hairs, then turns and unwittingly strikes a face-on, screen-test pose for the camera.

Perfect.

Vanya's back in the room now, her heels wobbling slightly on the squishy carpet as she walks to the chest of drawers and finds a condom. The gentleman takes off his jacket and hangs it on the back of the chair, then places his shoes neatly underneath. By the time Vanya has rolled the condom over her index finger and greased it thoroughly with Vaseline, the man is naked but for his calf-length thin black socks and has positioned himself on the bed, facing away from the camera, bearing his arse to it.

Vanya kneels behind him on the bed, still in her slip and shoes, and gently greases the QC's rectal area, accompanying the finger strokes with a softly murmured Croatian lullaby. *Mamu ti jebem u guzicu.* She gently eases the digit inside and begins finger-fucking the man, her Serbo-Croat mantra rising in volume as the pace of the thrusts quickens. *Picka. Mamu ti jebem u guzicu . . .* About one minute later the silver-haired gentleman, wanking furiously now, reaches his climax and the transaction is complete.

I press STOP.

Got the cunt.

Time to rewind.

The previous week—the previous millennium, in fact—I'd been at the River of Fire. The government had organized the Thames to be set on fire on the stroke of midnight. It was going to be an almighty twenty-stories-high flaming surge of orange-and-red pyrotechnic power bursting through the heart of the city at 800 miles an hour. *PM Turns Water into Fire; Elemental Alchemy on the Grandest of Scales.* But all anyone got were a few oversized candles fizzling away on some barges along a muddy river.

Not that I gave a fuck. Fabrication, fabrication, fabrication. I knew those sloganeering cunts would never deliver. I wasn't there for the show. I was there to steal stuff from unsuspecting thick cunts. And unsuspecting thick cunts do deliver. Copiously.

I wasn't doing it for the money—though some of the stuff I nicked did come in handy later. It just needed to be done. With all that sense of hope and expectation for the dawning of a new millennium, someone had to restore the balance. Inject a bit of reality into the situation. These people were supposed to be slick city folk, weren't they? Experts at the urban experience. *Come to London.* Where the people are such cunts they piss and shit and vomit on their own streets while a bunch of incompetent failed lawyers-turned-slogan-peddlers fuck them up the arse and make them pay for the pleasure.

So I put on my own show. Illegal performance art. A one-off special for a discerning audience of—me. Creative theft. Taking and giving. No one else would've got it anyway. It was a world away from the ham-fisted gippos and hood rats who worked Oxford Street and the tubes. Banging into tourists with an awkward fumble into their pockets and coming away with the odd one-day travel pass to sell on for two quid. The occasional mobile. No sense of style, no originality. No drama. Mine was a virtuoso performance—just me, my rucksack, and my pair of dextrous pals: Right-hand Man and his partner, Leftie. Dab hands, the both of them. Digitally precise, you might say. Got to keep them at arm's length though. You see? It's called style, cunt. Wit! Something those fucks will never have. I take and I give. It's art, fucking art.

True, the actual pickpocketing was pretty much the same as I'd done in my act a hundred times before. Same technically, anyway. And I'd picked pockets for real before, illegally that is, a couple of times. But it hadn't given me quite the buzz I'd expected it to. No sense of occasion. This was different though. The river bit might have been shit but there were still two million happy, stoned, drunk singing people all squashed up together. All mesmerized by a few colorful lights in the sky. And everyone happily embracing their fellow man, getting up close and hugging, like they didn't actually hate each other, like they weren't all cunts for one second. I'll give you "Auld Lang Fucking Syne," you twats. "Should auld acquaintance be forgot . . ." *Forgot to keep an eye on that, mate, thanks very much.* "And never brought to . . ." *Mind if I take that off you, sir?* "Should auld acquaintance be for . . ." *Gotcha!* "For the sake of auld lang . . ." *Signing off now, gotta go!*

All in front of about a zillion boys in blue. It was a good night. A new beginning. The way forward.

After the show I figured I'd go for a celebratory fuck. Vanya would still be working. I'd been going to her for about six months—since she'd come over from Croatia. She was very good value for money—extremely pretty face and a good body, but still reasonable rates. If she were English she'd probably have charged twice as much. Maybe three times. But then I guess that's one of the benefits of immigration. Cheap, efficient labor.

I started slowly working my way through the throng. Up the Strand, past Trafalgar, and on toward Piccadilly and Shepherd Market. Made up a little song on the way, to the old Robin Hood theme tune: *He steals from the thick/And gives* to the whore/Robbing's good!/Robbing's good!/Robbing's good! Sometimes, Jonathan Marcus Tiller, I thought, you really are the wittiest fucker in the world. In the fucking world.

I was just taking in Piccadilly Circus—the glitz of Burger King, the glamour of Dunkin' Donuts—when I was approached by an American tourist: "Hey there. Could you direct me to Piccadilly Circus?" He said the last two words uncertainly, as if no such place with that name could possibly exist.

I didn't reply, just announced the thing with outstretched arms, then turned to him with an expression I'd hoped conveyed: *What the fuck do you think that is, cunt? Now fuck off.*

It didn't work.

"Only, I'm kinda here to make this movie and I was told Piccadilly Circus was where to look."

I glanced up and down his face as he spoke.

"Look for what?" I said, mildly intrigued.

"To meet actors. Only, I'm filming the thing in my hotel tonight and I thought you might like to . . ."

Suck your cock? "Don't think so, mate. But yeah, this is the right area—just a decade or so too late . . ."

I left the Yank fruit to it and carried on up Piccadilly. Walked along the north side. It's lined with imposing gray-stoned edifices, like gigantic doormen keeping an eye on things, keeping the undesirables out. Raising a suspicious eyebrow at anyone who dares venture near the promised land of Mayfair. *Perhaps sir would be more comfortable taking a different thoroughfare? A street more suited to sir's . . . position, shall we say?*

Not tonight though. Tonight I wasn't being hassled by them. It was as if I'd passed some kind of test. Like I was okay now. They hadn't exactly handed me the keys, but at least they were going to turn a blind eye while I picked the locks for a while. It was definitely a new beginning.

I took a right down White Horse Street and into Shepherd Market, a twisty-turny little red-lit corner where all Mayfair's dirt had been swept to, out of sight. Like a mini Soho but better-spoken and wearing a blazer. By day, the place wasn't really that special—a bit too twee for my taste. But come night—proper night, that is, once the after-work lager's been drunk and the late-night diners have fucked off—that's when it happens. When it reveals its true identity. The perfect place for a discerning maverick street thief artist.

I stopped to hitch my rucksack up, then turned left, then right into Market Mews. Stopped at the open door marked *Model 1st Floor* and made my way up the stairs. Up the wooden hill to Shagfordshire. *Another good one, Jonny boy.* On the way up I waved at the CCTV camera on the wall and pressed the plastic doorbell helpfully labeled *Press*. Rita opened up. A short round woman with enormous sagging tits, bald but for a few patches of yellowy-gray hair. She was sporting worn-out pink slippers and a loose-fitting cream-colored tracksuit topped with an off-pink toweling dressing gown. Rita is Vanya's maid, the woman who welcomes the punters.

"Hello, Jonny love, she's with a gentleman at the moment, be about ten minutes, that all right?"

"Fine," I said, unhitching the rucksack and plopping myself on the foam two-seater sofa in the living room. The only other rooms in the flat are a tiny kitchen with a kettle and microwave and a small bedroom.

The TV was on so Rita and I sat watching the ITN news report of the millennium celebrations. I broke a Marlboro open to pad out a joint while Rita puffed on her B&H.

"Looks bitter out," she said, nodding at the TV images of

the crowds along the Thames. She got up to turn the thermostat to one hundred.

"Yes," I said, twisting the end of my newly constructed joint before lighting it up.

"Aren't you playing a show tonight, love? Thought you'd be busy tonight of all nights."

"Nah. I could've had a gig but I wanted to check out the River of Fire," I said, watching the end of my joint glow as I toked on it.

I'd often chat with Rita while Vanya was otherwise engaged. She thought I was a bit glamorous cos I was a magician.

"Been busy?" she asked.

I told her about the last gig I'd done—a Christmas party for an accounting firm in the city. I'd been booked with an illusionist called Damon Smart to entertain the staff before dinner. I'd worked with Smart before. His real name was Dave Smith. He was a cheesy cunt, but skillful.

We would approach a group of five or six of the accountants as they enjoyed some preprandial quaffing and introduce ourselves as so-and-so and so-and-so who'd just joined the firm. After a while Smart would start behaving oddly, grimacing and rubbing his stomach, complaining of indigestion. Then he'd do some pretend-wretching and—this is the particularly cuntish bit—start pulling a thread of razor blades from his mouth. Yes, it was that shit. Shitter, in fact, cos once his shtick was over I would then produce a selection of items I'd lifted from them while they were busy watching Smart hamming it up. "And I believe this watch is yours, sir . . ." I fucking hated it. I fucking, fucking, fucking hated the fucking fuck out of it.

Not that I let Rita know this though. She was happy to

think of me as some kind of Paul fucking Daniels, so I figured, why upset her? Nothing to be gained.

"So, yeah, it was a good night," I lied, and took another draw on my spliff.

"You'll be on the telly next," she said, nodding toward the box.

We watched the news coverage for another minute or so, then Rita nodded toward the bedroom door. "That'll be it then, love," she said.

She meant it was time for me to step into the kitchen—out of sight so the punter could leave without the embarrassment of seeing another male in the place. I don't know how the fuck she knew it was time—I hadn't heard a thing from the other room—but her orgasm-detector was spot on. I went into the kitchen and shut the door, leaving it open a tiny crack so I could see who was coming out without him seeing me. I always liked to get a look at the bloke Vanya had been with immediately before me. Just natural curiosity, I suppose.

Half a minute later Vanya appeared from the bedroom and left the flat for the communal toilet on the landing.

Then out he came.

I knew I knew him as soon as he came into view. Someone famous, but I couldn't think who. A newsreader maybe? No, not that well-known. An MP? Not sure, but someone . . .

He picked up the overcoat he'd left on the settee, then pulled out a tenner and handed it to Rita.

Rita smiled and took the tip. "Safe journey now, it's bitter out."

"My overcoat will guard me against the cold, my dear," he said. "And I shall savor your delicious non sequitur the length of my secure passage home."

The name hit me.

I waited till I heard his footsteps disappear down the staircase before coming back into the room.

"Do you know who that was?" I didn't wait for an answer. "Nicholas Monroe. The lawyer. He's . . ."

Vanya teetered back in from the toilet.

"He's famous. Well, for a lawyer anyway . . ."

"Fahmous? Fahmous who? Frederick?" Vanya asked, taking the £60 I had ready for her.

I followed her into the bedroom.

"No, yes—no—his name's Nicholas Monroe. He's always on the news. He got that gang off who killed that black kid in East Ham a couple of years ago. And that gangster from where you're from . . ."

"From Croatia?"

"Somewhere like that, I don't know. Albania maybe, it doesn't matter," I said, shutting the bedroom door. "The point is, he's fucking well-known, got shitloads of money."

"He's not from Croatia, silly, he's English," she said. "Very fine English man. Now what shall we do? Talking or fucking?"

"I mean, what the fuck's he doing here?" I said, ignoring the question.

Vanya plopped herself down on the bed and started inspecting her fingernails.

"If he wants a shag he could go to some discreet high-class place in Kensington or somewhere. What's he doing coming here?"

Her eyes narrowed. "He like me," she said. "He like the way I speak and how I—"

"What, has he been here before? He's a regular?"

"Yes, of course." She said it as if it was obvious, as if I was the stupid one. "He come to here every week nearly. I speak to him in Croatian and put my finger up his ass and he . . ."

Fuck me. "You put your finger up his arse?"

"Yes, of course, this is normal, what's wrong with this?"

"Fucking hell, Vanya—it's not what's wrong with it, it's what's *right* with it. He's rich. He can't afford this to get out. He'll pay us not to tell anyone."

Vanya had a habit of being a bit "kooky," like she wasn't quite all there. Like everything was a game, everything was happening in some surreal Eastern European kiddie film. But now she became more serious, more real. I felt a rise of something in my belly.

"Pay us? How much pay us?" she said.

"Dunno. Ten grand. Maybe more." *Fifty, at least.* "It's nothing to him. He can earn that in a week probably . . ."

"In a week? *Nemoj me jebat!*"

"Exactly." I spoke calmly now, took the tempo down a notch. "We just have to do it properly. Plan it right . . ."

I didn't know a lot about Vanya, but I knew she wasn't a whore by choice, that she hadn't known this was what she'd be doing when she was brought to England. And I knew that, like Anna and Katarina in the flats upstairs, she wasn't seeing much of the five grand or so a week she was earning for the management. She listened carefully as I went through the plan, nodding slowly as I showed her how to work the camcorder, where the record button was, and how to tell if it was on or not. Then I marked the exact spot on the wardrobe where she should put it next time Monroe visited. She would phone me as soon as he'd gone and I would come and collect the camcorder and tape and put Phase 2 into operation.

Ten minutes later I left. We hadn't even fucked but it didn't matter. This was better, I thought. Much better. As I left the place I became aware of the warmth again. Only now it was spreading, up through my chest and arms and down into my groin. This was proper, I could feel it happening now. The real thing. The way forward. The night's earlier performance was a mere prelude. A toccata to the fugue I was composing. I went home but couldn't sleep. Six spliffs and a bottle of wine later, I could . . .

I spent the next few days in my flat in Kentish Town planning Phase 2 and thinking about what to do with the cash. And afterwards too, the next job. Maybe some type of con. It had to be something elegant, stylish. After a few years I'd retire and write my memoir, get it published anonymously. Reveal myself to a select few, my own little magic circle.

The call finally came on Monday night, about 11. I left the flat and hailed a cab for Market Mews. Rita let me in and Vanya was there on the settee eating a Pot Noodle.

"Did you get it? Did it come out okay?" I said.

"Yes, of course."

"Where is it?"

Vanya put the plastic pot down on the carpet and pulled the camcorder out from under the sofa.

"Brilliant." I took it off her. "I'll give you a call. Gotta go. See you."

I left her to her MSG-flavored processed soya and caught a cab on Piccadilly.

"Kentish Town, please, mate."

The cabbie nodded and I got in and hit the PLAY button. It was all there. *Good girl. Perfect. Got the cunt.*

Back at the flat I fired up my Mac and started working on the blackmail letter. The title—*Blackmail Demands*—in twelve-point size, centered on the page. I used italics in the first draft but decided it was a bit too soft so opted for plain text. Then the font. That proved more difficult. Gothic Bold seemed like a good choice but it looked too melodramatic. I liked the sound of Chicago, a bit gangsterish, but it came across too friendly on the page. Then Typewriter. Quite sinister-looking, but more of a ransom-note font, I thought. In the end I went for Times New Roman. Simple. Serious. Businesslike.

Then the text itself. I spent a good few hours on this and was pretty satisfied with the results:

I have in my possession a videotape of you, Mr. Nicholas Monroe, QC, engaging in an act of depravity with a prostitute. The tape is three minutes and twenty-six seconds in length and you are clearly identifiable in it. I am prepared to sell this tape to you for a price of no less than £50,000 in cash. Otherwise I will take it to the newspapers. The fee is non-negotiable and there is only one copy of the tape. You will have to trust me on that last point. Bring the cash, alone, to the Printers Devil public house in Fetter Lane, 6 p.m. on Wednesday the 12th of January, and in return you will receive the tape, which will be in the video camera so you can see what you are getting. Looking forward to doing business with you, Jon X

After a couple of spellchecks I printed it out on a clean piece of white A4. It looked good but the vertical position of the text wasn't quite right so I moved it down slightly, then printed it out again. That was it. I folded it into thirds and sealed the letter in an envelope. *Strictly Private and Confidential. Nicholas Monroe, QC*, it said. I used my left hand to write it, just in case, then deleted the document from my Mac.

I looked over at the TV. *Countdown* was on—the early-morning repeat. It was about half an hour before the tubes started running so I watched the last fifteen minutes, waiting for the nine-letter conundrum bit at the end. I wanted to see if it would be *BLACKMAIL*. I had a feeling it would be. It wasn't.

At that time of day, it only took thirty minutes to get from Kentish Town to Chancery Lane, where Monroe's chambers were. I slipped the letter through the mailbox and went back to the flat to get some sleep.

It was 2 in the afternoon when the alarm woke me up. Wednesday. I shaved, took a shower, put my suit and overcoat on, and headed back Chancery Lane to the Printers Devil. I got there at 3:30 and the place was about half full, which was good. Bought a G&T and found a table with a clear view of the door. While I waited I went over what I was going to say to Monroe. He would walk in alone; I'd gesture for him to come and join me at the table and offer to buy him a drink. He was bound to be nervous and I wanted to keep it friendly. When I'd brought his drink back from the bar I'd say my piece: *Well, Mr. Monroe, I think we both know why we're here, don't we, so let's get down to business, shall we?* He'd probably just nod, I figured, be happy for me to do the talking so he could get the fuck out of there as soon as possible. After the exchange we'd shake hands and I'd leave him there and go and see Vanya to give her her five grand.

Except it didn't quite happen like that. For a start, Monroe was late. Very late. So late in fact that he didn't actually fucking bother to turn up. I phoned his office and was told he was in meetings all afternoon but would I like to leave a message. Would I like to leave a fucking message? What the fuck was going on here? Monroe was in no position to fuck with me. I had the tape; I was in control of the situation. My instructions were clear. The letter. He couldn't just ignore this. It wasn't going to go away. I had him by the balls and he had to deal with it. He had to. The arrogance of this cocky fuck—I couldn't believe it. Like I was some prick of a client he could keep on hold while he plays golf or gets finger-fucked or whatever else the cunt does in his spare time.

I needed to calm myself, so I had another drink and considered my options. There was only really one. Dominic. We'd been at Ampleforth together and had kept in touch since. Dom had taken up journalism and was working as a news sub-editor at the *Sunday* where his dad had worked. I'd sell the tape to them. It wouldn't fetch quite the same price, but what else could I do? If this cunt thought he could ignore me, he could think again. He'd been warned. It was all in the letter.

I phoned Dom from the pub and set up the meeting, a drink after work at the Prospect of Whitby in Shadwell, near the *Sunday*'s offices. I got there at around 6:30 and he introduced me to his workmate.

"Jon, this is Stuart," Dom said. "He's up for the Young Journalist of the Year award next month."

Really? Looks like a cunt to me.

"Nice to meet you, Stuart," I said. He looked in his late twenties. Had a shaved head and wore a black suit with a dark shirt, no tie. And his handshake was too firm.

"I've brought Stu along cos this is more his kinda thing," Dom explained. "I'm more on the editing side of things, not really a reporter, but Stu here—"

Is a cunt. "Brilliant," I interrupted, keen to get things moving. "Can I get you guys a drink?"

They both wanted lagers.

When I got back from the bar I launched straight into it. "So, what do you know about Nicholas Monroe, the QC?" I threw the question firmly at Young Cunt of the Year.

"Monroe, yeah, mate, what about him?" Shave-head said, picking up his pint for a gulp.

"Well, what if I were to tell you I have a video of him getting finger-fucked by a £60 whore in Shepherd Market?"

He put his pint down. "What—have you?"

"How much would the *Sunday* pay for it?" I asked.

"Have you got it with you?"

I played them the tape. A minute in and I could tell he was impressed—with the tape and with me. Once he'd seen Monroe's face on the vid, he shot me a look that said: *Okay, cunt—I can do business with you.* When it was over I pressed STOP and put the camera back in my overcoat pocket. Stu spoke first.

"It's good but we'd need the girl," he said bluntly.

"The girl? Why? It's all there . . ." I looked at Dom for some backup. It didn't come.

"It's all there, yeah, yeah," Stu said, "but it's more complicated than that. He's a very powerful guy, old Monroe. He knows half the fucking cabinet. Probably worked with them when they were still practicing."

"Stu's tried to do pieces on Monroe before, Jon," Dom chipped in.

"Yeah, but they always get spiked," the cunt continued. "He knows everyone. His old flatmate from law school is tipped to be the next DG of the Beeb." He took another gulp and held my gaze. *My move.*

"But he couldn't sue you when you've got him there on tape, clear as day," I said.

"Look, the guy likes to take chances, likes to think he's a

bit dangerous. But he's smart, he's fucking smart, covers his tracks. As I say, friends in high places. He's supposed to be on the Queen's birthday list for a knighthood."

"So what? He's untouchable?" I said. I could feel it slipping away.

"Mate, I'm not saying it's impossible. But I know Neil and he's going to be very wary of this."

"Neil's our editor, Jon," Dom said.

"And he wouldn't even consider it without the girl," Stu continued. "We'd need her, on the spread, telling her story—and prepared to testify, if necessary."

"I see. But how much— What's the story worth if I get her?"

"That's not really my call. Dunno, probably five figures though," he said.

Five figures, that's at least ten grand. It was still good, I thought. I downed my G&T, then made my excuses and left, as the tabloids say. Cabbed it to Shepherd Market, up the wooden hill, and pressed *Press*.

Rita answered the door. But this time there was no cheery hello. She would only keep the door ajar, wouldn't let me in. She just said: "Vanya's gone. She won't be back. You're not to be let in." And then the door.

What the fuck?

"What do you mean *gone*?" I said through the door. "Rita? Gone where? Rita?"

"Go on, hop it now or I'll have to call him," she said.

She meant Davor, the guy who owned the place.

I walked slowly back down the stairs, trying to make sense of what just happened. I'd never seen Rita look stern before. It was odd. And to threaten me with Davor or one of his thugs . . .

I went home and spliffed myself to sleep. Woke up in my clothes around noon the next day and started getting ready. The camcorder was still in the pocket of my overcoat. I put it on and left the flat to find a pay phone. Dialed the number.

"Put me through to Nicholas Monroe," I said.

"Mr. Monroe is in a meeting with a client at the moment, he can't—"

"It's urgent. He's expecting me to call."

"Sir, Mr. Monroe hasn't mentioned a—"

"Just tell him it's John X. It's extremely urgent."

The line went quiet, that electric nothingness you get when you're in phone-line limbo. Then a man's voice.

"Ahhh, Mr. X . . ."

He sounded relaxed, jovial even.

"This is your last chance, Monroe," I said. "I've been to the *Sunday* and they are very interested in the tape. They're prepared to run the story . . ."

"The *Sunday?* I see."

What the fuck is it with this twat? I was talking, you rude cunt.

"So the situation we find ourselves in, Mr. X," he said, each word measured, calm, "is that you have a firm financial offer from the *Sunday* newspaper and you're wondering whether I'm prepared to beat that offer. Am I correct?"

"Yes."

"Good. And may I ask how much their offer is?"

Five figures, Shavey had said. "Ten grand."

I regretted the words as soon as I said them. He would have expected me to come up with a figure twice what I was being offered. And why did I tell him which paper it was? I was fucking this up, I knew it. He was too calm and I couldn't deal with it. It wasn't what I was expecting.

"Mmm," Monroe said. "I can probably lay my hands on five thousand by this afternoon—will that do you?"

I suppose it'll fucking have to. Five grand. It was an insult. But I didn't really have a choice.

"Six o'clock in the Printers Devil on Fetter Lane—and don't be late." I put the receiver down.

I killed the rest of the afternoon in my local, trying to drink away what had happened, and left at 5 to meet Monroe. The platform at Kentish Town was fairly full when I got there—trouble on the Northern Line, as usual—but it was completely rammed by the time the train finally arrived. I fought my way onto the tube, southbound for Tottenham Court Road where I'd change for the Central Line and Chancery Lane. I managed to defend my own little corner by the doors as far as Camden Town, where about a billion people squeezed on and I was thrust into the middle, both hands holding onto the bar above to keep balance. I rarely got the tube, but even I knew that this was worse than normal. Pensioners, office workers, hood rats, tourists—almost every type of low-life London scum was pressed right up against me.

I felt the first risings of a panic attack coming on but pushed it away with a happy thought. I closed my eyes and relived my New Year's Eve performance, then Monroe, the tape and the letter, the money, the next job, the memoir . . . then what? . . . Monroe not turning up, the shavey-head cunt trying to make me look stupid, getting turned away by Rita . . . Davor . . . and then Monroe laughing at me on the phone, the arrogant fuck. How dare the cunt? Me with video proof of this fucker—this QC, no less, who knows the Cabinet, is in line for a knighthood—getting finger-fucked up the arse in his stockinged feet by a whore he's probably managed to have chased out of the country, and all I can get for it is a stinking £5,000, if the cunt shows up at all? He just didn't seem to give a fuck. It was a minor detail in another week's work. Hadn't he grasped the situation? I was in charge here—I was the blackmailer—I had the power.

I opened my eyes. Tottenham Court Road—needed to get off and change. I slowly pushed my way through the pensioners and hood rats, still gripping the bars for balance, and made it to the open doors, squeezing myself out of the carriage just in time before they shut behind me and the train moved off, leaving two dozen or so pissed off commuters to wait for the next one. A moment of *schadenfreude* consolation for me. I started moving toward the *Way Out* sign, patted my coat pocket for the camera. Nothing there. I checked the other outside pocket, then the lining one, panic surging through my body, then my trouser pockets, and back to the pocket where I knew I'd put it. Empty. Gone. I started running after the train as it moved along the platform, swearing, screaming at it as it disappeared down the tunnel. I covered my face with my hands.

"You all right, mate?" a voice said.

I let my hands drop to my sides and opened my eyes. It was a station guard.

"No. I've been pickpocketed."

That was six months ago now. I've never been back to the flat in Shepherd Market. But I did go to the Printers Devil—that same day, in fact. I don't know why exactly. Just to see Monroe there, I suppose. See without being seen. Thought I might be able to come up with another plan there and then. I waited till 7. He didn't turn up.

I got a text message from Dominic the next day, Friday,

saying sorry but they couldn't go ahead with the story, girl or no girl. He didn't say why.

I've been doing more gigs since then. My agency has got me a cruise thing lined up, starts in July, next month.

The funny thing was, though, a few weeks after it all happened I was looking on the web for porn when something caught my eye—a video clip. The description said: *Sexy brunette finger-fucks old guy up the ass—in his socks—funny.* I downloaded it, sent it out on a group e-mail—to the Law Society, three Cabinet MPs, and the Lord Chancellor's office. No text, just *Nicholas Monroe, QC* in the subject field.

Monroe didn't make it onto the Queen's birthday honors this year. He must be very disappointed.

I HATE HIS FINGERS

BY SYLVIE SIMMONS

Kentish Town

That's what she said. "I hate his fingers." I tugged open the freezer door—iced up, as usual; who the fuck ever had time to defrost a freezer?—and when I managed to pull the box out, it too was encased in solid ice. I stabbed at it a few times with the bread knife—more because it felt good than for any effectiveness it was having—then threw it into the microwave and put it on defrost. I opened a bottle and poured a large glass.

"You're supposed to let wine breathe."

I lit a Dunhill—only ten so far today, not bad.

"And you might consider letting me breathe as well," Dino coughed. He sounded like an old, gay Jack Russell with emphysema.

"Nice try," I said, "but I never did get the knack of emotional blackmail."

"Shame, or Kate might still be here and we might have something decent to eat."

"Fuck you," I smiled.

"In your dreams. A dangerous line to use on a Freudian," Dino giggled like a girl. "So, this patient of yours, I take it you thought of asking whose fingers and what she had against them?"

"I told you, that's all she said."

"*I hate his fingers?* For fifty minutes?"

"Apart from the forty spent saying nothing at all and the two spent telling me she was only here because her GP told her she was getting no more temazepam until she took some sessions with the practice shrink."

"Who's her GP? Philip?"

"Yeah. His letter said his best guess was OCD—obsessive-compulsive disorder—but it could be a weird phobia. He said he knew what a hard-on I got from those." Since I moved out of general practice into psychiatry—long story, and one I'd prefer not to go into here—I'd made a name, if I say so myself, with my papers on unusual phobias.

"Hating being touched is not unusual. Having your hand up my arse gives me the heebie-jeebies and I'm a hardened pro."

I chose to ignore him. "Yeah, haphephobia's pretty commonplace, but if it's fingers, *per se*—well, dactylophobia's a new one on me. But I don't know, from the look of her she might well have some kind of body dysmorphic disorder. She looked borderline anorexic. Like she weighed all of seven stone."

She was the kind of girl who leaves no footprints when she comes into a room, but makes a big impression, you know what I mean? She was small and delicate, looked about sixteen years old. Wore one of those little girl dresses, bare legs, short-sleeved cardigan. And big Bambi eyes, like one of those little urchin paintings the tabloids always say are cursed. Burn your house down the second you go out. Maybe they're right. Her medical records said she was thirty-five and married.

"Would it help if I sat in on a session?" Now and again I'd take Dino along—mostly when I was treating children. They seemed to relax around him. Opened up more. The microwave dinged. The cardboard box was wet and steaming. Smelled disgusting. I tore it off and put the plastic tray back in the oven. Dino was right about the food.

"I don't know," I said. "I'll see."

"I'll tell you what I see: a lump in your trousers." Damn if the little fucker wasn't right again. "Takes wood to know wood. And what I know I see is a man who wants this little girl all to himself."

When Dino got excited his voice became unbearably camp. Now he was chanting in a high, sour voice, "Doc has got a stiffie, Doc has got a stiffie."

"Right, that's it." I strode across the kitchen and put my hand around his throat, lifting him clean out of the chair. I carried him like that into the living room, and hurled him against the wall. Legs splayed, bow tie skewed, his jaw hinged open like a snake getting ready to swallow a rabbit, the dummy lay propped up against the TV set, staring at space.

For the first half hour of the second session she didn't say a word. Just chewed the hangnail at the side of her thumb and looked up and sideways at me through her eyelashes. That little-girl-lost look. It was like she was waiting for me to tell her what to do. I found myself reaching across the desk to comfort her, make it all right. Fortunately I stopped myself in time; that was all I needed, another incident. If it wasn't for my old friends at the practice—or more to the point, if it wasn't for what I had on my old friends at the practice—I would have been out on the street. Which is where Kate and her fucking lawyer wanted me. At the last minute, I pretended to swat an imaginary bug off the Kleenex box on her side of the desk.

Since she wouldn't talk, I did. I told her not to worry.

That she'd come to the right place. Phobias, I said, like American T-shirts, came in all different colors but just one size, extra-large. There's no such thing as being a little bit phobic. It's like being pregnant, you either are or you aren't. As I said that, in reflex, her knees pressed together tight. They were pink and rosy, like a little girl left out in the playground too long, but there was nothing at all childlike about the rest of those legs. They ended in a pair of expensive, black, strappy stilettos, with a half-moon cut out of the end of each one where her red lacquered toenails peeped through.

I found myself, and I don't know why, talking about myself, telling her about my automatonophobia. Fear of ventriloquist dummies. When she didn't seem that impressed, I admitted that it wasn't, of course, as socially debilitating as being finger phobic, since you're likely to run into more fingers on a daily basis than ventriloquist dummies. But the effects, I said—the panic, the terror, that black-ice, deep-gut nausea—they were exactly the same. A few years ago, I told her, I was in the Oxfam shop buying coffee when I saw an old wooden dummy staring down at me from the shelf behind the till. In the past I would have frozen in fear. But I was so over my phobia that I bought it and took it home. Since then we'd become something of a double act, at least in medical circles, me and Dino. Kate of course would have put it differently, but Kate wasn't here. Kate was fucking her lawyer, when she was colder to me than a Marks & Spencer microfuckingwave meal.

I assured her that she too could feel the same way about fingers.

"It's not all fingers I hate," she said. "Just my husband's."

Her husband's? We were getting somewhere. If I'd only

known where, I'd have run straight out of that door, down to Kentish Town station, and jumped on the first train going anywhere else.

My other half is a bitch. Did I tell you that? I'm sorry. I've been obsessing a lot lately, going over and over the notes. These are from our third session—the one where I looked across the desk at her and fell uselessly, impossibly, in love. It was raining like a dog that day. A typical black, filthy London day, I remember. Sunny when I left home at 7.30, though, or I would have taken the car. But I walked down the street and into a climate change. You'd think I'd be used to that trick by now, wouldn't you? The one God plays on the English almost every single fucking day: an hour of sun first thing in the morning to wake you up and get you off to work, then pissing on you mightily. I'm a slow learner, I guess.

It's a short walk to the surgery but not a pretty one. It gets uglier still the closer you get to Kentish Town Road. Shabby, shapeless old buildings, oddly bent, like they're about to collapse, though no one seems to notice or care. And those garish shop signs. The whole street looks like an old tart with osteoporosis. London's full of shabby old buildings, but you can look at them and see that once in their lives they looked grand. On Kentish Town Road, they look like they were built to look that shabby. And the people on the street have grown to look just like the buildings, the way people start to look like their dogs. It's no wonder half of Camden is on SSRIs; the other half are just too fucking depressed to go and fill their prescriptions.

It was still raining hard when she arrived at 3 that afternoon. Her bare legs were so badly splashed by passing cars they looked like Rorschach tests. Her short skirt was soaked right through. It stuck to her so tight you could see she wore no underwear. When she sat down, she tried pulling the thin fabric over her thighs, but realized it was hopeless. She covered her lap with her bag and gave me the sweetest, saddest smile. Then she furrowed her brow. I didn't have to say a word. She started talking right away.

"Doc," she said, "I'm telling you this because I think you're the only person who would understand. I feel like a stranger in my own life."

I'd heard this before, of course, or a thousand different variations, but coming from her, it shot through me like electricity. She told me she'd been married for eight years—I felt another stab, jealousy, envy, loss?—to, well, let's just say a famous rock musician. Or as famous as bass players are likely to get. Bass players are the overlooked band members. I've had a few of them sitting in that same seat in the past, trying to deal with not getting enough attention, not getting enough love. With nothing ever being quite big enough.

"Have you ever looked at a bass player's hands?" she asked. I couldn't say I had. She was looking at my hands now, so intimately it felt like a touch. "You have elegant fingers. Artistic. I'm sure a lot of people have told you that. Bass players' fingers are repulsive. They don't have joints like regular fingers. They bend at the knuckle and that's it. When they play the bass they just kind of throw themselves at the strings and bounce off—*thwack*. Like pork sausages on a grill. Like pigs throwing themselves at an electric fence." She illustrated it with an air–bass guitar solo. It made me smile, which made her frown again. "I hate his fingers," she said.

The rest of him, apparently, was all right. He was ten years older than she was, but that wasn't a problem. He had money and was happy to let her spend it. He spent most of his time in the studio he had near King's Cross. Their sex life had always been good, though it had tapered off in the past six months. She thought the reason for that was her bringing up the idea of children, but really she didn't care either way. Kate didn't want children—my children anyway. Though I got hold of her medical notes through one of my contacts and, what do you know, she's four months gone. Did she and her thieving-cunt lawyer think I was dumb enough to just sign it all over to them? She said the only reason she'd mentioned babies was because for a while she thought she might be pregnant. She would throw up every morning, usually when he tried to touch her. It had got to the point where all she could think of were the pigs. His fingers even smelled porky. They revolted her, to the point where she could barely eat . . . nor sleep, worrying about the morning coming and the fingers. That's why she needed the temazepam. It wasn't so bad if she took a couple of those.

The desk clock chimed. I couldn't believe fifty minutes had gone so fast. I didn't want to send her out into the rain and ugliness of Kentish Town. I wanted to make things all right for her. Somehow it felt like this was my one last chance to make things right for anybody—me in particular. That night I told Dino I felt there was a voice that wasn't mine inside me that kept on saying, *Drop it. Send her back to her GP. Give her the number of the divorce lawyer. It's not too late. Stop now.* I expected Dino to say something sarcastic about how he knew he had a voice inside him that wasn't his. But he felt how serious I was and didn't say a word.

I'll tell you what it was like. Like I'd dreamed about this so often that I wasn't sure what to make of the reality. One thing's for certain, it wasn't so real. Surreal, certainly, especially after our fifth session—but I'm getting ahead of myself.

It was session four when she came in, picked up her chair, and carried it around to my side of the desk. She sat down next to me, close enough that the smell of her shoulder made me light-headed. She opened up a large school satchel and said, "I've got something I want you to see."

It was a folder containing several sheets of A4 paper. Pictures printed from a computer. The first was a photograph of her husband. She looked at me expectantly, seeing if I recognized him. I didn't. Like I said, he was a bass player. Good-looking though. Tall, thin, angular, unkempt in a studied sort of way. A lot of hair for a man in his mid-forties. Very English face, upper-class; it had that distracted, vaguely inbred look. He stood by the front door of a house—theirs, I imagine— with his hands in his pockets, smiling. In the second picture he was onstage. The third was the same photograph zoomed in on his fingers, playing the bass guitar. She was right. They were ugly. Thick, pink, and rigid, like a glove-puppet's. The last picture was the most disturbing. It was another close-up, but this time so close-up and so fuzzy as to be almost impossible to make it out. It appeared to be his fingers, or the bottom half of them anyway. The top half had disappeared into something white and mottled like cottage cheese and at the same time dark and fleshy like meat.

"He's cheating," she said, and then she started to cry, loudly, like someone was gutting her. So loudly one of the practice nurses came in and put an arm around her. For the rest of the session I sat there helplessly, watching her sob. When I got home, Dino asked me if I'd seen the package under the front doormat. I hadn't, though I must have stepped on it coming in. It was an envelope, which I opened right up. Inside was a DVD. I poured a glass of wine while my laptop booted up. We spent the whole night, me and Dino, watching that DVD over and over on the computer screen. And again, not a single word of sarcasm. Not even about the cigarettes.

She turned up for session five in a pair of black jeans and an oversized Red Hot Chili Peppers T-shirt—mine, I recognized the bloodstain on the front, but that's another story. This one's about fingers. It was funny how boyish she looked. Beautiful though. Especially when she blushed, which she did when I told her that Dino had watched the DVD with me. Dino sat in this time. She told me she wanted to meet him. I asked her if it was shot in her husband's studio. She said she supposed so but she'd never been inside. If he wasn't on the road or with the band, he went there at 2 every afternoon, returning home at 8. He told her he was working on a "solo project" and didn't want to be disturbed.

In the film, the place had the look of a well-appointed office. A wood-paneled front room was hung with gold and platinum albums. There was a large, leather-top desk, an upright bass, three or four electric bass guitars on stands. A trestle table, almost as wide as the room, was packed with an assortment of computer and recording equipment. There must have been webcams everywhere, since you could pretty much see every corner. He selected one of the electric basses, and with that in one hand and a carrier bag in the other, he walked along a corridor that led to another room at the end.

This room was even larger. Most of the space was taken up by an enormous mattress stacked on two, maybe three divans. It was very high for a bed. Lying on top was an old woman. She must have been seventy years old if she was a day. It takes more than sixty-nine years to get that ugly. She was stark naked. And the fattest woman I had ever seen in my life.

He put the carrier bag on the bed and sat beside her. Out of the bag he took a cardboard box which was stuffed with cakes, the sort they sell in cheap bakeries, yellow sponge, bright pink icing. Tenderly he slotted a whole cake into her mouth. As soon as she finished one, he fed her another, until the box was empty. Every time a piece fell from her lips he would guide it back in with one of those broad fingers. When she was all done, he kissed her mouth, which was puffy and purple, hemorrhoidal. Then he tried moving her—with difficulty, but not unkindly—to the foot of the bed. One hundred and ninety kilos of human being, shifted centimeter by centimeter. He got her upright somehow and propped her against a mountain of cushions. She looked like a melting Buddha blancmange. He kissed her face, her breasts—the folds on her body made every part of her look like breasts—then eased her thighs apart. He aimed a remote control at the doorway. Recording equipment clicked on. Facing a camera, he began to speak. I was wrong about him being upper-class English, he was American.

"The music of the spheres. We've all heard that expression. Some of us—the true artists—have spent our lives trying to capture the mysterious, terrifying beauty of that siren sound, only to be dashed on the rocks. It was the scientists that discovered its source. It's the sound waves made when a black hole sucks in and swallows a star." At these words the old woman licked her lips and grinned. He thrust his right hand between her legs.

"There is no gain without pain. Nothing survives the black hole other than this hum, which is the deepest note ever recorded—a B-flat, oscillating to a B, but six hundred octaves deeper than anything my bass guitar can play." He pulled his hand out abruptly, grabbed his guitar, and started to play, wet fingers slapping the thick strings. The look on his face was ecstatic.

So. Her husband was a feeder. And a gerontophile. Married to a tiny woman who looked like a child, and whose face, on our sixth and last session, I had touched with my own finger, tracing the thin bones and the delicate chin, down her neck and across her beautifully corrugated sternum, all the while whispering that I was going to help her. The question, as I asked Dino when we got in the car was, who was going to help me?

"A *bass* solo? And that sniffing business? Yee-uk! This *dude*," Dino stretched the word out to a good six seconds long, "doesn't make snuff films. He makes *sniff* films. Snuffing them would have been kinder than a bass solo." Dino's eyes swung wildly from side to side. "What is *wrong* with Americans? Do you remember that couple Kate brought here for dinner who said they didn't think the statue on Nelson's column looked much like Nelson Mandela at all? And that *creature*—when he has a *princess* at home. It's Charles and Camilla, all over again." He rolled his eyes back in his head.

"You'd need far more sessions with a shrink than you'll get on the NHS to figure that out," I replied. "What was it Clint Eastwood said in *Unforgiven?* It's got nothing to do with deserves. It's all about betrayal and double-cross—my work, my life, her husband, my wife . . ." Maybe she'll betray me too. Burn the whole house down like one of those big-eyed urchin paintings until there's nothing left but a pile of ash. But if I wasn't going to get as iced up as that freezer, right now I needed that flame. Which is why, instead of heading home after my last appointment, Dino and I were in my car, inching along Leighton Road. I parked on Lady Margaret, picked up Dino and my briefcase, and walked around the corner to the tube. By the station, as always, there was a clutter of winos perched on the benches under the glass-and-iron canopy. It always struck me that there was something the-atrical about this spot. Like it was some kind of project Camden Council had for out-of-work actors. Putting those insane uplighters in the pavement to illuminate the puddles of puke and piss only added to the effect.

As I approached, one of the men looked up. "I'm working hard," he said, "although I appear to have the air of a holiday-maker." He patted the space on the bench beside him. "Take a load off, doc. How's it going?" I recognized him. Back in the day when I worked as a GP around the corner, he had been one of my patients. I sat down and took out the cropped headshot I'd printed from the DVD. A man at the next bench with a can of Special Brew came over and eyed me suspiciously.

"Are you a cop?"

My old patient cut in with, "How many cops have you seen with a ventriloquist's dummy? I know him, he's all right," he said, and the man with the Special Brew came over.

"I know her too." He pointed at the picture. "It's Fat Mary."

"Oh, my love," his companion laughed. "That it is, and in the prime of health. And I thought she was dead. She's not dead, is she?"

Mary, he told me, used to work King's Cross; she had a handful of regulars who'd come to her for years. The cops left her alone mostly, but then they brought in all those commu-nity officers who shifted the girls along York Way up to the park by the astroturf football pitch. Her clients stopped com-ing and the younger girls gave her a rough time. Around a year ago she disappeared. Which must have been when the bass player took her in. They told me they had no clue where she was, but I already had an idea. I picked up Dino and headed for the car.

It was easy. Surprisingly easy. All you need is a computer and the medical profession behind you. The hardest part was changing the appointments; patients, psychiatric ones particularly, don't like change. My secretary put a few of them off and crammed the real crazies into the mornings. That way I had the afternoons to myself. I didn't spend the whole of that time with her, even though her husband was at his studio and we could work on her problems at her place, undisturbed. Like I said, I had other things to do, people to track down, plans to make. I'd lost contact with David and Malcolm many years ago, but here we all were, e-mailing each other like old friends.

I'd worked with both of them closely, way back when. It was before I started specializing in phobics. My interest back then was fetishists. David was an accountant. He was also my first feeder. Jailed for locking up and fattening up an under-age girl from Poland who had answered his ad for an au pair. He said she lied to him about her age and, already on the chubby side, she looked much older than she was. He believed that she was happy with the setup. Maybe she was. It was clear he worshipped her; he waited on her hand and foot. When they sent me to see him, all he did was ask if I would look out for her and make sure she was all right. At some point after his release, when the Internet started to catch on, he set up a site for fellow fat-admirers; it might even have been the first in the UK.

He knew about Fat Mary—her picture had been posted

in a number of places. Feeders took pride in their work, and there was a lot of Mary to be proud of. Most of the feeders were possessive of their gainers, but not the bass player. According to David, Mary had asked the bass player to let her bring customers in once in a while so she could make some money of her own. She said she didn't want to spend his; the bass player apparently found that amusing. So he lent her out to some of the FA network; probably filmed them too. David told me to give him a week and he'd come up with an address and a key. He did. I left a message with the secretary to book me two days leave.

It's only polite to take a gift when you visit a woman. I took four. I hadn't realized I would be so spoiled for choice in Kentish Town. Since she came along, I had been taking more interest in my immediate environment than I had in years, if ever. I'd even defrosted the fridge. Though I hate to say it, and it's still no excuse, there might have been something in Kate's accusation about my work taking over everything. I bought flowers, of course, then I crossed the road to the bakery and bought her some of those cakes. I swung back over to Poundstretcher, which Lord knows how but I'd never noticed before, and came out of the place with two huge jars of chocolates and, while I was at it, a child's silver shell suit for Dino. The tux definitely need a trip to the dry cleaner's.

On the way back home I made another find. A couple of blocks past the station there was a weird old ladies' underwear shop—you'll know it if you've ever seen it. It's like the place that time forgot. The main feature of its window display is an absolutely colossal pair of knickers, almost as big as the window itself. Too small for Mary, though. Still, things might change.

When rush hour was over I picked up Dino and got in the car. I knew precisely when the bass player would be leaving. Sitting outside on a yellow line, I pretended to examine the *A-Z* when I saw him come out the door. He walked a few paces to the residential parking bay, aiming a device on his keychain at a gleaming Range Rover. It chirped and he stepped in. I waited another ten minutes after he'd driven off before I got out and walked up the front steps.

Apart from the cars, the street was empty, or as empty as any Central London street can be. I tried the first key in the lock, then the second. Neither seemed to fit. I dropped them, cursing, just as someone walked out of the building next door. He did not so much as look in my direction. When I picked them up and tried again, it worked.

The front door opened into what appeared to be a storage space. Other doors, all unlocked, opened onto rooms crammed with boxes and packing crates. On the left there was a fairly narrow staircase. There must have been a lot less of Mary when she first came here. I climbed the stairs until they stopped at a locked door at the top. The second key opened it without trouble and I stepped inside.

I knew this room so well from watching that DVD over and over. It was as preternaturally clean and tidy as it appeared in the footage. Not so much as a finger smudge on the paneled walls. I spotted the webcams and wondered if they were filming me. I must have considered, subconsciously at least, the possibility, since I knew I was looking pretty good. Kate didn't know what she'd thrown away.

And there was the corridor. I walked along it. I noticed another door off to the side that I didn't remember from the film. I opened it: a large bathroom, also spotless. The mirrors that covered every wall looked like they'd been rubbed harder and more often than a teenager's dick. I walked on to the end of the corridor and pushed open the door.

"Hello, doc," she said. "You got a little something for me?"

I opened my bag.

I didn't feel like going home. Malcolm wouldn't be here until morning, but I just wanted to sit awhile, take a load off. My shoes were hurting me so I kicked them off. We left her lying there, she looked so peaceful, and went back into the other room. When I passed by the upright bass I felt a compulsion to give the strings a twang, but I resisted. There was a chair by the window, and we sat there, me and Dino, just listening to the traffic go by. Did I tell you about Malcolm? My memory's been getting fuzzy lately. Maybe it's the temazepam.

Malcolm was a surgeon, another of my patients from the old days. An acrotomophiliac. Though Dino used to argue with me that he was actually an apotemnophiliac by proxy, didn't you, Dino? Either way, Malcolm took a keener than usual interest in amputation and amputees in and out of the hospital. Like I said, I know things about people; it's interesting work. Malcolm is still a surgeon, but it's all private practice now. Gets paid a fortune. His patients love his work. Mary's going to love it too. And the bass player—why can't I remember his name, I'm sure she told me. He's going to look so much better without those fingers. Mary first in the morning, and then the bass player's appointment at 2. Shame I didn't think of asking Kate to come along, there's plenty of time. Maybe I should call her. What do you think, Dino? Shall I call Kate? Tell her I've signed the papers and she can come by and pick them up? Tell her I don't need her. That I don't need anyone anymore? What do you say, Dino?

Dino's awfully quiet tonight.

PARK RITES

BY DAN BENNETT

Clissold Park

The black-haired lady jogger beat her way around the concrete path that circled the western edge of Clissold Park, passing the brick shed near the entrance. Enzo watched her come. He stood in his place by the bushes where the path forked up toward the pond. He'd known she'd be here: it was 4 p.m. and she was always here. The lady jogger had her routines.

She ran toward him, the way she always ran, with her elbows pushed out wide, her head bent to the ground, so she couldn't see anyone in front of her. She ran like she was the only one in the world. Once, Enzo had seen her jog right into a woman with a pushchair. She'd fallen, sprawling on the tarmac. Enzo had walked past as she staggered to her feet, a tear in her leggings showing a large gash. She had touched it gently, wincing, while the woman with the pushchair had asked her if she was okay. Enzo had forced himself to keep on walking, his head down, his hand steady in his pocket. But he was unable to resist one quick glance, thinking, "Yeah, and one day, lady, *I'll* be there."

The jogger made her way onto a stretch of path opposite the estate. She was very close now. Enzo breathed in and smelled the air. He was waiting for a sign that things were ready, that the time was right. The sky was a pale gray above the green of the trees, the air smoky from a fire on the other side of the park, the ground reeking of wet earth. A triangular pattern of geese crossed the sky, and suddenly Enzo knew that this was the final piece that defined the moment: the sign that the time was right. The lady jogger reached the straight track that led right down toward him. Enzo's left hand worked inside the torn pocket of his tracksuit, his hand squeezing his prick. It was time.

Enzo stepped from the bushes as the jogger approached. He felt very calm. He gave himself one more grasp and then removed his left hand, and placed his right into the pocket of his hooded top. The jogger was almost on top of him now, and Enzo could see the words on her blue T-shirt, *University of Kent*, stretched over her small breasts, the black lycra tight on her legs, her huge white trainers with fat tongues. She was such a *small* woman, she was perfect for him, with her black hair in long bangs that flapped as she ran, like the limp beat of blackbird wings.

Enzo tensed, his right arm ready. Suddenly, on the road beyond the railings, a car pulled up, a blue Ford. Enzo looked up to see a man step from the passenger door, saying loudly, "Yeah, well, maybe later, but I'm not sure about it," to whoever was driving the car. He was wearing a football shirt, red and white. It was all too much for Enzo: he glanced quickly at the woman jogger, thinking maybe, maybe, when the man beyond the railings turned and looked over and stared Enzo fully in the face.

It caused the slightest delay in Enzo's movement. It was enough to spoil everything (the birds had gone from his eyeline now and the lady jogger was just a few steps too close) and make the moment lose its rhythm. Enzo let his hand drop from his right pocket. He looked down at the ground, kicked at a stone, sucked his lips against his teeth. The jogger pounded past him, the soles of her trainers squeaking slightly as she took the turn up toward the pond. The man slammed the passenger door shut and stood waving as the car pulled away. The moment had sailed away from Enzo, and it was exactly like that.

"Yeah, but I seen you!" Enzo called out to the jogger's back. "I seen you running, lady. I'll catch you maybe on the next time round."

The jogger didn't hear him. Enzo watched her run up the slight hill that led toward the pond and the white house at the center of the park. He wondered if today was one of the days she'd decide to run another circuit, or if she would leave by the entrance on Church Street, making her way back through Stoke Newington, through the cemetery. It didn't matter to him anyway. It was spoiled. He put his hand back into his left pocket and squeezed himself a couple more times, his prick sore and hard and hot. But he didn't let himself finish, although he was so close now, he was ready. To finish now would spoil things even more. That wouldn't be right. Instead, he set out walking up the path the jogger was running along, although he wasn't following her now. Instead, he headed over to see the deer.

On the grass by the side of the path, a group of boys were playing football, imitating the game that was going on right now in Highbury Stadium over on the other side of Blackstock Road. Enzo recognized a few of the kids on the football pitch, a couple from school, a couple from his estate. Almost all of them were wearing the red-and-white shirts. Sometimes on match days like this when Arsenal scored, you could hear the crowd screaming in unison, like a choir. It haunted you, but could thrill you too: make you want to be the one to make the crowd scream. It was what all the boys on the park were imitating, and in his way, it was what Enzo was working toward himself. As he walked in the direction of the deer enclosure, the ball squirmed from the playing field and rolled across the path in front of him, but no one shouted for him to kick it back. Enzo let the ball roll into the gully by the side of the path.

Enzo hadn't been back to school since some black kid, some tall Somali, had called him a freak at break, and who knows what *he* had been trying to prove? Enzo had stewed on it for the rest of the day. They met up at the gates after school, and when the Somali kid came toward him, Enzo had sliced a split Coke can across the kid's eyeball, judging it just right. The kid had dropped onto his knees, no time to say anything, not even enough time to put a hand to his eye. He squatted on all fours, staring down at the ground. He couldn't stop himself from blinking and his eyeball parted with a slice that grew wider every time his eyelid flicked over it, yawning into wet blackness. This disappointed Enzo. He'd hoped it would bleed more.

Not much school for Enzo after that run-in: not many calls of freak either. No calls at all. Enzo spent a lot of time alone. He spent most of it in the park, because it was better than being at home. Back there, Ma stayed in the kitchen, Dad on the living room sofa, the Virgin beaming down at everyone from the picture above the TV, Jesus wherever you wanted to go looking for him. That was life back in the flat. But sometimes Ma and Dad didn't stay in separate rooms, and for whatever reason, it was a bit more violent. That was home.

The park was a mess this afternoon. During the week, London had suffered under record storms, blowing the TV aerials and skylight covers from the roof of Enzo's estate, and shredding the heads of the trees. The grass all around was covered with small branches and twigs, as well as rubbish from the bins. Those storms had made Enzo feel crazy; he'd been able to feel them in his prick, like a pulse. He'd come three times that night the winds had shrieked at his window, telling himself no, no, no, have to save it for the park, have to look out for the lady jogger with the black hair. He'd been unable to hold himself back. And all he saw when he was touching himself were the fangs of a wolf piercing raw red meat, blood on white fur, on teeth.

It didn't take him long to walk around to the deer enclosure, but when he reached it, he found a father and son standing by the rails. A deer stood close by on the other side. The little boy was offering the deer a handful of grass, the father bent low over him, the shape of him spooned around the little boy. Enzo gave the father a look that said, *Yeah, and don't think I don't know what* you'll *be doing when you get the chance.* The man must have seen the way Enzo was staring, and he must have known that Enzo knew, because, you know, Enzo had that power too, he had all kinds of power. Eventually, the man got the message and gathered the little boy up in his arms. "Come on, let's go," he said. "Let's go and find Mum."

When he heard there were animals in the park, Enzo had been disappointed to find only deer and goats. He wanted wolves. When he was a kid, Ma and Dad had taken him to the zoo. This was not long—a few months—after *that* day. Enzo had seen the wolves at feeding time. He'd watched as they gnawed on raw meat, the blood flicking over the white fur and teeth, and suddenly it all made sense to him. Enzo understood. That night, Enzo pulled himself raw thinking about the wolves. He pulled himself raw, even before anything could happen, thinking of white teeth plunged into red flesh, blood splashed on fur. He pulled himself raw until one night the sperm came, and then he knew he was ready. He rubbed it over his fingers, gummy and warm. Finally he was close. He'd been waiting for years.

Now Enzo was finally alone. He squeezed himself a couple of times before he pulled his left hand away, and again he pushed his right hand into the pocket of his hooded top. He moved close to the fence. The deer raised its head for a moment, surveying him with a large, bland steady eye, a black ball. If the light changes, Enzo said to himself, I will be in that eye. It will shine and I will be inside the deer. He breathed deeply, quivering as he exhaled. The deer bent its head and nibbled at a patch of grass by the fence. Enzo pulled his right hand from his pocket and flashed it into the flank of the deer, two, three, four times, the knife sliding in like a dream, the metal not catching the light at all. The blood burst from the fur, over the blade, and it was all Enzo could do to hold himself back and not finish right there. The deer brayed and kicked up its back legs, bucked away from the fence, and ran over to the rest of the herd, the wound leaking into the gray fur on its side. If I could just go *there*, Enzo thought, if I could just finish in there it would end everything, I know it. He stayed, despite himself, despite everything he had to get busy with, he stayed staring at that hole in the flank of the deer until it trotted behind a fallen log and disappeared from his sight.

Enzo started walking away from the enclosure quickly, and once he was far enough away, he broke into a run. He headed across the concrete in front of the bandstand, skater punks practicing moves, kids spinning around on bikes. He ran down beyond the pond, to the hedges that lined the northern edge of the park, bordering on a stretch of white houses. Every step that Enzo took made his prick bounce against his tracksuit bottoms, bounce dangerously. The bloody knife was hot in his hand. Enzo dashed around a wooden bench facing the duck pond and pushed himself between a green-barked ash tree and the hedge. He was careful, even though it was the last thing he felt like being. He checked the road behind the hedge first, and the path leading down by the pond. No one was approaching.

He fell down on his knees and rested his head against the bark of the tree, his cheek bitten by the weight of his body. The wood smelled green and bitter. *(That day, a man wearing a hooded parka dragged him into a small copse, pushed him up against a tree.)* Enzo touched the bark with his tongue, the way he had the first time, tasted the bitter green against his lips, flakes of it dirty on his teeth. *("You keep it quiet now, you keep your mouth tight and shut or I'll open your throat.")* Enzo screwed up his eyes tight and closed his lips, his left hand moving to his pocket. *(And the fur on the man's hood brushing against the back of his neck as he pushed into him.)* His eyes were screwed tight his mouth closed, the way he'd been told to keep it, his breath whistling down his nostrils. *(And the feel of the man inside him, pushing against his insides, stretching and pushing, an ache that seemed to rise up through his guts, out of his mouth.)* Enzo hardly had to touch his prick to come, it lashed out into his palms, a hot slap that seemed to explode from behind his eyes. *("You turn round, I'm gonna come and get you, cut your throat. Do you understand?")* He stayed for a moment, breathing through his nose, his cheek bitten by the green wood. He opened his eyes. That first time, he'd seen a couple of birds beating steadily in the sky. This time, there was nothing but a cloud.

He sat back on his heels and gently, carefully, pulled his left hand from his pocket and his right from his hooded top. Both palms were wet: the left with the white of his sperm, the right with the red of congealing blood. He looked down at them for a moment, feeling the power of what lay in his hands, all of birth and life right there for him to hold. He saw the red and white of the boys at Mass and the football strip of the boys in the park. He saw the white of the wolf's teeth in the flesh. He weighed them in his hands and then slowly squeezed them together. He looked once more at his palms, and the white lay on the red like a blister, a pinkish tinge in the place where they had mixed. Life was this color. It caused things to be born.

That day, when the man had gone, Enzo had reached behind him to touch where he'd been hurt, and his hand had come back covered with the white and the red. He'd wiped his hands in the earth to bury it. Now, he bent down to the ground and wiped his palms over the dirt at the base of the tree. He pushed his hands hard into the mud, his fingers clawed at the earth, coming up black under the nails. He tried to bury it again, but this time he was planting it in the earth of the park, making it grow.

Enzo sat back, breathing heavily. The mud was caked onto his hands. Beyond the pond, the routine of the park was continuing. The boys were still playing football. Dogs chased the cyclists. A kite of red silk throbbed in the sky. Enzo watched it, thinking how good it would have been if he'd been able to open his eyes to this afterwards, how it would have been almost perfect. It had become his place now, this park, he ruled it like a kingdom. It didn't matter that it wasn't this park where it had happened, that first time. It didn't matter that Enzo didn't really know where he'd been, that it was all in pieces, all sharp and bright in his head, like the upturned broken bottles they cemented into the walls to stop the kids climbing over. It didn't matter that Enzo didn't really understand the ritual of it. All he knew was that he had to do this, and keep on doing it, because if he fed the land with the red and the white, then maybe he'd grow stronger and one day *he* would be the wolf.

Later, Enzo walked around to cross the stream and head back over Church Street, back home. He passed the aviary as he crossed the bridge by the side of the house, and another lady jogger came pounding toward him, her blond hair wound up tight on her head. Enzo didn't even look at her, but the birds started shrieking in their cage. Enzo smiled. The birds knew that he was close to them. They knew what was about to come.

A tree had blown down. It had fallen over from the churchyard at the back of the park, bringing with it a section of the cemetery wall. Enzo stopped for a moment and looked down at the top of the tree, the leaves and shoots and buds. He felt like only a god could, seeing the tree like that, he felt like a giant. One day, he knew, it wouldn't be the storm that would blow down the trees. Enzo would tear through the city like a wolf, a great creature the size of a storm. Trees and houses would fall in front of him, and all the people would scream, a great noise rising toward him like a choir. And they would feel his breath upon them, and it would burn with the heat of the red, it would stink with the heat of the white.

TROUBLE IS A LONESOME TOWN

BY CATHI UNSWORTH

King's Cross

Dougie arrived at the concourse opposite the station just half an hour after it had all gone off. He'd had the cab driver drop him down the end of Gray's Inn Road, outside a pub on the corner there, where he'd made a quick dive into the gents to remove the red hood he'd been wearing over the black one, pulled on a Burberry cap he'd had in his bag so that the visor was down over his eyes. That done, he'd worked his way through the mass of drinkers, ducked out another door, and walked the rest of the way to King's Cross.

The Adidas bag he gripped in his right hand held at least twenty grand in cash. Dougie kind of wished it was hand-cuffed to him, so paranoid was he about letting go of it even for a second that he'd had trouble just putting it on the floor of the taxi between his feet. He'd wanted it to be on his knee, in his arms, more precious than a baby. But Dougie knew that above all else now, he had to look calm, unperturbed. Not like a man who'd just ripped off a clip joint and left a man for dead on a Soho pavement.

That's why he'd had the idea of making the rendezvous at the Scottish restaurant across the road from the station. He'd just blend in with the other travelers waiting for their train back up north, toting their heavy bags, staring at the

TV with blank, gormless expressions as they pushed stringy fries smothered in luminous ketchup into their constantly moving mouths. The way he was dressed now, like some hood rat, council estate born and bred, he'd have no trouble passing amongst them.

He ordered his quarter-pounder and large fries, with a supersize chocolate lard shake to wash it all down, eyes wandering around the harshly lit room as he waited for it all to land on his red plastic tray. All the stereotypes were present and correct. The fat family (minus dad, natch) sitting by the window, mother and two daughters virtually indistinguishable under the layers of flab and identical black-and-white hairstyles by Chavettes of Tyneside to match the colors of their footie team. The solitary male, a lad of maybe ten years and fifteen stone, staring sullenly out the window through pinhole eyes, sucking on the straw of a soft drink that was only giving him back rattling ice cubes. On the back of his shirt read his dreams: 9 *SHEARER*. But he was already closer to football than footballer.

Then there was the pimp and his crack whore; a thin black man sat opposite an even thinner white woman with bruises on her legs and worn-down heels on her boots. Her head bowed like she was on the nod, while he, all angles and elbows and knees protruding from his slack jeans and oversize Chicago Bulls shirt, kept up a steady monologue of abuse directed at her curly head. The man's eyes where as rheumy as a seventy-year-old's, and he sprayed fragments of his masticated fries out as he kept on his litany of insults. Sadly for Iceberg Slim, it looked like the motherfuckingbitchhocuntcocksucker he was railing at had already given up the ghost.

Oblivious to the psychodrama, the Toon Army had half of the room to themselves, singing and punching the air, reliving moment-by-moment the two goals they'd scored over Spurs—well thank fuck they had, wouldn't like to see this lot disappointed. They were vile enough in victory, hugging and clasping at each other with tears in their eyes, stupid joker's hats askew over their gleaming red faces, they might as well have been bumming each other, which was obviously what they all wanted.

Yeah, Dougie liked to get down among the filth every now and again, have a good wallow. In picking over the faults of others, he could forget about the million and one he had of his own.

Handing over a fiver to the ashen bloke behind the counter, who had come over here thinking nothing could be worse than Romania, Dougie collected his change and parked himself inconspicuously in the corner. Someone had left a copy of the *Scum* on his table. It was a bit grubby and he really would have preferred to use surgical gloves to touch it, but it went so perfectly with his disguise and the general ambience of the joint that he forced himself. Not before he had the bag firmly wedged between his feet, however, one of the handles round his ankle so if anyone even dared to try . . .

Dougie shook his head and busied himself instead by arranging the food on his plastic tray in a manner he found pleasing: the fries tipped out of their cardboard wallet into the half of the Styrofoam container that didn't have his burger in it. He opened the ketchup so that he could dip them in two at a time, between mouthfuls of burger and sips of chocolate shake. He liked to do everything methodically.

Under the headline "STITCHED UP," the front page of the *Scum* was tirelessly defending the good character of the latest batch of rapist footballers who'd all fucked one girl between the entire team and any of their mates who fancied it. Just so they could all check out each other's dicks while they did it, Dougie reckoned. That sort of shit turned his stomach almost as much as the paper it was printed on, so he quickly flipped the linen over, turned to the racing pages at the back. That would keep his mind from wandering, reading all those odds, totting them up in his head, remembering what names went with what weights and whose colors. All he had to do now was sit tight and wait. Wait for Lola.

Lola.

Just thinking about her name got his fingertips moist, got little beads of sweat breaking out on the back of his neck. Got a stirring in his baggy sweatpants so that he had to look up sharply and fill his eyes with a fat daughter chewing fries with her mouth open to get it back down again.

Women didn't often have this effect on Dougie. Only two, so far, in his life. And he'd gone further down the road with this one than anyone else before.

He could still remember the shock he felt when he first saw her, when she sat herself down next to him at the bar with a tired sigh and asked for a whiskey and soda. He caught the slight inflection in her accent, as if English wasn't her first language, but her face was turned away from him. A mass of golden-brown curls bobbed on top of her shoulders, she had on a cropped leopardskin jacket and hipster jeans, a pair of pointy heels protruding from the bottom, wound around the stem of the bar stool. The skin on her feet was golden-brown too; mixed-race she must have been, and for a minute Dougie thought he knew what she would look like before she turned her head, somewhere between Scary Spice and that bird off *Holby City*. An open face, pretty and a bit petulant. Maybe some freckles over the bridge of her nose.

But when she did turn to him, cigarette dangling between her lips and long fingers wound around the short, thick glass of amber liquid, she looked nothing so trite as "pretty."

Emerald-green eyes fixed him from under deep lids, fringed with the longest dark lashes he had ever seen. Her skin was flawless, the color of the whiskey in her glass, radiating that same intoxicating glow.

For a second he was taken back to a room in Edinburgh a long time ago. An art student's room, full of draped scarves and fake Tiffany lamps and a picture on the wall of Marlene Dietrich in *The Blue Angel*. This woman looked strangely like Marlene. Marlene with an afro. *Black Angel.*

She took the cigarette from between her red lips and asked: "Could you give me a light?" Her glittering eyes held his brown ones in a steady gaze, a smile flickered over her perfect lips.

Dougie fumbled in the sleeve of his jacket for his Zippo and fired it up with shaking fingers. Black Angel inhaled deeply, closing her bronze-colored eyelids as she sucked that good smoke down, blowing it out again in a steady stream.

Her long lashes raised and she lifted her glass to him simultaneously.

"Cheers!" she said, and he caught that heavy inflection again. Was he going mad, or did she even sound like Marlene too? "Ach," she tossed back her mane of curls, "it's so good to be off vork!"

"I'll drink to that," Dougie said, feeling like his tongue was too big for his head, his fingers too big for his hands, that he was entirely too big and clumsy. He slugged down half his pint of Becks to try and get some kind of equilibrium, stop this weird teenage feeling that threatened to paralyze him under the spell of those green eyes.

She looked amused.

"What kind of vork do you do?" she asked.

Dougie gave his standard reply. "Och, you know. This an' that."

It pleased her, this answer, so she continued to talk. Told him in that smoky, laconic drawl all about the place she worked. One of the clip joints off Old Compton Street, the ones specifically geared up to rip off the day-trippers.

"It izz called Venus in Furs," she told him. "Is fucking tacky shit, yeah?"

He started to wonder if she was Croatian, or Serbian. Most of the girls pouring into Soho now were supposed to be ones kidnapped from the former Yugoslavia. *Slavic* was a word that suited the contours of her cheeks, the curve of her green eyes. But how could that be? Dougie didn't think there was much of a black population in Eastern Europe. And he couldn't imagine anyone having the balls to kidnap this one. Maybe she was here for a different reason. Images raced through his mind. Spy films, Checkpoint Charlie, the Cold War. High on her accent, he didn't really take the actual words in.

Until at some point close to dawn, she lifted a finger and delicately traced the outline of his jaw. "I like you, Dougie." She smiled. "I vill see you here again, yes?"

Dougie wasn't really one for hanging out in drinking clubs. He was only in this one because earlier that evening he'd had to have a meet in Soho and he couldn't stand any of the pubs round there. Too full, too noisy, too obvious. This was one of the better places. Discreet, old-fashioned, not really the sort of place your younger generation would go for, it was mainly populated by decaying actors skulking in a dimly lit world of memory. It was an old luvvie who'd first shown him the place. An old luvvie friend of a friend who'd been ripped off for all his Queen Anne silver and a collection of Penny Blacks by the mercenary young man he'd been silly enough to invite back for a nightcap. Dougie had at least got the silver back, while the guy was sleeping off what he'd spent the proceeds of the stamps on. He really didn't come here often, but as he watched the woman slip off her stool and shrug on her furry jacket, he felt a sudden pang and asked, "Wait a minute—what's your name?"

She smiled and said: "It's Lola. See you again, honey." And then she was gone.

Dougie found himself drifting back to the club the next evening.

It was weird, because he'd kept to himself for so long he felt like his heart was a hard, cold stone that no one could melt. It was best, he had long ago told himself, not to form attachments in his line of work. Attachments could trip you up. Attachments could bring you down. It was better that no one knew him outside his small circle of professional contacts and the clients they brought. Safer that way. He'd done six months time as a teenager, when he was stupid and reckless, and had vowed he'd never be caught that way again.

He was mulling over all these facts as he found himself sitting at the bar. He didn't quite know what he thought he was doing there, just that he felt his heart go each time the buzzer went and a new group of people clattered down the steps. Lola had come into the place alone. He supposed he could ask the guvnor what he knew about her, but that didn't seem very gentlemanly. After all, he wasn't a regular himself, who knew how long she'd been making her way down here after the grind of an evening "huzzling the schmucks" under Venus's neon underskirts?

At half past 1:00 she had wound her way down the stairs toward him. A smile already twitching at the corners of her mouth, she was pleased to see him. One look up her long, bare, perfect legs to her leather miniskirt and that same leopardskin jacket and he felt the same.

"He-*looo*, Dougie," she said.

Dougie felt drunk, as he had ever since.

Gradually, over whiskey and sodas with the ice crinkling in the glass, she'd told him her story. It was all very intriguing. Her father was Russian, she said, ex-KGB, who since the fall of Communism had managed to create an empire for himself in electronic goods. He was a thug, but a charming one—he had named her after a character in a Raymond Chandler book that he'd read, contraband, as a teenager.

They had a lot of money, but he was very strict. Made her study hard and never go out. There was not a lot of emotion between him and her mother.

Her mother was an oddity, a Somalian. Lola didn't know how they met, but she suspected. Back in the old days, it was quite possible her father had bought her out of semi-slavery in a Moscow brothel. Her mother always claimed she was a princess, but she was also a drunk, so what was Lola to believe? She was beautiful, that was for sure. Beautiful and superstitious, always playing with a deck of strange cards and consulting patterns in tea leaves. She might have mastered dark arts, but never managed to speak Russian—probably she never wanted to. So Lola grew up speaking two languages, in one big, empty apartment in Moscow.

Right now, she was supposed to be in Switzerland. She

looked embarrassed when she told Dougie this. "At finishing school. Can you believe? Vot a cliché." Lola had done a bunk six months ago. She'd crossed Europe, taking cash-in-hand work as she did, determined to get to London. She wanted to escape while she was in the "free West" rather than go back to what she knew would be expected of her in Russia. Marriage to some thick bastard son of one of her father's ex-comrades. A life of looking nice and shutting up, just like her mother.

But she feared her father's arm was long. There were too many Russians in London already. Someone was bound to rat her out, the reward money would be considerable. So she had to get together a "traveling fund" and find somewhere else to go. Somewhere safe.

"Vere are you from, Dougie?" she purred. "Not from round here, eh?"

"What do you reckon?" he said archly. "Where d'you think I got a name like Dougie from, heh?"

Lola laughed, put her finger on the end of his nose.

"You are from Scotland, yes?"

"Aye," nodded Dougie.

"Where in Scotland?"

"Edinburgh."

"Vot's it like in Edinburgh?"

A warning voice in Dougie's head told him not to even give her that much. This story she had spun for him, it sounded too much like a fairy tale. She was probably some down-on-her-luck Balkans hooker looking for a sugar daddy. No one could have had the lifestyle she described. It was too far-fetched, too mental.

The touch of her finger stayed on the end of his nose. Her green eyes glittered under the optics. Before Dougie knew what he was doing, words were coming out of his mouth.

She had given him the germ of an idea. The rest he filled in for himself.

Venus in Furs was not run by an established firm, even by Soho standards. Its ostensible owners were a bunch of chancy Jamaican wide boys whose speciality was taking over moody drinking dens by scaring the incumbents into thinking that they were Yardies. Dougie doubted that was the case. They could have been minor players, vaguely connected somehow, but Yardie lands were south of the river. Triads and micks ran Soho. He doubted these fellas would last long in the scheme of things anyway, so he decided to help Lola out and give fate a hand.

Trying to help her, or trying to impress her?

It helped that her shifts were regular. Six nights a week, 6 till 12. Plenty of time to observe who came and went on a routine basis. Maybe her old man really was KGB cos she'd already worked out that the day that the Suit came in would be the significant one.

There was this office, behind the bar, where they did all their business. Three guys worked the club in a rotation, always two of them there at the same time. Lynton, Neville, and Little Stevie. They had a fondness for Lola, her being blood, so it was usually her they asked to bring drinks through when they had someone to impress in there. She said the room had been painted out with palm trees and a sunset, like one big Hawaiian scene.

Like everyone, Dougie thought, *playing at gangsters— they're playing* Scarface.

Once a week, a bald white guy in a dowdy brown suit

came in with an attaché case. Whichever of the Brothers
Grimm were in at the time would make themselves scarce
while he busied himself in the office for half an hour. One of
them would hang at the bar, the other find himself a dark
corner with one of the girls. Then the bald man would come
out, speak to no one, and make his own way out of the club.

Every Thursday, 8 p.m., punctual as clockwork he came.

That proved it to Dougie. The lairy Jamaicans were a
front to terrify the public. The bald man collected the money
for their unseen offshore master. With his crappy suit and
unassuming exterior, he was deliberately done up like a mark
to blend in with the rest of the clientele.

Dougie had a couple of guys that owed him favors. They
weren't known faces, and it would be difficult to trace them
back to him—their paths crossed infrequently and they
moved in different worlds. On two successive Thursdays, he
gave them some folding and sent them in as marks. They
confirmed Lola's story and gave him more interesting background on the Brothers Grimm. Both weeks, it was the same
pair, Steve and Neville, little and large. Large Neville, a tall
skinny guy with swinging dreads and shades who was always
chewing on a toothpick, sat behind the bar when the bald
man showed up. He practiced dealing cards, played patience,
drank beer, and feigned indifference to the world around
him, nodding all the while as if a different slow-skanking
soundtrack was playing in his head—not the cheesy Europop
on the club's PA.

Little Stevie, by comparison, always grabbed himself a girl
and a bottle and made his way over to the corner booth.
While Neville looked like a classic stoner, Little Stevie was
mean. He wore a black suit and a white shirt, with thick gold
chains around his bulldog neck. A porkpie hat and thick

black shades totally obscured his eyes. Ocassionally, like when the girl slipped underneath the table, he would grin a dazzling display of gold and diamond dental work. Neville always drank proper champagne—not the pear fizz served to the punters as such—and both Dougie's contacts copped the telltale bulge in his pocket.

Neville's booth was the one from which the whole room could be surveyed, and even while receiving special favors, he never took his eye off the game. The minute the office door clicked open and the bald man slipped away, he would knee his girl off him, adjust his balls and whatever else was down here, and swagger his way back over to the office all puffed-up and bristling, Neville following at his heels.

Yeah, Stevie, they all agreed, was the one to watch.

While they were in there playing punters, Dougie was watching the door.

The Venus was based in a handy spot, in a dingy alley between Rupert Street and Wardour Street. There was a market on Rupert and all he had to do was pretend to be examining the tourist tat on the corner stall. The bald man went the other way. Straight to a waiting cab on Wardour. Each time the same.

On the night it all happened, Dougie felt a rush in his blood that he hadn't felt since Edinburgh, like every platelet was singing to him the old songs, high and wild as the wind.

God, he used to love that feeling, used to let it guide him in the days when he was Dougie the Cat, the greatest burglar in that magical city of turrets and towers.

But now he was Dougie Investigates, the private eye for the sort of people who couldn't go to the police. He had changed sides on purpose after that first prison jolt, never wanting to be in close proximity to such fucking filth ever again. If you couldn't be a gentleman thief these days, he reckoned, then why not be a Bad Guys' PI? His methods may have differed from those used by the Old Bill, but Dougie had kept his nose clean for eighteen years, built up his reputation by word of mouth, and made a good living from sorting out shit without causing any fuss. Filled a proper gap in the market, he had.

His blood had never sung to him in all that time. He supposed it must have awakened in him that first night he met Lola, grown strong that night she'd finally allowed him back to her dingy flat above a bookie's in Balham, where she had so studiously drawn out the map of the Venus's interior before unzipping his trousers and taking him to a place that seemed very close to heaven.

Bless her, he didn't need her map. He didn't even need to know what Neville and Stevie got up to, only that they were good little gangsters and stayed where they were, in that little palace of their imagination where they could be Tony Montana every day.

He wasn't going to take them on.

All he needed was the thirty seconds between the Venus's door and Wardour Street. And the curve in the alley that meant the taxi driver wouldn't be able to see. All he needed was the strength of his arm and the fleetness of his feet and the confusion of bodies packed into a Soho night.

At the end of the alley he slipped a balaclava over his head, put the blue hood over the top of that, and began to run.

He was at full sprint as the bald man came out of the door, fast enough to send him flying when he bowled into his shoulder. The man's arms spread out and he dropped his precious cargo to the floor. Dougie was just quick enough to catch the look of astonishment in the pale, watery eyes, before he coshed him hard on the top of his head and they rolled up into whites. He had another second to stoop and retrieve the case before he was off again, out of the alley, across Wardour Street, where the taxi was waiting, its engine running, the driver staring straight ahead.

Dougie was already in the downstairs bogs of the Spice of Life before the cabbie was checking his watch to make sure he hadn't turned up early. Had pulled out his sports bag from the cistern where he'd stashed it and busted the lock on the attaché case by the time the cabbie turned the engine off and stepped out of the car to take a look around. Dougie's deftness of touch was undiminished by his years on the other side. He counted the bundles of cash roughly as he transferred them into his sports bag, eyebrows raising as he did. It was quite a haul for a weekly skim off a clip joint. He briefly wondered what else they had going on down there, then chased the thought away as excess trouble he didn't need to know.

By the time the cabbie was standing over the crumpled heap in the alleyway, he had put the attaché case in the cistern and taken off the blue hood, rolling it into a ball when he nipped out the side door of the pub. He junked it in a bin as he came out onto Charing Cross Road and hailed himself a ride up to King's Cross.

Dougie looked up from his racing pages. As if struck by electrodes, he knew Lola was in the room. She walked toward him, green eyes dancing, clocking amusedly his stupid cap and the bag that lay between his feet. Sat down in front of him and breathed, "Is it enough?"

"Aye," nodded Dougie. "It's enough."

He hadn't wanted there to be any way in which Lola could be implicated in all this. He'd had her phone in sick for two days running, told her just to spend her time packing only the essentials she needed, and gave her the money for two singles up to Edinburgh.

The night train back to the magic city, not even the Toon Army could ruin that pleasure for him.

"You ready?" he asked her.

Her grin stretched languidly across her perfect face.

"Yes," she purred. "I'm ready."

Dougie gripped the Adidas bag, left his floppy fries where they lay.

As they stepped out onto the road, St. Pancras was lit up like a fairy tale castle in front of them. "See that," he nudged her shoulder, "that's bollocks compared to where we're going."

His heart and his soul sung along with his blood. He was leaving the Smoke, leaving his life of shadows, stepping into a better world with the woman he loved by his side. He took her hand and strode toward the crossing, toward the mouth of King's Cross Station.

Then Lola said: "Oooh, hang on a minute. I have to get my bag."

"You what?" Dougie was confused. "Don't you have it with you?"

She laughed, a low tinkling sound. "No, honey, I left it just around the corner. My friend, you know, she runs a bar there and I didn't want to lug it around with me all day. She's kept it safe for me, behind the bar. Don't vorry, it von't take a minute."

Dougie was puzzled. He hadn't heard about this friend or this bar before. But in his limited experience of women, this was typical. Just when you thought you had a plan, they'd make some little amendment. He guessed that was just the way their minds worked.

She leaned to kiss his cheek and whispered in his ear: "Ve still have half an hour before the train goes."

The pub was, literally, around the corner. One of those horrible, bland chain brewery joints heaving with overweight office workers trying to get lucky with their sniggering secretaries in the last desperate minutes before closing time.

He lingered by the door as Lola hailed the bored-looking blond bartender. Watched her take a small blue suitcase from behind the bar, kiss the barmaid on each cheek, and come smilingly back toward him.

A few seconds before she reached him, her smile turned to a mask of fear.

"Oh shit," she said, grabbing hold of his arm and dragging him away from the doorway. "It's fucking Stevie."

"What?"

"This vay." She had his arm firmly in her grasp now, was propelling him through to the other side of the bar, toward the door marked *Toilets*, cursing and talking a million miles an hour under her breath.

"Stevie was standing right outside the door. I svear to God it was him. I told you, he is bad luck that one, he's voodoo, got a sixth sense—my mama told me about *sheiit* like him. Ve can't let him see us! I'm supposed to be off sick, the night he gets ripped off—he's gonna know! He's gonna kill me if he sees me."

"Hen, you're seeing things," Dougie tried to protest as she pushed him through the door, down some steps into a dank basement that smelled of piss and stale vomit.

"I'm not! It vos him, it vos him!" She looked like she was

about to turn hysterical, her eyes were flashing wildly and her nails were digging into his flesh. He tried to use his free hand to extricate himself from her iron grip, but that only served to make her cling on harder.

"Hen, calm down, you're hurting me . . ." Dougie began.

"There's someone coming!" she screamed, and suddenly began to kiss him passionately, smothering him in her arms, grinding her teeth against his lips so that he tasted blood.

And then he heard a noise right behind him.

And the room went black.

"Fucking hell." Lola looked down on Dougie's prone body. "That took long enough."

"I told you he was good," her companion pouted, brushing his hands on his trousers. "But I thought you'd enjoy using all your skills on him."

"Hmm." Lola bent down and prised Dougie's fingers away from the Adidas bag. "I knew this would be the hardest part. Getting money out of a tight fucking jock."

The slinky Russian accent had disappeared like a puff of smoke. She sounded more like a petulant queen.

"Come on." She stepped over her would-be Romeo and the pile of shattered ashtray glass he lay in. "Let's get out of here."

The car was parked nearby. As Lola got into the passenger seat, she pulled the honey-gold Afro wig off her head and ran her fingers through the short black fuzz underneath.

"I am *soooo* tired of that bitch," she said, tossing it on the backseat.

Her companion started the car with a chuckle.

"He fucking believed everything, didn't he?" He shook his head as he pulled out.

"Yeah . . . and you said he was a private detective. Well let me tell you, honey, you wouldn't believe what I suckered that dick with. My dad was a Russian gangster. My mother was a Somalian princess. I was on the run from Swiss finishing school. Can you believe it?"

Lola hooted with derision. "Almost like the fairy tales I used to make up for myself," she added. "You know, I thought he might fucking twig when I told him I was named after a character in a Raymond Chandler novel. But I couldn't resist it."

"Well," her companion smiled at her fondly, "you certainly made up for the loss of that Queen Anne silver. We've got enough to keep us going for months now. So where do you fancy?"

"Not back to Soho," Lola sniffed, as the car pulled into the slipstream of Marylebone Road. "I've fucking had it with those poseur thugs. I know. I fancy some sea air. How does Brighton sound to you?"

"The perfect place," her companion agreed, "for a couple of actors."

Dougie came around with his face stuck to a cold stone floor with his own blood. Shards of glass covered him. He could smell the acrid stench of piss in his nostrils, and from the pub above he could hear a tune, sounding like it was coming from out of a long tunnel of memory. He could just make out the lyrics:

"I met her in a club down in old Soho/Where you drink champagne and it tastes just like cherry cola . . ."

CHELSEA THREE, SCOTLAND YARD NIL

BY MAX DÉCHARNÉ

King's Road

Chelsea, July 1977.

They found him in the pedestrian underpass beneath the northern end of the Albert Bridge, a short walk down Oakley Street from the King's Road. He'd obviously been given a thorough kicking, and there was an orange shoved in his mouth, completely blocking the passage of air. Tied up like something in a butcher-shop window.

Didn't look like he was bothered, though. He'd been dead for a good few hours already.

There wasn't much about it in the local papers, but you could tell the police thought they were onto something. They'd been seen nosing around at Seditionaries the following afternoon, flicking through the racks, checking out the *Cambridge Rapist* T-shirts, clutching copies of the *NME* as if they were going to stumble over a clue in among the usual snarky jokes and record reviews. Who knows, maybe they thought they had, because there they were again later that day, looking very out of place at the rear of the spiky-haired crowd in the Man in the Moon watching Adam and the Ants.

Nosed around. Asked a few questions. Lowered the tone of the place. Something about bondage. Yeah, well, officer, what can I tell you? There's a lot of it about . . .

Didn't look like the gig was their kind of scene. They left halfway through the headliner, X-Ray Spex.

The following Saturday it was hot as hell. Usual collection of punky scufflers hanging around outside Town Records. Watching the passersby. Opening cans. Wandering off to check out the stalls at Beaufort Street Market. Keeping an eye out for the Teds or the Stamford Bridge boys. Regular King's Road scene that summer, ever since the *Jubilee* violence had flared up—*Punk Rock Rotten Razored*, all the tabloid column inches stoking the flames. "Pretty Vacant" was heading up the charts while "God Save the Queen" was just on its way down, but Boney M and ELP were both in the top ten, and the papers were saying that Warner Brothers had just issued a single featuring a group made up of the *Sun's* page three girls. Finger on the pulse, as always . . .

Davis got out of the tube at Sloane Square, picked up a copy of the *Standard* at the stall outside, and headed up past Smiths in the direction of the Chelsea Potter for a lunchtime pint. No word on that stiff they'd found the other week at the Albert Bridge, but now some posh woman had been discovered smothered to death in her bed in Cheyne Walk, just a few hundred feet away from the site of the last killing. Done in with a pillow. *Police are refusing to comment on possible lines of enquiry.* Yeah, sure. Unconfirmed reports of a message of some kind pinned to the body.

Davis looked out from his window seat and watched the nervous out-of-town kids heading for Boy a few doors away, heads down, expecting trouble.

Two killings in as many weeks. Not unusual for the Lower East Side, but this was Chelsea.

He rolled up the *Standard* and put it in his pocket, digging out the tatty copy of the *NME* he'd been dragging around for the past couple of days. Front page headline all about violence in the punk scene: *This* Definitely *Ain't the Summer of Love.* Turned to page forty-six and scanned the gig guide, looking for likely shows. Nothing much doing tonight. Pub-rock no-hopers in most of the clubs. Monday looked better—Banshees/Slits/Ants at the Vortex, or Poly Styrene's lot on Tuesday at the Railway in Putney. All good research material. Getting an article together on the upcoming rash of punk films currently in the planning stages. Russ Meyer farting about in Scotland with the Pistols, trying to get *Who Killed Bambi* off the ground. Derek Jarman rounding up his mates for something called *Jubilee.* Then there was the bloke who'd put some money into the last Python film and was now backing a disaster-in-the-making called *Punk Rock Rules OK.*

"Get out there and see what's happening," said his editor. Five thousand words on the punk film scene. Throw in a sidebar about Don Letts's 8mm footage they'll be showing at the ICA. Have a look round the clubs. Keep your eyes open. Nice little feature with a few shots of some of these punkettes in fishnet stockings and ripped T-shirts. Play up the punch-ups with the Teddy Boys as well. Sex and violence. *Must we fling this filth at our kids? Blah, blah, blah* . . . Get a quote from that GLC nutter, Brooke-Partridge, the one who reckons most punk rockers would be improved by sudden death. *Is this the future of the British film industry?* The usual bollocks, you know the form . . .

So there he was, knocking back a few pints in the Chelsea Potter, waiting to interview some idiot who claimed to be getting a script together about punk, but whom none of the bands or the managers on the scene that he'd spoke to had ever heard of. Probably a wasted afternoon, but what the hell. Even if the guy turned out to be a complete dingbat, he might provide some comic relief. A few stupid quotes. Ten years of interviewing some of the "giants" of European cinema for the magazine and listening to all their pompous arty bullshit had taken its toll. Egomaniacs, the fucking lot of them. Fellini's 8, Fellini's *Roma*, Fellini's talking out of his arse . . . Give him an out-and-out chancer or a total loser any day of the week. At least they might be funny.

In any event, the guy was a no-show. Two hours late and nothing doing, he was three pints down and had read both papers cover to cover, winding up back at that murder report in the *Standard*. Smothered to death sometime yesterday? Let's check out the scene. Mildly pissed but coherent, he pushed through the door and headed west along the King's Road. Turned left at Oakley Street, down past Scott's old house, with someone playing *Unicorn* by Tyrannosaurus Rex out of an upstairs window nearby, then round the corner to where Rossetti had kept wombats and peacocks in his Cheyne Walk back garden a decade before they even built the Albert Bridge.

Bored-looking copper on guard outside, bolting the door after half of Aintree had scarpered. Davis dug through his wallet and pulled out the press card he hardly ever used, knowing full well that it meant damn-all to most people. Still, you never knew.

"Afternoon, officer . . . Nothing much left to see, eh?" Offered the copper a fag but he turned it down. "Heard there was a note pinned to the body . . ."

"That's right. Not that it helps much."

"Guess he's hardly likely to have left his home phone number . . ."

"Sounded like a quote from a book or something."

"Oh yes?"

"They'll be putting out a statement this afternoon, so there's no harm in saying . . ."

"Saw it, did you?"

"Some people think little girls should be seen and not heard . . ."

July 21. Hadn't been a bad week. He'd seen the Only Ones at the Speakeasy on the Saturday. The Adverts and 999 at the Nashville on Monday, then that new bunch of Australians, the Saints, down in Twickenham at the Winning Post. Talked to a lot of people—punters, groups, managers. Bernie Rhodes refusing to let him talk to the Clash. Miles Copeland trying to convince him that some desperate bunch of ageing hippies calling themselves the Police were actually a punk band. Same old story. He'd also gone back to Chelsea again, to the Royal Court this time. Alberto y Los Trios Paranoias and their punk rock musical *Sleak!* with the annoying bloody exclamation mark on the end. The coppers were still sniffing around the scene, chasing some supposed connection with the two murders. As if killers are so eager to be caught they go around leaving clues, just like in the films.

Davis was wandering up the King's Road with a photographer in tow, looking for likely faces in the right gear who could help decorate the article. Fishnet stockings, the man wanted. Ripped T-shirts. Okay then. Sure, they'd already been down to the Roxy, but that was full of tourists—not like in Czezowski's day back in the spring. Ever since the Roxy live album had come out a few weeks back, you couldn't move down there for bandwagon-jumpers. Mind you, if today was any indication, the King's Road was suffering from the same disease. It was like a lot of people had been telling him at shows all week: Half the real punks had already bailed out of the scene, and the plastics were moving in. Still, the editor wanted photographs . . .

Saw a couple of likely looking prospects outside the Chelsea Drugstore, on the corner where Royal Avenue met the King's Road. Bought them a can of beer, slipped them a quid each, and they said it was cool to photograph them for ten minutes or so. Davis let them get on with it and wandered off a few yards away to sit in the sun. Before you knew it, more police, uptight about the camera.

Asking for ID. Getting aggressive. The photographer couldn't see what the fuss was about. Wasn't as if she was the first person trying to get some shots of punks on the King's Road that summer. Turned out it wasn't that at all. They'd found another body. Right there on Royal Avenue, early that morning. Milkman practically tripped over it.

When he came over to see what the fuss was about, Davis noticed that it was the same policeman he'd talked to outside the Cheyne Walk house.

"Aren't you the press man who was asking me questions about the previous murder?" said the copper.

He admitted that he was. Somehow, being seen taking photos a few yards away from the latest crime scene started the constable's antenna twitching. Davis agreed that he had a few minutes spare in which to come along and talk to the detective sergeant.

"Bit of a coincidence, isn't it? What's your interest in all this?"

"In the first one, pure curiosity. I'm a journalist. I read about it in the paper. I was round the corner having a drink. Thought I'd take a look."

"And today?"

"Shooting pictures of punks for a feature I'm writing. It's for a film magazine. They want coverage of some upcoming punk movies. I've been going around checking out the scene."

The sergeant thought about that for a while.

"So would you describe yourself as an expert on this type of music?"

"Not an expert, no. I'm way too old for this. Most of the punters are about sixteen. But I've been at a lot of the shows these past couple of months. Talked to some of the bands involved. Research. Building up a picture. Why, is there a connection between the punk scene and the murders?"

"That's one possible line of enquiry."

The sergeant produced a clear plastic evidence bag and held it out for inspection. Visible inside was a sheet of paper with the usual blackmail lettering cut out from newspapers which had fast become a punk cliché through overuse. There was just one short phrase written on it:

I wAnNA Be a sLAvE FoR yOU aLL

"Mean anything to you?" asked the sergeant.

"Found on the body, was it?"

"If you'd just answer the question, sir . . ."

"Yes, actually, it does."

"I see. And why might that be?"

"X-Ray Spex."

"X-Ray Spex?"

"The band . . ."

"I know who they are, sir. I had the *pleasure* of seeing them perform several songs at the pub up the road a couple of weeks ago . . ."

"All right then. Go down to Town Records, 402 King's Road. Get a copy of a new album called *Live at the Roxy*. X-Ray Spex track called "Oh Bondage Up Yours." I think you'll find it's part of the lyrics."

Early August. "I Feel Love" by Donna Summer blasting out from every pub jukebox. Pistols still at number four with "Pretty Vacant," just one place down from "Angelo" by Brotherhood of Man. Check out the record reviews in the *NME* and the two main albums featured were the new ones from the Grateful Dead and Soft Machine. These were strange times. Davis was finishing up his evening getting plastered at the Roebuck. Usual mixed crowd. A couple of the staff from Seditionaries getting the evil eye from some of the older geezers who took exception to the swastikas on their clothes. Francis Bacon wandering in, looking for who knows what. Two famous actors in the corner, saying nothing, seemingly miserable, and a smattering of underage drinkers keeping their heads down. Davis spotted a few of the punks he'd interviewed at a Rezillos show in the Man in the Moon a few days previously, then went up and bought them a drink on expenses to see if they had any likely tips for the coming week.

"How's it going, lads? Still getting hassled by the boys in blue?"

"Now and then. They were at the Spex gig at the Hope & Anchor the other day. Taking people outside. Going through your pockets. The usual crap."

"Did they say what it was about?"

"Nah. Don't need an excuse, do they?"

Apparently not. He went off to get some more cancer sticks and then pushed his way out through the doors and into the street. It was still bloody hot, but at least the tubes would still be running.

Now it was September. He'd finally finished that bloody punk films article, not that the editor had been particularly impressed. Easy to see why, really. The Pistols film with Meyer was shaping up to be a total fiasco and no one would even let him *near* that shoot—a sure sign of trouble. Nice idea on paper, but what would a director like that know about punk? Or care, for that matter . . . As for *Jubilee*—God help him—if he had to listen to much more of Jarman droning on about his plans to have some of the actors speaking in Latin, like his fucking unwatchable previous effort, then Davis would personally pay a group of King's Road Teds to show up on the set and batter people to death with copies of the script. At least that German bloke who'd shown up in town from Munich making a punk documentary a week or so back seemed to have the right idea. Go to the clubs, talk to the fans, talk to some of the music papers and shops. Capture it as it's happening.

Still, what the fuck, the article was done now.

As for the cops, they had rounded up some poor sod who was now "helping them with their enquiries." Three killings in four weeks. Must have made all the happy little ratepayers in their Chelsea Mews houses start screaming bloody murder at their local MP. No wonder somebody's been arrested. Can't have that sort of behavior in the neighborhood. The *Standard* didn't have much in the way of details, as per usual. Seems like the guy had been picked up after a show at the Nashville, following "information received." According to the way it played in the press, it sounded like they were hoping that they'd taken some kind of dangerous lunatic off the streets.

Innocent until proven guilty, of course . . .

What the hell. After a summer in which all the tabloids had spent their time running stories which claimed that the Sex Pistols cut up dead babies onstage and that your average punk was just as likely to bottle you in the face as say hello, hardly surprising that the cops would believe almost anything of someone who wore all the bondage gear. Was he guilty? Well, it seemed like he was their best bet . . .

Davis turned on the television, but there wasn't anything on the news about the killings. *New Faces* on LWT. Couldn't stomach that so he turned it over and got the last ten minutes of *Dr. Who* on BBC1, followed by Bruce Forsyth and the bloody *Generation Game*. Still, at least in the film slot there was a double bill later on of *House of Dracula* and Corman's *Fall of the House of Usher*, kicking off just after 10 p.m. Saturday night, though. What did they expect? Sometimes it looked as if they felt that anyone over the age of about fourteen or under the age of sixty would definitely be out and about having a wild time, so why bother?

He turned off the TV. All right then, if all else fails, do some work. Went to the fridge, dug out a beer, and sat down in front of the Olivetti manual typewriter. The neighbors never liked hearing the clatter it made, but then fuck 'em; their kids had been playing the sodding *Muppet Show* album all week at huge volume on what appeared to be continuous repeat, and when the father ever succeeded in commandeering the record player it changed to the fucking Allman Brothers and *The* Fucking *Road Goes On For*-fucking-*ever*. All of it. Several times. In the same evening.

Jesus wept.

No, a little typing at 7 p.m. was hardly enough to repay them for that kind of abuse.

The punk film article was done and dusted, due to hit the newsstands in a week or so, but he still had a piece to write for some arty French cinema magazine which was right up itself but paid surprisingly well. He supplied them with stuff written in English, which they then translated and printed in French. Who knows if they did a good job or not. He didn't care, and no one he knew ever saw the stuff. Mostly they wanted pretentious toss of the worst kind, and he was happy to oblige, under a pseudonym. This time, though, he'd sold them on the idea of a subject that actually interested him. Still, better not run this one under his real name either, all the same. Okay, the magazine only sold about 20,000 copies a time, virtually all of them across the channel, but you never quite knew who might be reading it, putting two and two together.

Another swig of beer. Light up a fag. In with a new sheet of paper. Here we go:

CHELSEA ON FILM

Next time you're in London on holiday, take a walk down the King's Road. Now notorious for the exploits of some of Britain's new 'punk rockers,' it also has much to interest the student of film history.

Did you know that Stanley Kubrick shot parts of A Clockwork Orange right here in the neighborhood? Try catching the underground to Sloane Square station, then walk down the King's Road until you reach number 49, the Chelsea Drugstore. Malcolm McDowell's character, Alex, picks up a couple of girls in the record shop here before taking them back to his flat for an orgy. Then, if you continue in the same direction up the road, turning left onto Oakley Street, you'll come to the Albert Bridge.

It's here, in the pedestrian underpass which runs beneath the northern end of the bridge, that McDowell is given a severe beating by a gang of tramps toward the end of the film.

While you're there, look back along the Chelsea embankment about a hundred feet and you'll see an imposing Georgian house which is number 16 Cheyne Walk. It was in one of the upstairs bedrooms that Diana Dors was smothered to death with a pillow in Douglas Hickox's hugely entertaining 1973 horror film, Theater of Blood, *starring Vincent Price as a homicidal Shakespearean actor.*

Retracing your steps back to the Chelsea Drugstore, turn off at the road leading down the side of it called Royal Avenue. Another fine Georgian house, number 30 Royal Avenue, was used as the location for Joseph Losey's 1963 film, The Servant, *in which Edward Fox treats his manservant Dirk Bogarde almost like a slave, until the latter starts to get the upper hand . . .*

He paused and sat back in his chair, consulting his notes. *Blow Up, Killing of Sister George, The Party's Over* . . . Yeah, there were enough other ones to pad out the article. Shame to waste all that research.

And anyway, how many coppers could read French?

PART III

GUNS ON THE ROOF

LOVE
BY MARTYN WAITES
Dagenham

L ove it. Fuckin love it. No other feelin in the world like it.

Better than sex. Better than anythin.

There we was, right, an there they was. Just before the Dagenham local elections. Outside the community center. Community center, you're avina laugh. Asylum-seeker central, more like. Somali center.

June, a warm night, if you're interested.

Anyway, we'd had our meetin, makin our plan for the comin election, mobilizin the locals off the estate, we come outside, an there they was. The Pakis. The anti-Nazis. Shoutin, chantin—Nazi scum, BNP cunts. So we joined in, gave it back with Wogs out an that, Seig heillin all over the place. Pakis in their casual leathers, anti-Nazis in their sloppy uni denims, us lookin sharp in bombers an eighteen-holers. Muscles like taut metal rope under skin-tight T-shirts an jeans, heads hard an shiny. Tattoos: dark ink makin white skin whiter. Just waitin.

Our eyes: burnin with hate.

Their eyes: burnin with hate. Directed at us like laser death beams.

Anticipation like a big hard python coiled in me guts, waitin to get released an spread terror. A big hard-on waitin to come.

Buildin, gettin higher:
Nazi scum BNP cunts
Wogs out seig heil
Buildin, gettin higher—

Then it came. No more verbals, no more posin. Adrenalin pumped right up, bell ringin, red light on. The charge.

The python's out, the hard-on spurts.

Both sides together, two wallsa sound clashin intaya. A big, sonic tidal wave ready to engulf you in violence, carry you under with fists an boots an sticks.

Engage. An in.

Fists an boots an sticks. I take. I give back double. I twist an thrash. Like swimmin in anger. I come up for air an dive back in again, lungs full. I scream the screams, chant the chants.

Wogs out seig heil

Then I'm not swimmin. Liquid solidifies round me. An I'm part of a huge machine. A muscle an bone an blood machine. A shoutin, chantin cog in a huge hurtin machine. Arms windmillin. Boots kickin. Fueled on violence. Driven by rage.

Lost to it. No me. Just the machine. An I've never felt more alive.

Love it. Fuckin love it.

I see their eyes. See the fear an hate an blood in their eyes. I feed on it.

Hate matches hate. Hate gives as good as hate gets.

Gives better. The machine's too good for them.

The machine wins. Cogs an clangs an fists an hammers. The machine always wins.

Or would, if the pigs hadn't arrived.

Up they come, sticks out. Right, lads, you've had your fun. Time for us to have a bit. Waitin till both sides had tired, pickin easy targets.

The machine falls apart; I become meself again. I think an feel for meself. I think it's time to run.

I run.

We all do; laughin an limpin, knowin we'd won.

Knowin our hate was stronger than theirs. Knowin they were thinkin the same thing.

Run. Back where we came from, back to our lives. Ourselves.

Rememberin that moment when we became somethin more.

Cherishin it.

I smiled.

LOVED IT.

D'you wanna name? Call me Jez. I've been called worse.

You want me life story? You sound like a copper. Or a fuckin social worker. Fuckin borin, but here it is. I live in the Chatsworth Estate in Dagenham. The borders of East London/Essex. You'll have heard of it. It's a dump. Or rather, a dumpin ground. For problem families at first, but now for Somalis an Kosovans that have just got off the lorry. It never used to be like that. It used to be a good place where you could be proud to live. But then, so did Dagenham. So did this country.

There's me dad sittin on the settee watchin Tricia in his vest, rollin a fag. I suppose you could say he was typical of this estate (an of Dagenham, an the country). He used to have a job, a good one. At the Ford plant. Knew the place, knew the system, knew how to work it. But his job went when they changed the plant. His job an thousands of others. Now it's a center of excellence for diesel engines. An he can't get a job there. He says the Pakis took it from him. They got HNDs an degrees. He had an apprenticeship for a job that don't exist no more. No one wants that now. No one wants him now. He's tried. Hard. Honest. So he sits in his vest, rollin fags, watchin Tricia.

There's Tom, me brother, too. He's probably still in bed. He's got the monkey on his back. All sorts, really, but mostly heroin. He used to be a good lad, did well at school an that, but when our fat slag bitch of a mother walked out, all that had to stop. We had to get jobs. Or try. I got a job doin tarmacin an roofin. He got a heroin habit. Sad. Fuckin sad. Makes you really angry.

Tarmacin an roofin. Off the books, cash in hand. With Barry the Roofer. Baz. Only when I'm needed, though, or seasonal, when the weather's good, but it's somethin. Just don't tell the dole. I'd lose me jobseeker's allowance.

It's not seasonal at the moment. But it's June. So it will be soon.

So that's me. It's who I am. But it's not WHAT I AM.

I'm a Knight of St. George. An proud of it. A true believer. A soldier for truth.

This used to be a land fit for heroes, when Englishmen were kings an their houses, castles. A land where me dad had a job, me brother was doin well at school, an me fat slag bitch of a mother hadn't run off to Gillingham in Kent with a Paki postman. Well, he's Greek, actually, but you know what I mean. They're all Pakis, really.

An that's the problem. Derek (I'll come to him in a minute) said the Chatsworth Estate is like this country in miniature. It used to be a good place where families could live in harmony and everyone knew everyone else. But now it's a run-down shithole full of undesirables an people who've given up tryin to get out. No pride anymore. No self-respect. Our heritage sold to Pakis who've just pissed on us. Love your country like it used to be, says Derek, but hate it like it is now.

And I do. Both. With all my heart.

Because it's comin back, he says. One day, sooner rather than later, we'll reclaim it. Make this land a proud place to be again. A land fit for heroes once more. And you, my lovely boys, will be the ones to do it. The foot soldiers of the revolution. Remember it word for word. Makes me proud all over again when I think of it.

An I think of it a lot. Whenever some Paki's got in me face, whenever some stuck-up cunt's had a go at the way I've done his drive or roof, whenever I look in me dad's eyes an see that all his hope belongs to yesterday, I think of those words. I think of my place in the great scheme, at the forefront of the revolution. An I smile. I don't get angry. Because I know what they don't.

That's me. That's WHAT I AM.

But I can't tell you about me without tellin you about Derek Midgely. Great, great man. The man who showed me the way an the truth. The man who's been more of a father to me than me real dad. He's been described as the demigog of Dagenham. I don't know what a demigog is, but if it means someone who KNOWS THE TRUTH an TELLS IT LIKE IT IS, then that's him.

But I'm gettin ahead. First I have to tell you about Ian.

Ian. He recruited me. Showed me the way.

I met him at the shopping center. I was sittin around one day wonderin what to do, when he came up to me.

I know what you need, he said.

I looked up. An there was a god. Shaved head, eighteen-holers, jeans, an T-shirt—so tight I could make out the curves an contours of his muscled body. An he looked so relaxed, so in control. He had his jacket off an I could see the tats over his forearms an biceps. Some pro ones like the flag of St. George, some done himself like Skins Foreva. He looked perfect.

An I knew there an then I wanted what he had. He was right. He did know what I needed.

He got talkin to me. Asked me questions. Gave me answers. Told me who was to blame for my dad not havin a job. Who was to blame for my brother's habit. For my fat slag bitch mother runnin off to Gillingham. Put it all in context with the global Zionist conspiracy. Put it closer to home with pictures I could understand: the Pakis, the niggers, the asylum-seekers.

I looked round Dagenham. Saw crumblin concrete, depressed whites, smug Pakis. The indigenous population overrun. Then back at Ian. An with him lookin down at me an the sun behind his head lookin like some kind of halo, it made perfect sense.

I feel your anger, he said, understand your hate.

The way he said hate. Sounded just right.

He knew some others that felt the same. Why didn't I come along later an meet them?

I did.

An never looked back.

Ian's gone now. After what happened.

For a time it got nasty. I mean REALLY nasty. Body in the concrete foundations of the London Gateway nasty.

I blamed Ian. All the way. I had to.

Luckily, Derek agreed.

Derek Midgely. A great man, like I said. He's made the St. George Pub on the estate his base. It's where we have our meetins. He sits there in his suit with his gin an tonic in front of him, hair slicked back, an we gather round, waitin for him to give us some pearls of wisdom, or tell us the latest install-ment of his masterplan. It's brilliant, just to be near him. Like I said, a great, great man.

I went there along with everyone else the night after the community center ruck. I mean meetin. There was the usu-als. Derek, of course, holdin court, the foot soldiers of which I can proudly number myself, people off the estate (what Derek calls the concerned populace), some girls, Adrian an Steve. They need a bit of explainin. Adrian is what you'd call an intellectual. He wears glasses an a duffelcoat all year round. Always carryin a canvas bag over his shoulder. Greasy black hair. Expression like he's somewhere else. Laughin at a joke only he can hear. Don't know what he does. Know he surfs the Internet, gets things off that. Shows them to Derek. Derek nods, makes sure none of us have seen them. Steve is the local councillor. Our great white hope. Our great fat whale, as he's known out of Derek's earshot. Used to be Labour until, as he says, he saw the light. Or until they found all the fiddled expense sheets an Nazi flags up in his livin room an Labour threw him out. Still, he's a true man of the people.

Derek was talkin. What you did last night, he says, was a great and glorious thing. And I'm proud of each and every one of you.

We all smiled.

However, Derek went on, I want you to keep a low profile between now and Thursday. Voting day. Let's see some of the other members of our party do their bit. We all have a part to play.

He told us that the concerned populace would go leafletin and canvasin in their suits an best clothes, Steve walkin round an all. He could spin a good yarn, Steve. How he'd left Labour in disgust because they were the Pakis' friend, the asylum-seekers' safe haven. How they invited them over to use our National Heath Service, run drugs an prostitution rings. He would tell that to everyone he met, try an make them vote for him. Derek said it was playin on their legitimate fears, but to me it just sounded so RIGHT. Let him play on whatever he wanted.

He went on. We listened. I felt like I belonged. Like I was wanted, VALUED. Meetins always felt the same.

LIKE I'D COME HOME.

The meetin broke up. Everyone started drinkin.

Courtney, one of the girls, came up to me, asked if I was stayin on. She's short with a soft barrel body an hard eyes. She's fucked nearly all the foot soldiers. Sometimes more than once, sometimes a few at a time. Calls it her patriotic duty. Hard eyes, but a good heart. I went along with them once. I had to. All the lads did. But I didn't do much. Just sat there, watched most of the time. Looked at them. Didn't really go near her.

Anyway, she gave me that look. Rubbed up against me. Let me see the tops of her tits down the front of her low-cut T-shirt. Made me blush. Then made me angry cos I blushed. I told her I had to go, that I couldn't afford a drink. My job-seeker's allowance was gone an Baz hadn't come up with any work for me.

She said that she was gettin together with a few of the lads after the pub. Was I interested?

I said no. An went home.

Well, not straight home. There was somethin I had to do first. Somethin I couldn't tell the rest of them about.

There's a part of the estate you just DON'T GO. At least not by yourself. Not after dark. Unless you were tooled up. Unless you want somethin. An I wanted somethin.

It was dark there. Shadows on shadows. Hip hop an reggae came from open windows. The square was deserted. I walked, crunched on gravel, broken glass. I felt eyes watchin me. Unseen ones. Wished I'd brought me blade. Still, I had me muscles. I'd worked on me body since I joined the party, got good an strong. I was never like that at school. Always the weak one. Not anymore.

I was kind of safe, I knew that. As long as I did what I was here to do, I wouldn't get attacked. Because this was where the niggers lived.

I went to the usual corner an waited. I heard him before I saw him. Comin out of the dark, along the alleyway, takin his time, baggy jeans slung low on his hips, Calvins showin at the top. Vest hangin loose. Body ripped an buff.

Aaron. The Ebony Warrior.

Aaron. Drug dealer.

I swallowed hard.

He came up close, looked at me. The usual look, smilin, like he knows somethin I don't. Eye to eye. I could smell his warm breath on my cheek. I felt uneasy. The way I always do with him.

Jez, he said slowly, an held his arms out. See anythin you want?

I swallowed hard again. Me throat was really dry.

You know what I want. Me voice sounded ragged.

He laughed his private laugh. I know exactly, he said, an waited.

His breath was all sweet with spliff an alcohol. He kept starin at me. I dug my hand into my jacket pocket. Brought out money. Nearly the last I had, but he didn't know that.

He shook his head, brought out a clingfilm wrap from his back pocket.

Enjoy, he said.

It's not for me an you know it.

He smiled again. Wanna try some? Some skunk, maybe? Now? With me?

I don't do drugs. I hardly drink. An he knows it. He was tauntin me. He knew what my answer would be.

Whatever, he said. Off you go then, back to your little Hitler world.

I said nothing. I never could when he talked to me.

Then he did somethin he'd never done before. He touched my arm.

You shouldn't hate, he said. Life too short for that, y'get me?

I looked down at his fingers. The first black fingers I'd ever had on my body. I should have thrown them off. Told him not to touch me, called him a filthy nigger. Hit him.

But I didn't. His fingers felt warm. And strong.

What should I do then? I could hardly hear my own voice.

Love, he said.

I turned round, walked away.

I heard his laugh behind me.

At home, Dad was asleep on the sofa. Snorin an fartin. I went into Tom's room. Empty. I left the bundle by his bedside an went out.

I hadn't been lyin to Courtney. It was nearly the last of me money. I didn't like buyin stuff for Tom, but what could I do? It was either that or he went out on the street to sell somethin, himself even, to get money for stuff. I had no choice.

I went to bed but couldn't sleep. Things on me mind but I didn't know what. Must be the elections. That was it. I lay starin at the ceilin, then realized me cock was hard. I took it in me hand. This'll get me to sleep, I thought. I thought hard about Courtney. An all those lads.

That did the trick.

The next few days were a bit blurry. Nothin much happened. It was all waitin. For the election. For Baz to find me some more work. For Tom to run out of heroin again an need another hit.

Eventually Thursday rolled round an it was election day. I went proudly off to the pollin station at the school I used to go to. Looked at the kids' names on the walls. Hardly one of them fuckin English. Made me do that cross all the more harder.

I stayed up all night watchin the election. Tom was out, me dad fell asleep.

Steve got in.

I went fuckin mental.

I'd been savin some cans for a celebration an I went at them. I wished I could have been in the St. George with the rest but I knew us foot soldiers couldn't. But God, how I WANTED TO. That was where I should have been. Who I should have been with. That was where I BELONGED.

But I waited. My time would come.

I stayed in all the next day. Lost track of time.

Put the telly on. Local news. They reported what had happened. Interviewed some Paki. Called himself a community leader. Said he couldn't be held responsible if members of his community armed themselves and roamed the streets in gangs looking for BNP members. His people had a right to protect themselves.

They switched to the studio. An there was Derek. Arguin with some cunt from Cambridge. Least that's what he looked like. Funny, I thought people were supposed to look bigger on TV. Derek just looked smaller. Greasy hair. Fat face. Big nose. Almost like a Jew, I thought. Then felt guilty for thinkin it.

It's what the people want, he said. The people have spoken. They're sick and tired of a government that is ignoring the views of the common man and woman. And the common man and woman have spoken. We are not extremists. We are representing what the average, decent person in this country thinks but doesn't dare say because of political correctness. Because of what they fear will happen to them.

I felt better hearin him say that. Then they turned to the Cambridge cunt. He was a psychologist or psychiatrist or sociologist or somethin. I thought, here it comes. He's gonna start arguin back an then Derek's gonna go for him. But he didn't. This sociologist just looked calm. Smiled, almost.

It's sad, he said. It's sad so few people realize. As a society it seems we base our responses on either love or hate, thinking they're opposites. But they're not. They're the same. The opposite of love is not hate. It's indifference.

They looked at him.

People only hate what they fear within themselves. What they fear themselves becoming. What they secretly love. A fascist, he gestured to Derek will hate democracy. Plurality. Anything else—he shrugged—is indifference.

I would have laughed out loud if there had been anyone else there with me.

But there wasn't. So I said nothing.

A weekend of lyin low. Difficult, but had to be done. Don't give them a target, Derek had said. Don't give them an excuse.

By Monday I was rarin to get out of the flat, was even lookin forward to goin to work.

First I went down the shoppin center. Wearin me best skinhead gear. Don't know what I expected, the whole world to have changed or somethin, but it was the same as it had been. I walked round proudly, an I could feel people lookin at me. I smiled. They knew. Who I was. What I stood for. They were the people who'd voted.

There was love in their eyes. I was sure of it.

At least, that's what it felt like.

Still in a good mood, I went to see Baz. Ready to start work.

An he dropped a bombshell.

Sorry, mate, I can't use you no more.

Why not?

He just looked at me like the answer was obvious. When I looked like I didn't understand, he had to explain it to me.

Cos of what's happened. Cos of what you believe in. Now don't get me wrong, he said, you know me. I agree, there's too many Pakis an asylum-seekers over here. But a lot of those

Pakis are my customers. And, well, look at you. I can hardly bring you along to some Paki's house and let you work for him, could I? So sorry, mate, that's that.

I was gutted. I walked out of there knowin I had no money. Knowin that, once again, the Pakis had taken it from me.

I looked around the shoppin center. I didn't see love anymore. I saw headlines on the papers:

RACIST COUNCILLOR VOTED IN TO DAGENHAM

Then underneath:

KICK THIS SCUM OUT

I couldn't believe it. They should be welcomin us with open arms. This was supposed to be the start of the revolution. Instead it was the usual shit. I just knew the Pakis were behind it. An the Jews. They own all the newspapers.

I had nowhere to go. I went to the St. George, but this was early mornin an there was no one in. None of my people.

So I just walked round all day. Thinkin. Not gettin anythin straight. Gettin everythin more twisted.

I thought of goin back to the St. George. They'd be there. Celebratin. Then there was goin to be a late-night march round the streets. Let the residents, the concerned populace, know they were safe in their houses. Let everyone know who ruled the streets.

But I didn't feel like it.

So I went home.

An wished I hadn't.

Tom was there. He looked like shit. Curled up on his bed. He'd been sick. Shit himself.

Whassamatter? I said. D'you wanna doctor?

He managed to shake his head. No.

What then?

Gear. Cold turkey. Cramps.

An he was sick again.

I stood back, not wantin it to get on me.

Please, he gasped, you've got to get us some gear . . . please . . .

I've got no money, I said.

Please . . .

An his eyes, pleadin with me. What could I do? He was me brother. Me flesh an blood. An you look after your own.

I'll not be long, I said.

I left the house.

Down to the part of the estate where you don't go. I walked quickly, went to the usual spot. Waited.

Eventually he came. Stood before me.

Back so soon? Aaron said. Then smiled. Can't keep away, can you?

I need some gear, I said.

Aaron waited.

But I've got no money.

Aaron chuckled. Then no sale.

Please. It's for . . . It's urgent.

Aaron looked around. There was that smile again. How much d'you want it?

I looked at him.

How much? he said again. An put his hand on my arm.

He moved in closer to me. His mouth right by me ear. He whispered, tickling me. Me heart was beatin fit to burst. Me legs felt shaky.

You're like me, he said.

I tried to speak. It took me two attempts. No I'm not, I said.

Oh yes you are. We do what our society says we have to do. Behave like we're supposed to. Hide our true feelings. What we really are.

I tried to shake me head. But I couldn't.

You know you are. He got closer. You know I am.

An kissed me. Full on the mouth.

I didn't throw him off. Didn't call him a filthy nigger. Didn't hit him. I kissed him back.

Then it was hands all over each other. I wanted to touch him, feel his body, his beautiful black body. Feel his cock. He did the same to me. That python was inside me, ready to come out. I loved the feeling.

I thought of school. How I was made to feel different. Hated them for it. Thought of Ian. What we had got up to. I had loved him. With all me heart. And he loved me. But we got found out. And that kind of thing is frowned upon, to say the least. So I had to save my life. Pretend it was all his doing. I gave him up. I never saw him again. I never stopped loving him.

I loved what Aaron was doing to me now. It felt wrong. But it felt so right.

I had him in my hand, wanted him in me body. Was ready to take him.

When there was a noise.

We had been so into each other we hadn't heard them approach.

So this is where you are, they said. Fuckin a filthy nigger when you should be with us.

The foot soldiers. On patrol. And tooled up.

I looked at Aaron. He looked terrified.

Look, I said, it was his fault. I had to get some gear for me brother . . .

They weren't listening. They were staring at us. Hate in their eyes. As far as they were concerned, I was no longer one of them. I was the enemy now.

You wanna run, nigger-lover? Or you wanna stay here and take your beatin with your boyfriend? The words spat out.

I zipped up my jeans. Looked at Aaron.

They caught the look.

Now run, the machine said, hate in its eyes. But from now on, you're no better than a nigger or a Paki.

I ran.

Behind me, heard them laying into Aaron.

I kept running.

I couldn't go home. I had no gear for Tom. I couldn't stay where I was. I might not be so lucky next time.

So I ran.

I don't know where.

After a while I couldn't run anymore. I slowed down, tried to get my breath back. Too tired to run anymore. To fight back.

I knew who I was. Finally. I knew WHAT I WAS.

And it was a painful truth. It hurt.

Then from the end of the street I saw them. Pakis. A gang of them. Out protecting their own community. They saw me. Started running.

I was too tired. I couldn't outrun them. I stood up, waited for them. I wanted to tell them I wasn't a threat, that I didn't hate them.

But they were screaming, shouting, hate in their eyes.

A machine. Cogs an clangs an fists an hammers.

I waited, smiled.

Love shining in my own eyes.

SIC TRANSIT GLORIA MUNDI

BY JOOLZ DENBY

Bradford

We put six black plastic bin bags of stuff in that Rent-A-Wreck transit van; that's what we took, and we left another twelve or so of rubbish in the house. We'd cleaned up too—or at least what we thought of as cleaning; though it's no good excuse, you'd have needed an industrial steam-cleaner to shift the muck in that kitchen. And we left a note, taped to the spotted mirror in the front room:

> *Dear Mr. Suleiman,*
> *We are very sorry to run away and not pay what we owe you for the rent. One day we will come back and settle up, we promise.*
>
> *Yours sincerely,*
> *The tenants at no. 166*

And we set off in the middle of the night, an old transistor radio and tape deck wedged on the filthy dashboard, the rain smearing the windscreen as the wonky wiper jerked spastically across the glass and we put "Babylon's Burning" on at full distort and we laughed and you floored the pedal until the engine howled.

Oh, man; running away from Bradford in the lost, gone,

and sadly not-forgotten '80s. Running into the great spirit gold of the rising sun and the hot rush of cutting loose at last from the viscous, clinging mud of small-town England; every weekday the dole and just enough coarse cheap food to keep you alive, every Saturday night the same round of drinking, fighting, and dreaming, every Sunday a long smashed afternoon of everyone droning on about how shit it was and how if only they had the breaks, cha, just watch 'em, they'd be rock stars and axe heroes and *Somebodies*.

If they had the breaks, yeah. If some god on high did it all for them and made it all for them, they'd be off to London in a trice, because that, we all knew, was where everything was. That's where über-cool parties were a dazed haze of glitter-floating beautiful people with clothes from boutiques so hip even their names were a transgression, where even the lowliest shop-girl was such a counterculture punkette pinup she got her pic in *Sounds*, and the streets were paved with cocaine and the gutters ran with Jack in a fumey vapor of sweet decadence; rich boy's piss, the blood of rock 'n roll. We all knew this to be 110-percent true because what journalist ever wrote paeans to the punk night at Queen's Hall, Bradford, or eulogies to some darktime niterie in say, oh, Chester? No, it was London; everything, everyone, every luminous, lush, and longed-for treat was stashed in the belly of that old beast. It was a fact. We'd read it in every newspaper, Sunday arts supplement, music journal, and fashionable novel since forever. It was the way it was and we were the huddled peasant masses crouching on our savage hills gazing up in the torch-lit dark at the divine superstar that was London, London, London.

So we sat in the van as it hurtled down the M1, wired out of our skulls with adrenaline and burning with messianic passion, white hot and calamitous. We weren't kids, oh no; we weren't teen escapees, you see; we were genuine artists, gone twenty-five and *almost* possessing a record contract with EMI; cash-poor we might be, but we'd worked like dogs and earned our turn at the table—so no pallid, plump, dumb fuck of a corporate recording executive was going ruin our Big Chance. We would be there in the thick of it, in London, in control. We weren't going to be throwaway tinsel two-bit popstrels, oh no—we were going to change the face of music, of literature, of art, of life, *forever.* Those decadent, air-and-arse kissing Londoners would be forced to welcome us with open arms because we were the future, we were the *Warriors of the New.* Strapped into our armor of hand-stitched leather and raggedy black, we looked in my tattered old tarot cards and saw rapture rising behind us like a prophecy.

It had to be that way. We'd told everyone it would be. We'd been princes and princesses in Wooltown, now we were going to live like kings and queens in the Smoke. We'd chanted the spell, we'd invoked the gods. It was a done deal.

All that winter six of us slept on the spare bedroom floor of our singer's sister's shoe-box flat in the Northerner's ghetto of London, Highbury New Park. Done up like chrysalides in our stinking doss-bags, we waited for spring when we'd be turned into butterflies. At night the floor heaved like a living carpet and the air was sucked clean of oxygen, but it was too cold and grimy to open the window. They'd never said how tumble-down, litter-strewn, and dirty London was in those magazines and on the telly; the muck was terrible. Put on a clean T-shirt and it'd be black-bright in ten minutes of being exposed to the exhaust-fume leaden reek of the monstrous crawling traffic. Blow your nose and the snot was black; clean your makeup off and the grease was shot with gritty gray that wasn't mascara. The dirt had its own smell too, sour and rank, hanging in the unmoving air like a filthy veil.

Back home, we'd think—each to ourselves and not letting on for fear of being thought soft—the cold, fresh wind off the moor unrolled through the canyons of gothic sandstone buildings, embroidered with the faint scent of heather and the sweet dust of the craglands, scouring the crooked streets and lighting wild roses in your cheeks.

But it was no use thinking like that. We were here to stay, to make our mark. So we'd shake ourselves back to the now and think, hey, who cares about *Wuthering Heights* when we can go to Heaven, guest-listed on the strength of the last article in the *NME* about our meteoric rise to cult stardom, or my snarling mask adorning the front-cover of *Time Out*—Kabuki-style, rebel-girl eyes sparkling incandescent with unreason and fury. Fame, we thought, never having been taught to think otherwise, was better than bread—and infamy was preferable to anonymity. We didn't have to stand in line with the other runaways outside whatever nightclub was in that week, listening to the chopped vowels and singsong drawl of the North, the West, or all the other great cities that netted the country—what Londoners called "the provinces" in that particular tone of voice that made you want to spit in their eyes.

So we walked past the Liverpool whine or the Brummie choke of the queuing hordes, and strode in a cloud of patchouli, crimper-burnt hair, and Elnett, into the dreamland they could only hope for. A London nightclub; wow. The carpets patinated with muck, spat-out gum, and marinated in beer slops and puke. The glasses plastic and the watered-down drinks a fortune, the toilets a slick tsunami of bogwater and busted, stinking, scrawled-on, paperless cubicles flapping with broken-locked doors. You never really got anything for nothing in London, see; proved how sharp they were, proved no one got anything over on a real Londoner.

Not that we ever met a real Londoner. Not one born and bred, like. Maybe they were out there somewhere, but we never found them. Certainly not one who could truly say he'd entered this vale of tears to the cheery clamor of Bow bells, the coarse comforting din of the old pub pianner belting out "Miybe It's Becorse I'm a Lunnoner," and the smiles of pearly royalty handing out platters of jellied eels and cockles. No, folk said they were from London, but there was always somewhere else hidden in the dusty folds of their fast-forgotten past; they'd lived in London, oh, now, you know, God, forever. But they came from Leicester or Bristol or Glasgow or Cyprus or Athens or Berlin or Ankara. They came to be famous, but until that bright day they washed dishes, threw plates of greasy nosh about in caffs, or struggled round the heart-and-soul-breaking savagery of the infamously brutal London dole offices.

Oh, aye, it was a cold coming we, and many like us, had, and no mistake. But what did we care? If we felt heartsick or homesick, we stood ourselves up straight, wiped our eyes if we were girls, unset our rock-hard jaws if we were boys, and commenced afresh our sure-to-be-stellar careers in the world of art. We would show them, we would not be broken and crawl off home like yellow, sag-bellied curs—we had a meeting with EMI tomorrow where we'd tell 'em how it was, and tonight there was a Happening at an old warehouse by the river, promising an installation featuring a naked model-girl embedded in a tank full of jelly created by the latest cutting-edge performance art duo, a clutch of ranting skin-punk poets, and a couple of hot new London bands cobbled together from the tatterdemalion remnants of last year's hot new London bands.

How many of those Happenings did we go to, expecting the dark whirligig of cruelly brilliant excess and getting instead a half-cocked mock-up in a rickety-rackety drafty squat where some anorexic pilled-up slapper was toted round in a rusty wheelbarrow slopping with lime Chivers by two public schoolboys whose aristo boho dads had been Hampstead artists in the '60s, and people we recognized from magazines cooed about authenticity and artistic daring as they wiped their coke-snotty noses and patted each other on the back? They always, always all knew each other from school and from their families and they didn't know us—but suffering Jesus, we knew them, because we knew what real really was and they. Did. Not. Still don't, as it goes. Anyway, all these evenings ended in fighting, in smack-and-thunder brawls driven by our frustration and our rage at those whited sepulchres and their great stitch-up. How we frightened them, the faux-Londoners, how we shook their skinny trees. Yeah, yeah, yeah—all that talk of voyeuristic ultra-violence and the thrill of the street evaporated like oily vapor off a stagnant pond when they saw the lightning we were. They never knew us, no, they never did. They never saw us weep.

Oh, it was all such a shill, a sell, a sham; while we ripped ourselves apart searching for the pure, beating heart of things, believing we could, by telling the truth, by tearing the old lies apart at the seams, set ourselves and all our tribe free, London rolled on, a tottering juggernaut of blind and desperate delusion, all the little mannequins trying to find the tailor who made the emperor's bee-yoo-ti-ful new clothes, so they could ape the great cockalorum and maybe, maybe grab a tiny bit of reflected glory. It was a nonstop dance macabre and we didn't realize how bone-tired we were becoming.

Then, for us, it all came down in twenty-four hours.

First, we woke up and knew that yet again we wouldn't be able to see the sky. Might not sound like much but it finally got to us, hemmed in and overshadowed as we were by the ugly gray buildings crouching over us, the exhalations of air-cons and extractor fans panting rancid fast-food farts into the starving air, choking us. In Bradford, you see, the skies constantly scroll above us in a massive cloudscape, as free and ever-changing as the wild pulse of nature—the sandstone of the city is buttery amber, lit from within by a million prisms when the light hits it at sunset. We live in a flame, in a painting by Turner, in Gaia's Lamp. In London, we were dying for lack of light.

That morning, well, we knew it would be another London day, and lo! It was. And that night it was my thirtieth birthday, and I wasn't a kid anymore. I had decided to have a party. It was to be at the Embassy Club, private, just for the tribe, and it would be a suitable send-off to my disheveled youth. I spent hours with the crimpers and the kohl pot and I looked like the priestess at Knossos, but I covered up my breasts out of modesty. The snakes, well, I had them tattooed on; easier that way.

How long did my birthday party last in that tatty mold-smelling red-velvet cellar before the scavenging liggers arrived, cawing over the booze they stole, screeching and cackling at us, the barbarians? How long was it before one of them abused the wrong soldier in our little army, and bang-bang it went? Not long, believe me. Then there were cracked noses, plum-black eyes, split lips swelling fat in an instant over sharp-chipped teeth, and the shrill screams of speed-skinny harridans egging on their leathery men-folk to try and "fuck that bitch up." *That bitch* stood as the maelstrom rolled around her in a sparkle of broken glass and the red stitch of blood, and thought, ah, *enough*. So that bitch—which was me, of course, naturally—picked up a tall bar stool and, raising it overhead, smashed the great mirror by the bar into a blossom of shards so I wouldn't have to see my reflection backdropped by that screeching mess.

Then it went quiet, and all you could hear was breathing and a fella coughing where he'd been whacked in the gut. And the mangy jackals slunk off as the bouncers—late as ever—bulked into the room and tried to get lairy and failed, no one having the energy left to take them seriously.

And I went to the bar manager and said I was sorry for breaking his expensive-looking glass, and he said I hadn't.

So I said, no, it was me, I'll pay for it, fair's fair, somewhat nervous though, as I was mortally skint as usual.

And he said, no, it wasn't you.

But it was, I said. It was.

No, he said, it wasn't, you didn't do it, it's nothing; you're famous, we all know you, *people like you don't have to pay for what you do.*

And an abyss opened up in front of me that reeked sulphurous of what I could become, of what was in me that rubbed its corrupted hands together and murmured about fame, power, and hubris, which would be the end of freedom and the death of my spirit, and I knew too that a million wannabes would think me the biggest fool living for not pricking my thumb pronto and signing on the dotted line. So I threw some money on the bar—without doubt not enough—and walked out of that shabby shithole, my pretty golden boot-clogs crunching the broken mirror-glass, and I felt a great disgust at the sorry, sordid smallness of the sellout offered me. For if I was going to trade my immortal soul, brothers and sisters, would it be for the entrée to crap clubs and pathetic parties in a slutty run-down frazzle of a city in a small island off the coast of Europe? Oh, I think not, I really think not, as it goes. Only the universe would be enough to satisfy *my* desire, and I'm still working on that.

So we left London and returned to Bradford double-quick before we had time to think too hard. We rented another stone house terraced on the slopes of our crazy secret city's hills and breathed the good air with profound relief and paid Mr. Suleiman what we owed, and more, and he said he knew we'd come back one day and we all shook hands, straight up. Then we set ourselves to write our own histories in songs and stories, make our own testaments in paintings and books, which we have done and are still doing and will do forever and ever, amen; stronger and stronger, brighter and brighter. And I'm grateful I saw what I saw when I did, before I was blinded by habit and despair, like so many I know who are lost now, beyond recall.

Twenty years have passed since that night, and I ask myself what it really was we all hated most about our sojourn in the Great Wen. What was the grit in the pearl in the oyster, the time-bomb ticking heart of it? I've heard all the stories of loneliness and fear, of self-harm and suicide, of madness and addiction, from others who finally limped home to lick their wounds—but it wasn't any of that for us. No. What finally, finally finished us with London wasn't the corruption or the scandals, nothing so interesting, nothing so bold, nothing so grand.

Sic transit gloria mundi—so passes away the glory of the world.

London, that braggart capital, passes away without glory, you see. Without greatness, without any kind of joy, without passion or fire or beauty. In the end, you see, London was such a pathetic bloody *disappointment*.

And you know what? It still is.

That's all.

NEW ROSE

BY JOHN WILLIAMS

New Cross

Years ago Mac had read this interview with a British soul singer whose career had had its share of ups and downs. The guy was asked whether he felt he'd been a success. "Well," he said, "I've never had to go back to mini-cabbing." It was a line that came into Mac's head quite regularly these days as he delivered a fare to the Academy or hung around the office playing cards with Kemal, the night controller.

Not that Mac minded cabbing particularly. There were a lot worse things to do, he was well aware. And it fit pretty well with his lifestyle. Not just the working at night but the fact that you could drop it just like that when something better came along. Though it was a bit of a while since something better had come along. It had been three months since he'd finished a stint road managing for the Lords—a bunch of re-formed Aussie punks he'd known from back in the day. And it had been a good six months since anyone had asked Mac to get his own band back on the road. Mac had been in one of the original class-of-'76 punk bands but one that had somehow missed out on becoming legendary. They had a bit of a following in Italy, and most of the places that used to be Yugoslavia, but that was about it.

Five a.m. a call came in for a trip to the airport, Heathrow. Kemal looked over at Mac, who sighed then nodded. It was 7:15 by the time he made it home, a council maisonette in Gospel Oak. Jackie was just getting up, making some tea and yelling at the kids, teenagers now both of them, to get themselves out of bed.

"Hey," he said flopping down on the couch, absolutely knackered.

"Hey yourself," said Jackie.

"Good time last night?" Jackie had been out with a couple of mates from the school.

"Yeah," said Jackie, "nice. Listen, there was a message for you when I got in. From someone called Etheridge. Wants you to call him. Sounds like it might be a job. Etheridge, why does that name ring a bell?"

"Used to manage Ross, you remember?"

Jackie pulled a face. "Oh, him."

"Yeah," said Mac, "him. He's doing all right these days, has his own label and management company. Did he leave a number?"

"Yeah, by the phone."

"Right," said Mac, stretching and heading for bed. "I'll call him later."

"So," said Jackie at teatime, her turn to sit on the couch looking knackered, after a day spent looking after special-needs kids at the school. "What did he want, this Etheridge?"

"Ah, he wants me to talk to someone."

"Oh yeah, any particular someone?"

"Yeah, someone he wants to do a gig, and he's heard I'm the man who might be able to talk this someone into doing one, or at least sober him up enough to get him on stage."

"Oh Christ," said Jackie, "not bloody Luke."

"Yeah," said Mac, "bloody Luke is exactly who he wants.

It's this label's twenty-fifth anniversary and they're having a whole series of gigs to celebrate and they really want Luke to be there, as he was the guy who started it all for them. There's some decent wedge in it for me and all, if I can get him on stage."

Jackie shook her head. "Well, just as long as you don't bring him round here again. Not after last time. Not if he's still drinking."

"Oh," said Mac, "it's a pretty safe bet he's still doing that."

Luke North was another old-timer, another feller who went all the way back to '76/'77, had played all the same speed-driven, gob-drenched gigs as Mac. Only Luke's crew had found favor with the all-important John Peel on the radio, and a bit of a cult had grown up around them over the years. Every decade or so a new band would come along and say their heroes were Luke and his mob, and then there'd be a feature in the *NME* about his dissolute genius or whatever.

All that dissolute genius stuff sounds fine when you read about it in the paper, of course. It tends to be a bit different when you get up close, though. The truth of it was that Luke was a fuck-up, and one who had the knack of fucking up anyone who came in his orbit. But to be fair, he had charm, charisma even, and, given that Mac wasn't planning on sharing his life with the bloke, he'd always got on with him okay. They'd been close for a while right back at the beginning, drifted apart as you do, then become mates again after they'd both been touring Slovenia at the same time a few years back, both of them at a low ebb. Since then, Luke would call up once a month or so and they'd go out, have a drink or whatever.

A few times Mac had brought him back to Gospel Oak

but Jackie wasn't too keen. Said she sort of liked him, you know, she could see what the attraction was, but there was something about him that creeped her out. Mac hadn't really known what she meant till the last time he'd come round. He'd been really drunk, maybe something else going on as well. He hadn't eaten a thing, stubbed his fags out in the food, all that kind of shit which was bad enough, but this time Mac had really known what Jackie meant. There was something—not evil, that was overstating it—but rotten, something definitely rotten coming off him. And since then, that was three, four months ago, Mac had only seen him once.

But apparently that was more than anyone else had done, and if Etheridge was going to pay him a grand "consulting fee" just for getting him on stage, well, Mac was in no position to turn it down.

Calls to the couple of numbers he had for Luke proved fruitless, so Mac decided to cruise around a few of his known haunts in between fares. A run down to Soho gave him a chance to check out the Colony and the French; Luke liked those old-school boho hangouts. No sign of him though, which wasn't much of a surprise, no doubt Etheridge would have found him already if he was hanging around Soho. Same went for Camden Town. Mac checked the Good Mixer and the Dublin Castle just in case, but once again no sign, nothing but Japanese tourists hoping for a glimpse of someone who used to be in Blur. This was ridiculous, Mac decided, there had to be a million drinking holes in London and the odds of finding Luke at random were next to zero. Even if he was in a pub at all and not crashed out in some flat in Walthamstow or Peckham or God knows where else.

He'd just about given up on the idea when a fare took him to London Bridge station and he had a bit of an inspiration. Years ago, Luke had a kid with a woman who ran a pub just down the way. Well, she hadn't run a pub back then, but she did now. Luke had taken him in there a year or so back. He was from Bermondsey, was Luke, originally. Over the years, he'd become all international rock and roll, but scratch deep enough and there was a bit of barrow boy lurking in there. And for years, when he was starting out, he'd had this girlfriend who came from the same background as he, London Irish, Linda her name was.

The pub was tucked underneath the railway line, a real basic boozer with a pool table and jukebox and bunch of old fellers sitting at the bar.

Linda was playing darts when Mac walked in. She was a tall woman, what you'd call handsome rather than pretty, chestnut hair and good bones, looked like she could sort you out herself, no problem, if you started any trouble. He waited till she finished her turn, then said hello.

"All right, darlin'?" he said, and she looked at him uncertainly for a second, then broke out a big smile, came over, and hugged him. Women liked Mac, always had, he was big and solid and he kept his troubles to himself. Plus, in this particular case, there was a little bit of history. It was a long time ago, so long ago that Mac had kind of forgotten it till he felt her arms around him, but once, must be twenty years ago, they'd had a bit of a night. Nothing serious, just a bit of a laugh when Luke had been driving her crazy.

"So," she said, leading him over toward the bar, "what brings you down this way?"

"Well," said Mac, "pleasure of your company, of course."

"Oh, aye?" said Linda, and gave him a bit of a look, one

that said she didn't believe him for a moment, but she'd let it slide for now. "So how's the family?"

"Good. Growing up, you know. How's your boy?"

Linda shook her head. "In prison."

"Oh," said Mac, who wasn't inclined to rush to judgement, he'd done his own time in his wild youth. "Anything serious?"

Linda scrunched her face up. "Not really, just some E's and intent to supply."

"What? They sent him down for that?" He looked at Linda, saw the little shake of her head. "Oh, not a first offense then."

"No," said Linda, "not exactly." Then she mustered up a bit of a smile. "Like father, like son, eh?"

"Yeah, well," said Mac, "he was always a bit of a boy, your Luke, that's for sure. You seen him recently?" Felt like a bit a bastard slipping that in.

"Luke? Yeah, now and again, you know how he is." She paused, took a slug of the drink she had on the bar. Could just be Coke, though Mac wouldn't have bet on it. "You know what I used to think, back when?"

"No," said Mac, remembering her back then, a sharp girl in a ra-ra skirt, worked as a barmaid in the Cambridge. Ha, funny to think of it, but she was the only one of them who had managed to advance her career in the meantime, barmaid to landlady definitely had the edge on punk rocker to punk rock revivalist and part-time cabbie.

"I used to think you two were like twins. Like Luke was the good one and you were the evil one."

"Me?" said Mac, affecting an expression of mock outrage. "Evil?"

"Well," said Linda, "you had just come out of Strangeways when I first met you."

Mac shook his head. It was true. The band he'd been in, in Manchester, they were all proper little hooligans, got all their equipment by robbing music shops. Nothing subtle either. Just a brick through the window in the middle of the night and leg it with whatever you could carry. It was no wonder he'd ended up inside.

Linda carried on. "Then later on I thought I'd got it arse backwards, you were the good one and I'd picked the evil one."

Mac just looked at her, didn't say anything. The business they were in, you didn't play by the usual rules. You were in a band, no one expected you to behave properly. A woman went out with you, it was taken as read there'd be others. At least when you went on tour. Had Luke been worse than him? He didn't really know. He'd never really been one for judging other people. Certainly not back then.

"I chucked him in the end, you know. Well, of course you know. I just got tired of it. And I thought about you now and again. How I should have chosen someone like you."

Mac shook his head, started to say something, "You don't know . . ."

Linda waved his words away. "Yeah, I know. I realized it last time I saw you. A year or two back, when Luke brought you here. I saw you both then and I realized you were the same, just blokes. You just want what you want, all of you."

Mac had a sudden urge to protest. Was he the same as Luke these days? He didn't like to think so. Since he'd been with Jackie, god, getting on twenty years, he'd been a reformed character, responsible.

Well, up to a point. He'd tried to be responsible, he'd give himself that, but there were plenty of times he'd failed, plenty of times he'd strayed. Slovenia, where he'd met up with Luke again, that was a case in point all right. This girl called Anja. Yeah, Linda was close enough to the truth of it. Though he kind of hoped there was a sliver of difference in there somewhere, like the gap between Labour and Tory or something, tiny but just big enough to breathe in.

"So," he said "you know where I might find my evil twin?"

Linda leaned forward reached out a hand and took hold of Mac's chin, turned his face till he was looking right at her, and she at him. "See what I mean?" she said. Then she laughed and let him go and said, "Dunno, exactly, but you could try New Cross. He's got a new girlfriend, she's at Goldsmiths there."

"A student?"

"No, a bloody lecturer. What d'you think? Course she's a student. You think some grown woman's going to take Luke on?"

Mac put his hands up in surrender, then leaned forward and gave Linda a quick kiss right on the lips before heading back out to the car, where he could hear Kemal squawking on the radio.

"Hey," he said, "calm down man. Look, I'm going off the radar now for a couple of hours, but I'll work through till morning. All right?"

He switched the radio off before he could hear Kemal's no doubt outraged reply and headed for New Cross.

Jesus Christ, Mac remembered when New Cross was a nice quiet place to drink, basically dead as anything with a bunch of big old Irish boozers. Now it was like a dank and ugly version of Faliraki, all-disco pubs with bouncers on the outside and liquored-up sixteen-year-olds on the inside. He'd tried Walpole's, the New Cross Inn, and Goldsmiths. No sign of

Luke. He tried the Marquis of Granby, which was a slight improvement, a standard dodgy South London Irish boozer where you could at least hear yourself think. Tired and thirsty, he drank a quick pint of Guinness, tried to remember where else there was to drink in this neck of the woods, and was struck by an unwelcome thought. Luke had always been a Millwall fan.

Reluctantly he dragged himself back out to the car and drove round some back streets that had done a pretty good job of escaping gentrification till he got to the Duke of Albany. He'd been there once with Luke for a lunchtime pre-match session. Hardcore wasn't the word.

From a distance it looked as if it had closed down. The sign had fallen down and most of the letters of the pub's name had gone missing. But there was a light showing behind those windows that weren't blacked out, and Mac sighed and headed on in. He was rewarded by the sight of a dozen or so hard cases giving him the eye, England flags all over the place, and a carpet that immediately attached itself to his feet. He had a quick look round. No sign of Luke. The locals didn't seem to appreciate his interest. Still, Mac knew exactly how to handle these situations these days.

"Someone order a cab?" he said brightly.

"No, mate," replied the barman, and Mac shrugged and grimaced and got out of there.

Back in the car, he checked the time. Eleven, closing. He was about to turn the radio back on when he was struck by a memory. Years ago, he'd played a few gigs at a pub in New Cross. What the hell was it called? The Amersham Arms, that was it. Heading down toward Deptford. Maybe it was still there.

It was, and practically the first person he saw when he

walked into the music room was Luke North—he was slumped on a banquette with his arm around a ghostly pale redhead.

"Hey," said Mac, "how you doing?"

"Hey," said Luke, his eyes taking a moment to focus, "big man. How you doing?"

Better than you, thought Mac. Luke looked ravaged. Way back when, he'd been tall and blond and slightly fucked-up looking. Now he was still tall and blond but more than slightly fucked-up looking: His hair was receding and thinning, his face, even in the light of the pub, was mottled and flaking, and his hard drinker's belly was stretching his shirt underneath a black suit that looked like someone had died in.

Luke pulled the girl to him, turning her attention away from the band, if that's what you called a bunch of art-student types hunched over record decks and laptops, silent films playing on a screen behind them. "Sweetie," he said, "this is Mac, an old mucker of mine. Mac, this is Rose, she's the best thing ever happened to me."

Christ, thought Mac, just how pissed is he? Rose smiled at him enthusiastically. She was very pretty in a Gothic sort of way. Extraordinarily pale skin, set off by hair dyed blood-red, skinny as a rake under a long-sleeved black top.

"Nice to meet you," said Mac. "You want a drink?"

"No," said Luke, standing up suddenly and banging the table as he did so, sending a glass tumbling to the floor. "Let me get them. Guinness, Mac, yeah? You sit down there and talk to Rose."

Mac nodded and watched Luke sway his way toward the bar, then seated himself across the table from Rose.

She smiled awkwardly at him and mumbled something.

Mac gestured to indicate that the art students were making too much of a racket for him to hear, and she leaned forward. "You're a friend of Luke's?" she said.

"Yeah," said Mac, and paused for a second, then said what was on his mind. "Is he all right? He looks terrible."

Rose just gave him a look, like she had no idea what he was talking about, and leaned back and turned her eyes to the band. As she did so, her top rode up and Mac couldn't help noticing how terribly thin she was, not just skinny but full-on anorexic thin. Oh lord. Well, what sort of a girl did he think would want to go out with someone like Luke? She reminded him of someone. Anja the Slovenian. He'd fallen for her big-time. Typical midlife-crisis number, he supposed. Made him blanch to think of it now. He'd have given up Jackie for her, given up his whole life for her if she'd have had him. Thank Christ she hadn't been interested. He'd been an experience for her, that was all. A learning experience. Maybe that's all Luke was to this Rose. He hoped so, but her cuts gave him pause.

Moments later Luke hoved to, with a mineral water for Rose, a Guinness for Mac, and a pint and a large whiskey chaser for himself. Mercifully, the art students decided to pick that moment for a break in proceedings, and Mac figured he might as well make his pitch while the volume level permitted and Luke was still conscious.

He ran through the deal. The twenty-fifth-anniversary show. At the Festival Hall. Everyone was going to be there. All Luke had to do was twenty minutes. Could lead on to a whole lot of other stuff—Meltdown, All Tomorrow's Parties. Mac had no idea whether any of this was true or not, he was just spouting the same bullshit Etheridge had given him.

"He'll even sort out the band for you, if you want. Or you

can use your own, if you've got one at the minute."

"Fuck that," said Luke, and slumped back in his seat. "Fucking wankers."

Mac wasn't sure who the wankers were—his band, Etheridge, the whole crew of post-punk entrepreneurial types with their post-modern music festivals in out-of-season holiday camps. Personally, he was quite happy to agree that the whole lot of them were, indeed, wankers. But that wasn't going to get the bills paid.

"There's good money in it."

Luke just shook his head, but Mac knew him well enough to see something feral appearing in his eyes.

"Five grand," said Mac, "twenty minutes work. Not too shabby."

Luke rolled his eyes like five grand was neither here nor there. Then he leaned forward and grasped Mac's hands in his. "I don't give a shit about those wankers, Mac, you know that. But if you want me to do it, I'll do it. I love you, man."

Jesus Christ, thought Mac, wondering what chemicals Luke had imbibed along with the lake full of booze.

Mac hesitated for a moment. Say he delivered Luke to Etheridge, got him on stage with the right combination of chemicals inside him to impersonate sobriety—or at least sentience—for twenty minutes. What would be the upshot? Five grand for Luke—probably enough to kill himself. A grand for Mac—probably enough to pay off Jackie's credit cards.

Shit, why was he feeling guilty? They were all grown-ups, weren't they? Mac had enough to deal with in his own life, hadn't he? And anyway, we all had a few too many once in a while, didn't we? He looked at Luke trying to maneuver the pint of lager to his mouth without spilling it. It was blatantly obvious that he had passed the point of no return, social-drinking-wise. Dylan Thomas had that line about how an alcoholic was someone you didn't like who drank as much as you did. Well, Mac had been fond of quoting that in his time, but he could see the shallowness of it now. Thomas's drinking killed him, after all. Luke needed help. It was as simple as that.

"Look, I want you to promise me one thing. You do this gig, yeah? You'll spend the money on rehab."

"Sure," said Luke. "I love you, man."

Just then Rose got up to go to the loo. Luke watched her go, then leaned forward to Mac. "Isn't she gorgeous?"

"Yeah," said Mac, "she seems very nice, bit young though, eh?"

"Yeah," said Luke, "goes like a fucking firecracker, though." He knocked back his whiskey, then leaned forward again, motioning Mac to do the same. "Got some nice friends and all, if you're interested."

Mac was appalled to find himself considering it, by the unwelcome knowledge that somewhere inside him was the capacity to say yes, set me up with an anorexic waif of my own. Linda's line about them being like twins was running through his head. It struck him now that it was the evil twin she liked, she wanted. It let her off the hook. Maybe he should just give in to his dark side, maybe that actually made it easier for everyone. No self-repression, no hypocrisy. Just get down in the dirt.

He looked at Rose, heading back from the toilet, stopping at the cigarette machine, all young and fresh and damaged, saw Anja in her place, remembered how much he'd wanted Anja the first time he saw her at that club in Ljubljana. He saw Luke staring at Rose, eyes full of lust and lager, saw himself in Luke, embracing death. He felt like there was no air in the room. He took a deep breath, sucked in as much as he could. Then tilted his head back and stared at the ceiling, wondering how he got to this pass. Maybe he could retrain as a social worker or something. Something useful. Something that would stop him from taking his place in the tableau in front of him. He shook his head hard and the fog seemed to clear momentarily.

He became aware of the record that was playing, some old punk thing by the Damned, probably the art students were playing it ironically. It didn't sound ironic to Mac though, it sounded like his youth. It reminded him viscerally of what it had felt like being young then, nearly thirty years ago, playing this stupid fast music for no other reason than the sheer rush, the sheer pointless, joyous momentum of it.

And it reminded him that he wasn't young anymore, and no matter how many Anjas or brand-new Roses he picked up, he would be nothing more than a vampire, not magically returned to the loud stupid kid he'd once been. He tilted his head back down and looked at Luke. Then it struck him, the difference between them. Luke was still the loud stupid kid he had been, still a selfish, pleasure-seeking child. Ah well, good luck to him, he supposed.

"Sorry, man," he said, shaking his head, "not my scene."

"Your loss," answered Luke. "I tell you, she's a fucking firecracker, that one. Another pint?"

"No thanks," said Mac, but Luke was already up and lurching bar-wards again. As he did so, Rose ran over to him, threw her arms round him, and kissed him like she hadn't seen him for a week. He said something in her ear and she nodded and reached into her bag, took out her purse, and handed him a twenty. Luke trousered it and turned toward the bar before suddenly seeming to convulse. And then, slowly and oddly gracefully, he collapsed on the floor, banging into the legs of a couple of his fellow drinkers.

"You fucking wanker!" shouted one of the drinkers, and wound up to throw a punch, before realizing that his opponent was already down and out.

Mac looked on transfixed, his attention entirely gripped by Rose, who calmly knelt down on the floor next to Luke and cradled him against her, stroking his head with one hand, a flame-haired, flat-chested Madonna and her debauched infant.

Later, sitting in the cab, resigned to being a grown-up, earning his money the hard way, he found the words "damned" and "blessed" jostling for space in his brain.

The following afternoon he was woken up by the phone. It was Etheridge on the line. Mac paused for a moment, wondering what to say. He wasn't sure he really cared what Luke did, but the thought of taking a finder's fee for tracking him down felt weirdly unclean, seemed to somehow make him complicit in Luke's grim debauch. On the other hand, it was undoubtedly an easy grand.

Before he could make the decision, Etheridge started talking. "Look," he said, "not to worry about tracking down old Luke."

"Oh," said Mac, "decided against risking him on stage, have you?"

"No, no, not at all," explained Etheridge, "people love a bit of drama, don't they? No, his manager's been in touch so it's all sorted out. I just thought I'd let you know."

"Manager?" said Mac.

"Oh yes, delightful young woman by the sound of her,

name of Rose. Sounds like she's got him right under her thumb. So there we are. Well, thanks again."

"No trouble," said Mac and put the phone down.

The next morning he finished his shift deliberately early and got home in time to find Jackie still in bed. After they'd had sex he was happy to realize that for the first time in a long while he hadn't thought about Anja at all.

PENGUIN ISLAND

BY JERRY SYKES

Camden Town

Eamonn Coughlan had lived in Camden Town all his life, and from as far back as he could remember there had been packs of teenagers roaming the streets: from the wartime cosh gangs that had operated during the blackouts to the hippies in the '60s . . . from the punks of the '70s through to the . . . Well, he didn't know what they were called these days, but whatever they were called he had never come across a group of teenagers that had marked out their territories with as much determination as the current crop. Of course, he knew that graffiti had been around forever, ever since an unknown caveman had first picked up a piece of sharpened flint and scratched into the walls of his cave pictures of the animals that he had killed that morning. But it seemed that in the last few years almost every building in Camden Town had been marked with some kind of multicolored lettering or sign. He knew that it had something to do with drugs, an ongoing turf war, and that the signs were forever changing because of the constant battle for the rights to deal drugs to the thousands of tourists who flocked into the area around Camden Lock each weekend, but the subtleties of the different signs were lost on him.

For the last eighteen months, the dominant piece of graffiti on the wall beside the lift in his building had been a large picture of a castle in red and blue. But as Coughlan pushed through the door that late spring morning, he saw that the castle had been covered over with black paint and that a couple of boys were now creating a new motif in its place. The new design was still little more than a sketch, he could just about make out three big letters outlined in red and orange—*YBT*, it looked like—but before Coughlan could see more, one of the boys caught him looking and turned and raised a hard chin in his direction.

"Yo, what d'you think you're lookin' at," snarled the boy, his neck stretching out of his collar. From the rest of his face he looked to be no more than thirteen or fourteen, but his eyes were cold and hard, aged before their time. He had a greased-down, straight-fringed haircut that made him look like a little Caesar, and the skin around the corners of his mouth was studded with cloves of acne. The other boy continued to paint, his head rising and falling to some music that no one else could hear.

Coughlan shook his head and let the door fall closed behind him. Averting his eyes, he shuffled across to the lift, Little Caesar following him with narrowed eyes, his breath loud and coarse through his mouth. As Coughlan pressed the button to call the lift, the other boy turned to see what his friend was looking at, and Coughlan recognized him at once as Pete Wilson, a boy from the building that he had known since he was a toddler. From what Coughlan could remember, he must have been about twelve now.

Pete's pupils went wide as he recognized the old man and his hands whipped behind his back, hiding the paint can.

"What do you think you're doing, Pete?" asked Coughlan, but as soon as the words were out of his mouth he felt his shoulders tense. He had never been one for making a fuss, and his outburst had scared him almost as much as it had surprised him.

Pete hesitated for a moment, torn between his childhood links and the new alliance of his fresh and future independence.

"I bet your mother doesn't know what you're up to," Coughlan persisted, brave now. "What do you think she'd say if she knew you were down here vandalizing your own building?"

Discovering that the decrepit old man in front of them knew his friend, Little Caesar's mood lightened and he sniggered and punched Pete on the arm. Pete grunted and punched him back, glad for the distraction. From further up the stairs the sound of someone cursing and kicking the lift door could be heard.

"I hope you're going to clean that mess up before you go home," said Coughlan, pointing a crooked finger at the wall.

"I was just painting over the castle," protested Pete.

"With black paint on a white wall? And what's with the red and orange letters? What's that supposed to mean?"

"That's YBT," replied Pete, smiling. "You Been Torched."

"I don't understand," replied Coughlan, frowning.

Pete opened his mouth to speak, but before he could do so, Little Caesar hit him on the shoulder again. "You know we're not supposed to tell no one about that."

"It's not a secret," protested Pete, holding his arm tight where Little Caesar had punched him.

"Fuckin' child," snapped Little Caesar, snatching the paint can from Pete's hand and storming out of the building. Pete watched him go and then, after taking a quick glance at the unfinished graffiti, followed him. At the door, Pete cast a look back at the old man, and Coughlan thought he detected the hint of an apologetic word in the nervous stutter of his lips.

Coughlan watched them disappear around the edge of the building, Pete trailing the other kid like a sibling desperate to please his elder brother. He waited a couple of seconds to make sure there was no return, and then felt a long hot breath leave his chest. He had not realized that he had been holding his breath. He turned back to the lift and pressed the button again.

A couple of minutes later, an old woman in a blue raincoat appeared at the foot of the stairs, panting as if she had just walked up them and not down. "I hope you're not waiting on the lift," she managed to gasp on a cloud of smoke, a cigarette burning in her fist, before she too disappeared through the door.

Coughlan took a deep breath and started up the stairs.

Back in his flat on the fourth floor, he filled the kettle and dropped a teabag into a mug. Waiting for the kettle to boil, he rested his hands on the edge of the sink and looked out over the estate toward Kentish Town Road, toward a couple of phone booths. Behind the booths was a low brick wall where it was common knowledge that a number of drug dealers practiced their trade, their customers either walking up or pulling up on the street in their cars to pick up their goods. There was a dealer out there at the moment, and another one strolling up and down the street, gesturing with a pointed finger at the cars that passed. It had become such a common sight, part of the threadbare fabric of the estate, that it no longer triggered an emotional response in Coughlan. But as he let his attention drift across the rest of the estate, his heart filled with sorrow as he spotted Pete and his friend sitting on the back of a bench no more than fifteen feet from the phone booths, watching the drug dealers in silent fascination.

Later that night, stretched out on his bed, Coughlan listened with grim acceptance to the sound of his neighbors arguing, the rise and fall of drunken tongues and slurred insults. On the weekend it was like this most nights, along with the rumble of music through the wall that reminded him of the night during the war when a German bomb had reduced their neighbor's house to smoking ash and rubble. The bomb had buckled the foundations of their own house, and the front door had never fit the frame after that, still letting in a draft when the council had moved them out of the house and into the Castle Estate the same summer he retired. And it was on nights like this that he wished his neighbors, his imagined enemies, could be bombed all over again.

A week later, Coughlan was walking across the estate to the newsagent's on Castle Road when he saw Pete with another boy at the side of the building. It was the first time he had seen him since the afternoon near the lift. The other boy was not the same one who had been with him that time. No, this one looked to be more like one of the lads that hung around the phone booths, older, all cold skin and hand jerks. The two of them were talking, but there was something odd about their body language. Pete was nodding and grinning as the older boy spoke, as if the older boy was telling him a long joke, although from the look on the older boy's face he seemed to be more annoyed than amused. Coughlan tried not to watch, but he kept glancing up as he walked past, and when Pete caught him looking, the grin fell from the boy's face and his once innocent cheeks flushed with something approaching shame. The other boy caught the change in his features and, after peering across at Coughlan, jabbed Pete on the shoulder and asked him who the old man was. Pete attempted to shrug off the question, but the other boy jabbed him again on the shoulder, harder this time, and Pete's mouth sprung open. Coughlan turned his head aside and hurried on, but not before he caught his name in the tumble of words that spilled from Pete's mouth.

The following afternoon, struggling home from the super-market—since arthritis had calcified the knuckles in his hands, he was unable to load more than a few items into his bag at a time and so had to go shopping each afternoon—Coughlan ran into Pete again. As Coughlan was crossing the junction at the foot of the estate, a line of impatient cars pushing at the red light, Pete came rushing out of the green-grocer's with a loaf of bread under his arm and bumped straight into the old man. Coughlan stumbled but did not fall, though he did drop his shopping bag, and a tin of processed peas rolled into the gutter.

"Whoa, watch where you're going," squealed Pete, and then pulled up as he noticed that it was Coughlan he had bumped into.

Coughlan frowned at him and shook his head, and then stooped to pick up his groceries.

"Here, let me get that," said Pete, crossing to pick up the peas from the gutter. He held out the tin to Coughlan and the old man took it and put it in his bag with the other things.

"Sorry about that," Pete continued. "Look, why don't I carry your shopping home for you? The lift's not working again." Without waiting for an answer, he took the bag from Coughlan's hardened and aching hands and started walking.

Pushing through the door of the building, the boy hold-ing it open with the back of his heel, Coughlan noticed that Pete headed straight for the stairs without so much as a casual glance at the mess of graffiti on the wall. It had not been touched since Coughlan had stumbled across Pete and his friend with fresh paint on their hands, but he thought that Pete would have at least sneaked a look at it. Or perhaps that was the reason behind Pete helping him with his shopping . . .

Upstairs in the flat, Pete put the shopping bag on the kitchen counter, took out his own loaf of bread that he had put in there for safekeeping, and then turned toward the door. But he appeared to be in no great rush to leave, his lips mouthing silent words as if he had something on his mind.

Coughlan thought he knew what it was. "Don't worry about it, son," he said, smiling. "I'm not going to tell your mum about the graffiti or anything, if that's what you're worried about . . ."

"Oh no, that's not the reason I helped you," insisted Pete, shaking his head. "No, that's got nothing to do with it. I just saw you struggling across the street and I thought . . ."

"I know, I know," Coughlan assured him, patting the air in front of him with his palms. "And I do appreciate it. It's just that . . . Look, can I get you a drink of squash or something?"

"No, that's all right," said Pete, shaking his head. "I better get this bread home or my mum'll be wondering where I am."

"All right," said Coughlan. "Well, thanks again, Pete."

The boy offered him a brief smile and then turned and disappeared back down the stairs.

The following afternoon, Pete was waiting for Coughlan when the old man came out of the supermarket, and once again offered to help him with his shopping. Coughlan was surprised to see him after the awkwardness of their last meeting, but he knew enough to keep his mouth shut if it meant that much to the lad. And on the walk back to the estate, it did seem that Pete had forgotten all about it, chatting about his school and his teachers.

Over the following couple of weeks, Pete helped Coughlan with his shopping a number of times, and soon Coughlan found that he was timing his trips to the supermarket to coincide with Pete coming home from school. Sometimes Pete would accept the old man's offer of a drink, gulping it down, but more often than not he would decline, telling him that he had to get home.

And then one afternoon, an hour or so before Coughlan was due to leave for the supermarket, there was a knock at the door. When he opened it he was surprised to find Pete standing there with a couple of bulging shopping bags in his hands. "These weigh a ton," he gasped. "Are you going to let me in or what?"

Startled and amused, Coughlan stepped aside to let him across the threshold. "What've you got in there?" he said, trailing Pete down the hall and into the kitchen.

Pete left the question in the air as he hefted the bags onto the counter. He let out a great breath, and then turned and rested against the counter, smiling and shaking his head.

"I don't understand," said Coughlan, frowning.

"The teacher was sick, so we got let out of school . . . I thought I might as well pick up your shopping for you."

"But that lot must've cost you a small fortune," said Coughlan, stepping forward and peering into the bags. "You didn't pay for it yourself, did you?" He had no idea how much pocket money Pete got each week, or whether he had a paper round or some other job, but, whatever, he should have been spending it on himself, not on an old man. "You must let me give you the money."

Coughlan moved into the front room, the fire turned down low, and returned with his wallet. He took out a ten-pound note and handed it to Pete. "Is that enough?" he asked, looking at the remaining note in his wallet, a fiver. He felt that he should give the boy more for his thoughtfulness, but the fiver was all he had until he claimed his pension at the end of the week.

"Ten's fine," replied Pete. He took the crumpled bill from the outstretched hand and folded it into his front pocket.

"It was very kind of you, anyway," said Coughlan. "Very thoughtful."

"Look, I was thinking," said Pete, hesitant. His cheeks were flushed pink, and there was a fine sheen of perspiration on his forehead. "Why don't you let me do this all the time, get your shopping for you on my way home from school. I know it must be difficult for you, what with your hands like that . . . It's no problem, honest, especially as you always eat the same things."

Coughlan felt tears prick the back of his lids. "That's a great idea," he said. "Thanks."

"And then you can pay me when I get here," Pete added.

"But what if I'm not in?" said Coughlan, sniffing.

"Well, I don't know . . ."

"I might want to go out. I don't want you getting my shopping for me and then not being here to let you in."

"I don't suppose you've got a mobile phone, have you?"

"Er, no. No, I haven't . . ."

"Well, I don't know then," said Pete, his forehead crinkled in thought. "What about if you let me have a key or something? Or how about leaving it with one of the neighbors?"

Coughlan thought about his neighbors, the born fighters. "I'll go down and get you one cut in the morning," he replied.

"Sorted," said Pete.

The new arrangement suited them both fine. But then Coughlan found that he was just waiting in for Pete to arrive, and not getting out and about as much as he would have liked. He let this go on for some time, until one afternoon, as he was looking out the window, the clouds above the estate parted, the solid shapes of the buildings started to soften around the edges, and he realized that he was just being ridiculous and decided to go out for a walk. Pulling on his jacket, he left the estate and headed down Castle Road toward the center of Camden Town, past the boarded-up pubs, the shops that sold little more than international phone cards, and the cafés with names in languages that he did not even recognize let alone understand. As he walked, he saw a number of walls and bridges littered with both the castle and YBT graffiti, the castle artwork faded and peeling while the YBT letters shone with a brittle freshness. It did not cross his mind for one second that perhaps Pete had been one of the artists.

At the junction in front of Camden Town tube station there was a traffic island, a triangular slice of concrete and paving stones that for as long as Coughlan could remember had been known as Penguin Island. In the street behind the tube station, there was a Catholic church that back in the '50s had been frequented in the main by the Irish families who lived in the immediate area. After the regular Sunday morning Mass had finished at 11:30, the men would gather on the traffic island to wait for the pubs to open at noon, while the women would go home to prepare lunch. Standing there in their uniform black suits and white shirts, with their hands in their pockets, shuffling around on impatient feet, the men had resembled nothing so much as a squadron of penguins stranded in the middle of a sea of traffic.

Coughlan smiled at the remembrance, but then another more potent image appeared beside the first one: Coughlan himself walking back from the church with his wife at his side, wanting to be on the island but not having the courage to tell his wife that that was what he wanted. It had been the tale of his life, and he wondered if he would ever now get to Penguin Island. He pushed his hands deeper into his pockets and walked on.

When he returned to the flat an hour later, Coughlan was surprised to hear voices coming from the living room. At first he thought that Pete had arrived and turned on the TV to amuse himself while he waited, something that he had done before, but when he stepped through into the living room, he found Pete and another boy standing in front of the mantelpiece.

At the sight of Coughlan, Pete cast a quick glance toward his friend and then turned to look at Coughlan again, his mouth open in a mask of timid shock. The friend caught the apprehension in Pete's face and pushed back his shoulders and looked over toward Coughlan with a slow grin on his face.

"Yeah, this is . . . this is Keith," stammered Pete. "It's all right for me to let him come in and watch TV with me?"

"Well, I suppose so," replied Coughlan, distracted.

Coughlan looked across at Keith, took in the knowing look and the stance that told him that he was just as comfortable, if not more so, in Coughlan's home than the old man himself.

"Hello, Keith," said Coughlan, nodding.

Keith said nothing, just kept up the grin in response.

"I've put the shopping away," said Pete. "And I got you another one of those pork-and-pickle pies you like."

"Thanks, Pete."

"It was reduced so you might have to eat it today."

"Yes, thanks, Pete," muttered Coughlan again, embarrassed at discussing the state of his finances in front of a stranger. "Anyway . . . look, Pete, I don't mind you bringing your friends round here. But in the future, can you ask me first?"

"I'm sorry, I thought you'd be in," replied Pete.

"That's all right, no harm done this time," said Coughlan.

Pete kept a low profile for a short time after that, but when Coughlan came home late one afternoon a week later—to appear less needful he had taken to being out sometimes when Pete was due to call with his shopping—he found that Pete had not one but several friends with him. When Coughlan poked his head through the door, curious at the noise, there was a group of four or five lads sitting around the living room. One of them looked to be about the same age as Pete, but the others appeared to be about two or three years older, tufts of soft hair coloring their chins and their long limbs barely under control. Pete was sitting in the middle of the sofa and looked to be more at ease than he had been the time before, staring at the TV. He did not seem to have noticed Coughlan, but then none of them appeared to have noticed him, and Coughlan felt a tumble of emotions pass through him. On one hand, he felt that he should pull Pete out of the room and ask him to ask the others to leave, but then he did not want to embarrass the lad in front of his friends again. Without waiting to see if he had been spotted, Coughlan made a gesture as if he had forgotten something, and then turned and left the flat.

He walked up to Parliament Hill, through the park past the athletics track, and back down to Camden Town, his mind adrift on children and the past. When he reached home again, Pete and his friends had gone, but the smell of cigarettes and something else still hung in the air. Coughlan opened the top windows to clear the room and then closed the door tight and headed for bed.

Later that night, stretched out on his bed, unable to sleep because of the noise coming through the wall from his neighbors, Coughlan felt himself returning to the thoughts that had been troubling him during his walk earlier. He and his wife had not been able to have children of their own, and so he was not sure how he should have handled the situation with Pete. Instinct told him that he had done the right thing, but he wished to God that he had more than instinct on which to base his reactions.

In 1945, a short time before Coughlan had started courting his wife—he had known her since junior school, and in their teens the pair had lived just three streets apart—she had had a brief but intense affair with a married American soldier stationed in London. When the American had broken off the affair to return to his wife and home in West Virginia, she had just shrugged it off as if he had meant no more to her than a pair of old shoes. But then two months later she had fallen into a deep depression and not ventured out of the house for another three weeks. When at last she came out again, she had been a different person, as quiet in her new skin as she had been the life and soul in her old skin. And she had also then had some time for Coughlan, too, the quiet and dependable kid in the corner of the neighborhood. Of course, there had been rumors that it was not depression that had kept her in the house all that time, the strongest of which was that following the American's departure she had undergone a backstreet abortion that went wrong and left her barren. Coughlan had ignored all the rumors at the time, grateful for her attention, and had maintained a closed ear even when she had failed to become pregnant throughout their long marriage. Even now, more than a decade after her death, he still refused to believe that the rumors were something other than malicious gossip, putting their childlessness down as something that was just meant to be.

The following afternoon there was a group of boys in his flat again, but this time Pete was not with them. There were just the three of them, smoking and watching *The Jerry Springer Show*.

"What are you doing here?" asked Coughlan, doing his best to sound indignant but finding a touch of fear holding him back.

The boys ignored him, grinning as the TV pumped out a hard rattle of cheers and applause.

"How did you get in?" said Coughlan, stepping further into the room.

The boys continued to grin and ignore him.

"I said, how did you get in?" repeated Coughlan, stepping in front of the TV.

"Your boy gave us his key, man," replied one of the boys at last, scowling, his pale face shrouded in the hood of his sweatshirt, arching to look around Coughlan at the TV.

"You mean Pete gave you his key?"

"If that's what his name is," sniggered the boy.

"Well, he shouldn't have done that," said Coughlan, reaching down to turn off the TV. "So I'd like you all to leave."

"I was watching that," complained one of the other boys.

"Yo, he gave us his key, man," said the first boy. "Gave us his key and told us to wait here for him. Said he had to do some shopping for you or something. You can't ask us to leave."

"Yeah, what's he going to say when he gets back here and finds us gone?" said the second boy. "What's he going to say when he gets back here and finds you kicked us out?"

"Well . . . that's different then," said Coughlan, taken aback. "You should have said." And all at once he felt shrunken, as if he had betrayed Pete. He felt all the boys looking at him, judging him, making him out to be the villain of the piece. He did not know what to do, feeling like even his breathing was further condemnation, and after a few moments of just staring into space, he turned and walked through into the kitchen to look out across the estate, a terrible weight hanging in his chest.

Pete at last turned up half an hour later, but the next time that Coughlan came home to find a group of his friends watching TV in his living room, Pete was again not with them. There was still no sign of him an hour later, either, and so Coughlan climbed down from his stool in the kitchen, shuffled through into the living room, and asked them to leave. This time the boys did so without much bother, clucking tongues and dragging feet, but it left the old man feeling confused and hurt.

The time after that the lads had the TV up loud and, despite Coughlan asking them a couple of times to turn it down, the noise remained constant. Coughlan did not have the strength to argue with them and kept to himself in the kitchen. After waiting for Pete for over an hour, he could take it no longer. He slipped on his jacket and headed out into the night.

He sat on a bench in the center of the estate, watching people come and go. It was a warm evening and he felt comfortable out there, more comfortable than he did in the light, the twilight hiding the geographical sins and scars of the estate.

He sat for another few minutes and then decided to go for a walk. When he got home again about half past 10, the gang was gone but had left a mosaic of trash behind in his front room: crushed beer and Coke cans, fried chicken boxes, cigarette butts, neon bottles with chewed straws poking out of their lips. He tidied up as best he could and then went to bed, determined to confront Pete and ask him to give him his key back.

But Pete did not appear the following afternoon, or the one after that, and when he had still not turned up on the third afternoon, Coughlan felt his fragile resolve start to waver. Then one lunchtime, as he was looking for some tinfoil to wrap a half-eaten sandwich in, the ongoing tension had made him lose his appetite, he found something that fired him up again.

Standing on a chair in the kitchen, he was reaching into the top cupboard where he was sure there was some tinfoil, when he felt a cool plastic bag there. He could not see into the cupboard so he shifted his arthritic fingers around, attempting to make out what it was. An old carrier bag, stuffed with some linen napkins, perhaps. He tried to find purchase on the bag but his fingers kept slipping off. After a few failed attempts, he managed to catch hold of a corner of the bag and started to ease it out of the cupboard. Moving it a couple of inches at a time, he pulled it toward the edge of the shelf. And then there was a shift and a tumble, and a cascade of small plastic bags and little foil envelopes fell out onto the floor in a solid splash. A black bin liner followed like a winded kite. Coughlan looked at the mess in astonishment. There must have been at least two or three hundred little bags and envelopes spread across the kitchen floor.

It took him a minute to get there, but Coughlan had seen

enough police shows on TV to know that he was looking at drugs. Hundreds, perhaps thousands of pounds worth of drugs. He climbed down from the chair and sat for a moment looking at the hellish pile on the floor, wondering what to do with it all. He checked his watch and saw that it was almost 5 o'clock, Pete's usual time for coming around. Sighing at the situation, he levered himself down onto the floor, scooped all the small packets back into the bin liner, and hefted it up onto the table.

Fifteen minutes later he heard Pete's voice out in the hall, and then another voice behind the first. Coughlan held his breath, his heart beating loud in his chest, as he waited for them to walk along the hall and into the front room. He heard the TV being switched on, a quick pulse of canned laughter, and then seconds later a kid with black hair stepped into the kitchen. He saw Coughlan sitting at the table with the full bin liner in front of him and his pupils went dark and wide in anger.

"What the fuck d'you think you're doing with that?"

"I might ask you the same question," replied Coughlan.

"It's none of your fuckin' business."

"It's my flat," said Coughlan. "It's my home."

At that moment Pete walked into the room, lured in by the raised voices.

"Did you know anything about this?" asked Coughlan, pointing at the bin liner.

Pete glanced at the other boy, looking for the right words.

And then without warning, the other boy stepped up to Coughlan and punched him hard in the face.

Coughlan felt a great bolt of pain shake his spine and nail him to the chair. Tears sprang across his face and diluted the blood that bubbled from his nose. His head spun for a second, and then he fell unconscious face-first across the bag of drugs.

"You've killed him," squealed Pete. "You've killed him."

"He's not dead," said the other kid, poking Coughlan hard in the shoulder so that his head lolled back and forth. "Look, he's still bleeding. Dead people don't bleed like that."

"But he might be dead soon," said Pete, his face turning white and his tongue sticking in his throat.

"Don't be fuckin' stupid," said the other kid, stepping forward and giving Coughlan a hard shove. The old man slid off the table and dragged the bag of drugs onto the floor with him, spilling its contents across the battered linoleum.

Pete just stared at the old man, the spread of drugs.

"Well go on then, pick 'em up," said the other kid.

Pete hesitated for a second, his limbs telling him to run, but then did as he was told. He gathered the drugs together and tried to see if Coughlan was breathing all right.

"Come on, come on," snapped the other kid, tapping Pete in the side with the toe of his trainer.

Pete hurried to scrape up the remainder of the packets and stuff them back into the bin liner. He gathered the neck of the bag together and then tried to hand it to the other kid. But the other kid just told him to put it back in the cupboard.

"But what about Mr. Coughlan?"

"He's not goin' to be telling no one," came the response.

Coughlan came round moments later, more shocked than hurt. Drifting back into the here and now, he remained on the kitchen floor for a short time, listening for signs of other people in the flat. It all appeared to be quiet, and he was sure that it had been the slamming of the door that had stirred him. He ran a hand across his upper lip, wiping at the blood there. It had started to harden and it felt like his nose had stopped bleeding. He climbed to his feet and shuffled across to the sink. He turned on the tap and let it run until it got as cold as it was going to get. Cupping his hands together, he filled them with water, and then held his nose in the water until it had all leaked through his hardened fingers. He repeated the action. As the center of his face started to numb, the numbness spreading out from his nose, he felt his strength returning and his mind clearing. He knew that he should go to the police, but he also knew that would be a mistake. He had seen what had happened to people who stood up for themselves, and he did not want to go through that himself. Rather than bringing an end to their torment, it had more often than not meant an escalation.

He shuffled through into his bedroom and changed into a fresh shirt, throwing the bloodstained one into the waste bin behind the door. There were a few splashes of blood on his trousers, but as he had just bought them a few weeks earlier, he was reluctant to throw them out too, and decided to keep them on. Once he had finished dressing, he walked into the bathroom to inspect his injuries in the mirror. He used a flannel to wipe the dried blood from his skin and then leaned in to the mirror to get a closer look. There was a small scratch on the side of his nose, and the beginnings of a bruise, but apart from that the damage appeared to be minimal, at least on the outside.

He went back into the bedroom and put on a thick sweater. Despite the warmth of the evening, the assault had left him feeling cold and he had goosebumps on his arms. Then he went back into the kitchen and looked at the blood on the floor, the bloodied handprints from the floor to the sink like the footprints of some great lost beast. The sight of it made him feel a little sick, and he told himself he would clean it up later. He turned and left the flat, closing the door behind him.

He walked through Camden Town, through the streets he had walked since childhood, feeling that he no longer knew them. His mind was all over the place, dislocated and lost within the familiar maps of his life. Earlier he had been quite prepared to confront Pete about letting his friends use the flat, but now he felt like he just wanted to forget that he had ever met the boy.

He tried to eat an omelette at a café on Chalk Farm Road, pushing it around his plate until it got lodged in the cooling grease, and then walked up to Parliament Hill fields. There, he sat on a bench overlooking the athletics track, watching a group of girls messing about in the long jump pit. At one point, one of the girls ran across to the steeplechase water jump. There was no water in it, but she still jumped in and pretended to be drowning, waving her arms around and screaming. Her friends just ignored her and at last she returned to the sand pit.

The girls left when it started to get dark, but Coughlan felt too tired to walk home just then and stretched out on the bench to rest for a few minutes before setting off. The brittle summer stars spreading across the darkening ceiling of the world reminded him of a time during the war when he had dragged his mattress onto the roof of the outhouse to listen to the bombs dropping on the East End. Despite the noise and the threat of the bombs getting closer, he remembered it as being a time of calm for him, a time before he had met his wife, a time before the neighbor's house had been crushed. He let his lids fall, so tired and with a persistent headache, and when at last he opened them again it had started to get light. Surprised, he rubbed hard at his face to wake himself up and then climbed to his feet. His back ached but the pain eased up as he started walking toward the gate. When he checked the clock outside the jeweler's store on Kentish Town Road he was surprised to see that it was 5 o'clock in the morning.

He let himself into the flat and stood for a few moments in the hall, just holding his breath and listening. Minutes passed but all he could hear was the regular sounds of the flat creaking. He appeared to be alone, but to make sure he went round each of the rooms, checking in cupboards and behind doors, before going back to the front door and locking it. Then he went back into his bedroom and climbed into bed, still in his clothes.

When he woke again it was after 4 in the afternoon, a dull rectangle of orange light spread across the bed beside him. For a moment he did not know where he was, and then he remembered falling asleep on the bench and it all came back to him. But in that fleeting moment of not knowing, he had felt at peace with the world. And now the knot was back in his stomach. He looked at his watch again to check the time. Pete or some of his friends would be around soon and he did not want to be here for that. He went into the bathroom to check on the wound, and then back into the bedroom to dress in a set of thicker and more comfortable clothes. In the kitchen he took his pension book from the drawer, slipped it into the back pocket of his trousers, and headed back out- side. He took a quick glance at the drug dealers sitting near the phone booths, then turned and headed back up toward Parliament Hill fields, calling in at a corner shop to purchase a couple of small pies and a carton of milk.

There were a few pensioners out on the bowling green, and a middle-aged couple were struggling to hit the ball over the net on one of the tennis courts. Coughlan stopped for a moment to watch them, aching inside at their casual grasp of the ordinariness of their lives, and then continued on to the bench where he had slept the night before. As he turned from the fence bordering the court, he started to panic at the thought that someone else might be sitting there. But when he reached the top of the rise and saw that there was no one else there, the feeling of relief that flooded his senses was just as great as if he had returned to his flat and found that Pete and his friends had decided to leave. He stepped up his pace until he reached the bench, took his seat, and then looked around, blinking in the high afternoon sun. There was no one on the athletics track, no one messing around in the long jump pit, nothing for him to watch and help pass the time. But on the main path there was a woman out walking her dog, and when Coughlan offered her a cheerful hello he was rewarded with a brief smile. It was the greatest reaction he'd had had in a long time, the greatest acceptance.

Through the birch trees on the far side of the track and the cranes that seemed to be forever stalking the streets of London, Coughlan watched the sun go down until he became shrouded in darkness. The shroud felt a little colder than it had the night before, so he pulled his coat tight around his chest. A slight wind had also started to blow across the hill, and he thought that perhaps he might be too cold on the bench. He tried to think of somewhere else he might be able to sleep. There was a small café near the tennis courts, and he thought that perhaps he might be warm snuggled up there at the back of the kitchen. But then he remembered the bandstand further back. Not the usual kind of bandstand with a wrought-iron railing circling the stage, but one with a solid wall facing the path. Whenever the bandstand was in use, the audience would sit on the hill to watch. If he crept in there he would be sheltered from both the wind and people passing on the path. Taking one last look across the track toward the failing light, Coughlan bundled himself up inside his coat and headed for the bandstand.

Within an hour he was asleep. He dreamed of black-and-white creatures diving from a concrete island and swimming free, at ease with both themselves and their surroundings. From the opposite bank he stood and watched them for a long time before summoning up the courage to dive in and join them. His arms and legs felt awkward at first, stiff and making little progress, but soon he too was swimming free. At first the other creatures kept their distance, but after a few minutes he was accepted into their fold, and when the swim was over the creatures let him climb out onto their concrete island. When he looked back at the place from where he had dived into the water, it had disappeared.

The following morning he awoke feeling like he had just had the best night's sleep of his life, and he set off back to the flat with something approaching a spring in his step.

Walking across the estate, he saw that the door to his flat was wide open. Fearing that he had been burgled, he picked up his pace and hurried up the stairs. But as he approached the door, the fear was replaced with something else: huge relief that at long last he had no responsibilities and could do just as he pleased. On reaching the door, he stopped and listened for a moment, and then pulled it closed and carried on walking.

PART IV

LONDON CALLING

SHE'LL RIDE A WHITE HORSE

BY MARK PILKINGTON

Dalston

A hundred wary eyes watched his approach through the yellow-stained sodium twilight. The cats were all around him, frozen as if ready to pounce, though whether toward him or away from him, he couldn't tell. Heldon considered himself a cat lover, but their stares forced a shiver of unease.

The pinpoints of light punctured the night—under trolleys and cars, on corrugated roofs, though most of them, attached to near-identical scrawny brown bodies, surrounded an overturned plastic barrel that had spilled a neat chevron of part-frozen meat and bone onto a torn newspaper headline: *Iran: Allied Generals Are Ready.*

By day, Ridley Road Market is the heart of Dalston. A heaving babel of traders and shoppers—East End English, West African, Indian, Russian, Turkish—squeeze past each other in a permanent bottleneck. The stalls—Snow White Children's Clothes, Chicken Shop, Alpha & Omega Variety Store—offer exotically colored fabrics and cheap electrical goods alongside barrels of unidentifiable animal parts, unfamiliar vegetables, and unlocked mobile phones.

But at night the market belongs to the cats. They are everywhere. They don't need to fight, there's always plenty of food to go round; they just wait their turns in the shadows.

At least they keep the rats away, thought Heldon, in a

transparent attempt to console himself. A foot-long rodent scuttled behind a wheelie bin. The cats' eyes remained fixed on the larger intruder. "Don't mind me," he said out loud, "just keep eating your dinner."

"Ignore the cats, they're just keeping an eye out for troublemakers."

The deep, careful African voice came from a closed stall within a concrete shell on the other side of the road; a tired-looking sign above a closed wooden door read, *Bouna Fabrics Afr*, before trailing off into decay.

The cats returned to their business. Heldon crossed the road and opened the door.

"Hello, Ani. You've got yourself a few more cats since I was last here."

"Yes, my friend. At least they keep the rats away, eh?"

Aniweta smiled and the men shook hands. A Nigerian barrel of a man with a gold-ringed grasp to match, his strong dark hand engulfed Heldon's puffy pink-white flesh. He claimed to be in his forties. But his watery eyes and leather-tan skin made Heldon think he was older than that.

"It's good of you to see me," said Heldon.

"Well, it's not as if I have a choice, eh? Come, let's go out back, this place gives me a headache." Aniweta turned, pushed his way through the lurid yellow and green fabrics hanging from the ceiling, and disappeared.

A thick black curtain veiled a door leading into a small, dimly lit room. Lined shelves held rows of unlabeled glass jars containing dried plants, powders, and things too deformed to be identified as animal, mineral, or vegetable. A heavy wooden desk, its surface covered with what could just as easily be scientific or magical debris—scales, tongs, a pestle and mortar, stains, scorch marks, and candle wax—stood near the wall facing the entrance.

Aniweta sat down on a sturdy wooden chair and looked expectantly at Heldon.

The sickly aroma of faded incense, over-ripe vegetables, and old meat reminded Heldon of the first time he'd been down here. That was almost five years ago. Then he had been a little afraid, though he would never have admitted it at the time. Now he was just angry.

"There's been another one, Ani. But I suppose you know that already."

"Yes, I know. A girl this time. No doubt you will call her Eve."

Heldon knew the market well. You had to, working in this neighborhood. Mostly it looked after itself, a closed system, and it was best not to get involved. The force had their own people in there, and the market presumably had its own people in the force. Recycled mobiles and other stolen goods were one thing. They could be dealt with quietly. But there were other things that could not be ignored. As the trade in guns and drugs got a little too casual, like it did every year, a few stalls were inevitably raided, as was the old pub on the corner of St. Mark's Rise, which was now less popular, though more peaceful, as a beautician's.

But all this was regular police work, and so no longer Heldon's business.

At first, bush meat was his business. Chimps mostly, but also the odd gorilla, brought in from the Congo and Gabon. An Italian punk girl had almost fainted on seeing a huge, dark, five-fingered hand fall out of brown paper wrapping as it was passed to a customer at the Sunny Day Meats stall.

The raids found no whole animals, only parts—heads, feet, genitals, hands—most too precious for food and sold only for *muti* or *juju*. Medicine. Magic. They turned up something else too. The squad at first thought the bag contained parts of a baby chimp: fingers stripped of skin, a dark and shriveled penis and scrotum, teeth. But forensics found otherwise. They were human.

The stallholder was arrested.

Heldon's team had kept the details from the press, but Aniweta had known. As a *sangoma*, a witch, he knew many things. Heldon knew very little about him, however, except that he had emigrated to London from Nigeria in the 1970s, had a UK passport, and no criminal record. He had always proved a reliable source of local and traditional knowledge, and his calm manner, coupled with a dark sense of humor, had commanded Heldon's respect and, on occasion, fear.

At first Heldon had assumed the parts were imported. That was until September 21, 2001, the autumn equinox, when a boy was fished from the Thames outside the Globe Theatre. The five-year-old's body was naked, apart from a pair of orange shorts, put on him, it turned out, after he had been bled to death. Then his head and limbs had been severed by someone who knew precisely what they were doing.

They named him Adam. It was sickening to keep referring to him as "the corpse" or "the torso." They initially thought he was South African, but an autopsy revealed otherwise—inside the boy's stomach was a stew of clay, bone, gold, and the remains of a single kidney-shaped calabar bean. The calabar bean was like a neon sign to the investigation. The plant grows in West Africa, where it's known as the "doomsday plant" because of the number of accidental deaths it causes. It's also used to draw out witches and negate their power—once a bean is eaten, only the innocent survive. The shorts were another clue. Bought in a German Woolworth's, they were coral orange for the *orisha* spirit Ochun, the river queen of the Yoruba religion: the great diviner who knows the future and the mysteries of women.

The calabar would have caused his blood pressure to rise painfully, followed by convulsions and conscious paralysis; his screams imbuing the magic with a rare and terrible strength. Then his throat was slit and his torment ended by a final blow to the back of the head. Once dead, the butchery began. The blood was drained from his body and preserved; his head and limbs removed, along with what is known in *muti* as the atlas bone: the vertebra connecting his neck to his spine, where the nerves and blood vessels meet.

The boy's genitals, still intact, suggested that it wasn't his body parts the killer was after. It was his blood, drained slowly and carefully from his hanging corpse. Adam died to bring somebody money, power, or luck. Perhaps the slave traffickers who brought him to London. His journey probably began when he was snatched or sold in Benin, and continued through Germany before reaching these shores, his final destination.

Somebody had cared for Adam before he died—there were traces of cough medicine in his system. Who knows whether he was brought here with sacrifice in mind, but had he not been marked for death, he might have ended up working as a slave, or as a prostitute. At least then he'd have had a chance.

Despite arrests in London, Glasgow, and Dublin, and prosecutions for human trafficking, nobody was convicted of the boy's murder. Heldon had burned with frustration for months, but he had managed to keep it together, unlike others in the team. The three-year investigation had taken its toll on O'Brien, the detective in charge. He'd quit the force a nervous wreck at what should have been the peak of his career. Heldon had been his deputy on the Adam case; he'd seen the strain, the shards of paranoia puncture O'Brien's hardman armor.

And now there was another corpse.

Aniweta was right. They had called her Eve.

The girl had been mutilated like Adam, her torso wrapped in a child's cotton dress; white with red edging. Dustmen had tipped her out of a wheelie bin on December 5, four days ago, outside a dry cleaners on White Horse Street, near St. James's. She was probably six years old.

"What can you tell me, Ani?" Heldon asked the *sangoma*.

"I can tell you that this one is different."

"So far, forensics suggest that she was killed the same way as Adam."

"Yes, but she is different. Powerful." Ani nodded his head, impressed. "The red and the white on the dress are for Ayaguna. He is a young *orisha*, a fighter. You know him as St. James, and when he comes, he rides a white horse. Now she rides with him. He likes the girls, you see, he likes them young like this. Their blood is clean. This is strong *juju*. You'll find things inside her: clay, gunpowder, silver, maybe copper."

"Anything else?"

Ani, who had been staring at the stains on his tabletop, turned to look directly at Heldon.

"Yes, my friend, I can tell that you're not sleeping well."

Heldon was caught off guard. "Well, you might say I'm taking my work home with me."

"Like O'Brien?"

"No. And I don't intend to end up like him. But yes, this has shaken me up. I didn't expect another one so soon. And then I suppose there's the war."

"There is always war, that is Ayaguna's business. But there will be no war where this girl came from. She is one of their own. A peace offering."

"I was talking about Iran, but yes, we think the girl was another Nigerian."

"No, she is not one of ours. She is from the Congo," replied Ani, with a certainty that Heldon could not question. "That's where the trouble is. But for now there will be no war. She died to end the fighting. She will keep Ayaguna happy for a while. How long depends how well the *sangomas* know him. If they know him well, she will have died with six fingers and six toes. Her skin cut six times with a blade and burned six times with a flame."

"If she died to prevent a war, why was she killed here and not in her home country?"

"The *sangomas* don't like war. It upsets the balance. So much death creates problems for everybody. Now the smart ones are over here."

"Makes sense. I don't like war either. Okay, thanks, Ani. We'll be in touch."

Heldon returned to the night. The cats were gone.

Forensics showed that Ani was right. Mineral analysis of her bones revealed that she was indeed Congolese. The girl had swallowed, or been forced to swallow, a mix of gunpowder, silver, copper, and clay. She had been bound and stabbed several times, then scorched with a burning twig from the iroko tree. They had not found her limbs, so they couldn't count her fingers and toes; but Heldon suspected that if they ever found them, there would be six of each.

African newspapers revealed that the Congo had been on the brink of another bout of bloodshed, but in the past few days an agreement was reached between the warring factions. With over three million already dead, you would think they were tired of killing.

The story hardly made the UK nationals; the situation in Iran was worsening, despite the fact that things in Iraq had hardly improved since the Allied pullout eighteen months earlier. And now they were regrouping, preparing to flex their muscle against a defiantly hostile Iranian leadership. The mid-term government disingenuously declaring that the opportunity for peace lay in the hands of the Iranians, not the combined forces amassing at the nation's borders.

More dead children.

Rather than desensitizing him to death, Heldon's work had revealed to him its full horror. He knew what a bullet meant: the torn, seared flesh; the shattered bone; the screaming; the smell of blood. He had no children of his own, but he knew that the statistics of war weren't just numbers. They were a thousand Adams, a thousand Eves. Blasted, mutilated, lying in rivers, in puddles, in the arms of their parents; caught in the camera's lens, denied over breakfast, ignored on the train.

As an inevitable war loomed once again, the antiwar protests had grown incandescent, seething with fury and frustration. Heldon took part as often as he could. He didn't tell his colleagues, just as he didn't tell them everything that Ani had told him. It was easier that way.

He didn't tell them about his other research either. There was no need. And he hadn't told Ani. Again, why bother? He probably already knew all about the killings anyway. They had occurred throughout Europe and Africa over the years. Many, like Adam, were for power. Terrible as they were, they no longer interested Heldon. He was only interested in the others; the others like Eve. They were different. And they had worked. The evidence was there on the record—brief respites in long histories of warfare. Powerful *juju*.

She is one of their own . . . different . . . powerful.

Ani's words drove Heldon onward as he strode through the car park behind Kingsland Shopping Centre. Smooth, smothered by concrete, a no-man's-land between road and rail. Few people entered the mall through this back way. Once past the main entrance to Sainsbury's, the shops tail off into a mirror of what's available outside on Kingsland High Street.

A gray mid-morning on a school day. Any kids around now are avoiding something.

Now she rides with him.

He found her under the outdoor metal stairwell. Hood up. Not doing anything.

She was one of our own.

He had thought about this moment over and over again. Can a death ever be justified? Is one unpromising life worth ten thousand others? If it works, then yes, it is. Suddenly, Heldon knew exactly what he was doing.

"Hi. Shouldn't you be in school?"

"What's it to you? You a teacher?"

A flash of his card. "No, I'm a policeman. And I think you should come with me. Don't worry, you're not in trouble. I have a very important job to do, and I need your help. How would you like to ride a white horse?"

Without protest, the girl left with him.

SOUTH

BY JOE MCNALLY

Elephant & Castle

As an incomer to London, I have—almost inevitably—found myself enchanted with the city, in more than one sense of the word. I have enthusiastically thrown my hat in with those who purport to read the city; I have picked and hunted for the obscure volumes which I hope will allow me to enter their hallowed halls through recitation of the *Sacred Names of the Lost Rivers*, and gestured endlessly toward the notions which underpin their fictions.

For the most part, my own experiments in drift have been confined to the northern shores and, due to a specific confluence of geographical happenstance and the practicalities of car-engine maintenance, to the mysterious islets of the dead between Maida Vale and Ladbroke Grove; ghost country, the lands of the west. Too dead even for Ballard.

Think London as *Mappa Mundi*: wealth and comfort in the west, wealth and sterility in the far north, squalor and industry in the east (less of the latter these days—heritage docks, churches turned Starbucks), and in the south, a cliché *Heart of Darkness*. Incongruous strips of pristine brickwork along the river, a seething, churning mess we'd rather not think about.

It's uncharted territory, our own little Third World, just a little too feral for the tame psychogeographer. Not the heritage poverty of the East End, this is the real thing, waving a shattered bottle in your face and ranting a cloud of whiskey fumes before smacking you down and stripping you to your frame. There's a reason sorcerers don't cross running water; down here, they'd be trading your scrying glass for rocks within the hour.

But then it hits me, walking from tube to Thameslink at the Elephant, the peak of the delta—Old Kent Road another Nile, tarmac khem, its length vanishing off toward an unknown source in the mythic lands supposed to exist outside the M25. And here at the peak of the delta are the tunnels.

This could have been built for us, the self-styled cultists of the city still reeling from our frantic initiations of acid-fueled underground trips, coke-blasted long marches across the city trailed by gibbering crackheads waiting to fire up the crystal snot on our cast-off tissues, graduation only by turning up some new obscurity to which the metropolisomancers can nail a thousand mad-eyed theses. Here, a series of far-sighted planners, true inheritors of the Dionysiac mantle, conspired or were somehow moved by unseen forces to create a playground for those unable to travel through an underpass without pausing to attempt to decode the hidden patterns brought to half-life by every patch of crumbling concrete and piss stain.

It starts as soon as you vanish back underground after emerging from the tube. (No, it starts with the name: Elephant & Castle. Gnomic, at first quaint, then taking on sinister overtones. The Guild of Cutlers, ivory and steel. Bone and knife blade, a union still celebrated here more nights than not.) The subterranean walkways, with their vandalized or opaque signs, are an immediate hook, an obvious nod to Crete—passages which seem carefully planned to evoke the dread that some bellowing theriomorph might lurk behind each blind turn, pure *panic*.

At some point, in a misguided attempt to defuse these chthonic terrors, murals have been added showing imagined scenes from some non-history of South London, jungle scenes, subaquatic fantasies. Sharks patrol these walls. But the *genius loci* won't be denied. It rots the cheer, warps it over time into mania. Each grin now takes on a sinister aspect, the jolly street traders and their well-fed horses projecting an air of vague unease, like nursery drawings on the walls of a burned-out house. Crumbling and fading, they have become a desperate illustration of something that can only be hinted at in the most oblique symbolism, a private, autistic blend of Hoffman and Ryder-Waite.

Between the two stations, I stop to talk to a homeless woman sitting cross-legged with her back to one of the walls. She could be five or six years younger than me, but looks ten older. She has an immense paperback open in front of her, and I ask what she's reading, steeling myself to be polite about Tolkien or worse. Instead, it's an anthology of classic detective stories—Chandler, Willeford, Himes—with the words *Pulp Fiction* blazing across the cover. She explains that she bought it because she thought it was something to do with the film. She's about halfway through it now. I give her a pound and tell her to put it toward another book.

A pound's the least I can do; she's already shading into fiction, working her way into the web of metaphor, a fate not to be wished on any human or bestowed on them without recompense. It's a kind of death, after all. There was a real woman sitting in the underpass, reading a real book, I did stop, I did speak to her, I did give her the money, but by reducing her to this incident I triumphantly deny her the rest of her life, all the while patting myself on the back for my razor-sharp literary instincts and dreaming of Mayhew.

She was drawn into the book—her anthology, not this fiction, I'm the only one on this particular voyage just now—expecting something other than what she got, but now realizes that she's better off with what she did get. Enter the labyrinth and confront . . . The pat answer is usually some reassuringly bleak psychobabble borrowed from half-heard, never-read Freud or, worse, George Lucas—yourself, your parents, your dark side. The truth is that you're confronting the labyrinth itself, the ultimate manifestation of the journey that becomes its own destination. Anything you may find is a function of the maze.

An information bauble surfaces from the *Fortean Times* days. A piece by Paul Devereux on a South American temple which was designed as a shaman machine. The initiate would be fed hallucinogenic cactus, then sent into the temple. Each part was set up to accentuate some aspect of the psychedelic experience—walls that went from echoing to acoustically dead, water channels designed to create apparently sourceless sounds, weird lights.

The cactus they used, San Pedro, is now widely available in Camden and Portobello Road. But bang a couple of slices of that and venture in here, and I don't like to think what you'd get. Certainly not the sort of mantic howler in the outer darkness who lands regular spots in the LRB. Any signs one could read here would sear the brain with revelation, a freebase hit of pure kabbalah, rebridging the divisions between left and right cerebral hemispheres and turning the reader into an ambulatory conduit for the voice of the labyrinth.

It continues. I stride edgily through the shopping center to the Thameslink. The whitewashed concrete hallway feels like an abandoned bunker somewhere deep in Eastern Europe. The floor is inches deep in rainwater, with helpful yellow signs to point out this fact. Nobody is there. The nearest thing to human contact comes from the monitors, relaying information keyed in hours ago in some other location, a cathode ray phantom, news from nowhere. I have an hour to wait for the next train. I've missed its predecessor by seconds as a consequence of my chat with the homeless woman. (See: She doesn't even get a name, but the entire narrative really hangs on her; without her, you would not be reading this, or at least not in this form.)

I make for the bus stop, where the bus I need appears within seconds of my discovering that I need it. Another omen, another metaphor. This is a fertile zone; tiny possibility bombs detonating and sending ripples through the various levels of my mind. The people milling around the shopping center (the pink shopping center, a Little England nightmare made of concrete—dusky colonials and the taint of lavender) become a personal message to me from something beyond.

Once on board, I set my eyes on a mysteriously empty seat, one of three unoccupied places around a dozing bulk. It's a long haul into *terra australis incognita,* and I'll be needing my strength later. The instant I sit, I realize why the seats have not been taken up by any of my traveling companions. The man at the center of the exclusion zone smells. No, this barely does him justice. A truly heroic stench hangs around him, displaced each time he moves, sweeping out in almost visible curls before and behind him with every disturbance in his dream.

I deal with it for as long as I can, but eventually change

seats (being a good middle-class boy, I wait until I am absolutely sure he is asleep; there is, I reason, no possibility that he is unaware of his miasma, and I have no desire to remind him of it again). From my new vantage point, I see that, in fact, the earlier journey through the tunnels was just a decoy, a warm-up. This, though, is the real deal. There are no signs to help me here, no friendly guides clutching books full of familiar names to ground me. I took my eye off the road and left it without even noticing.

I look briefly at each of the other passengers. Eventually, there is no one left to look at and I am compelled to turn my attention to the man in front of me.

He is sitting back yet leaning forward at the same time. A great buffalo hump squats on his back, forcing his head toward the space between his knees. A woolly brown suit of indiscernible vintage helps add to the air of something bovine. Sagging expanses of flesh the colors of corned beef—complete with waxy marbled patches of fat—droop from an acromegalic frame and turn his face into a system of soft caves. His eyes are almost buried beneath overhanging folds of puffed skin, which threaten to fuse with his cheeks: a wax-work Auden rescued, too late, from a conflagration. Messy spikes of hair protrude from his scalp like a crown of feathers. He is between sleep and waking, and the bus' occasional stops and starts make him jerk, sending a shudder through his body, which is echoed and enlarged by corresponding movements in the mephitic cloud that clings to him like a swarm of locusts. The breath flaps out of him from behind crimson jowls.

He seems not to belong here, a refugee from a Grosz painting suppressed as too terrible for public consumption. There would be something comical about him were it not for his awesome vastness and the animal reek around him. It's an *ur*-stench, building from base notes of piss, shit, and sweat to encompass subtle undertones of days-old baby vomit and rank meat that linger in the brain much longer than in the nostrils.

I find myself rapt with wonder at him, barely able to contain my authorial glee. I am working heavy *juju* here; I set out telling myself that something worth putting down on the page would happen tonight, and it seems that I have managed to conjure this flesh golem out of pure narrative requirement—a notional space hitherto marked LOCAL COLOR HERE fills out with something truly strange, an authentic and unfakeable encounter that a better author would have the sense to condense to a paragraph or even a phrase.

But I can't leave well enough alone, and my mind races to find some way I can steal this creature and tame him for my own purposes. The fact that he is clearly dreaming, his physical appearance, his foulness, these are all good. I wonder for a moment if there is some way he can be shoe-horned into some sort of fiction, some easy way I can turn this to my own advantage.

As I wonder on all this, he stirs and begins to gather his belongings to leave the bus at the next stop. Assaulted by the inevitable accompanying spread of his insulating cloud, I turn back to the book I've been concealing myself behind (Maurice Leitch, *The Smoke King*) and desperately try to avoid attracting his attention. He is, after all, my creation and I do not want to be held responsible for the consequences should such a perfect beast gaze by accident into the eyes of his creator.

The bus stops, and as the doors open he shudders toward them, white plastic bags flapping from each wrist, stirring up tornadoes which disperse his spoor to the four corners of the vehicle. I steal a sideways glance at him when he blusters out onto the pavement. As he steadies himself from a sideways lurch, one of the bags swings and hits the glass beside me with with a noise I do not like. A pattern of darkness within momentarily resolves itself into what I pray is not a face, and the minotaur is gone.

WHO DO YOU KNOW IN HEAVEN?

BY PATRICK McCABE

Aldgate

R ight," I said, and phoned the cops.

"May I ask who's calling?" she says.

"Edgar Lustgarten," I said. "You might remember me from *Scales of Justice*. Then again, you mightn't."

"No, as a matter of fact, I don't," she says.

Not that it mattered, for I was gone.

The next thing you know, there's Feane on the *Daily Mirror* with an anorak over his head. But it was him all right—the two-tone shoes.

The worst thing about Mickey Feane was his relentless bragging. "Look at me—*I'm super-volunteer.*"

Never liked them Belfast bastards. Too cocksure.

He'd have all the time he wanted to brag now—any amount in Brixton prison.

Poor old Feane—yet another in a long line of slope-shouldered Irish felons in Albion, detained at Her Majesty's pleasure.

In the beginning it had been good—there can't be any denying that.

I think I'll go to London, I thought. Off I'll go and I won't come back.

"Goodbye cows," I said, "and streets—farewell."

Up your arse may they happily go and the rest of this miserable country as well.

After all, it was 1973. The whole fucking place was an outhouse deserted.

"Goodbye, Daddy, Mammy. Goodbye other kiddies. I hope you die," I said as I skipped.

I had met some very good friends indeed. They really were quite jolly good fellows. They wore zig-zag tops and half-mast jeans.

The very first day I arrived in off the boat, Harrods blew up. Two cops stopped me and said, "Hello, hello." Believe it or believe it not, it's absolutely true. I gave them an envelope with the old man's name on it. They weren't too happy with that, they declared.

"You could get into a lot of trouble over here," they went on. "These are odd and hair-raising times, my wide-eyed little Irish friend."

I was tripped out of my skull for most of the journey. I drank a few pints with an old chap sporting a face like a ripe tomato.

"Do you know what the English did?" he said to me. "Hung decent fellows outside their own doors."

I had never in my life quite seen such a face. *The Incredible Melting Man from Tipperary*, that was the only name I could think of which might suit.

"I'll tell you something about London," he says, but I never heard what it was, for the next thing, *slurp*, down he goes right into the ashtray with a sprig of red hair sticking up like a flower.

As soon as I was sure there was no one looking, I reached into his inside pocket and effortlessly removed his bulging wallet. Inside there's a bunch of *in memoriam* cards with a small square picture of this big farmer smiling. That, I assumed, was the recently deceased brother.

There was a good fat roll of money in there—all tied up with an elastic band. Consummate cattle-dealer style.

Away I went in the direction of Piccadilly. I turned a corner and there it flashed—*CINZANO*, on-off.

I stood there looking at it—truly mesmerized. The reason for that was, it was on our mantelpiece at home. As a matter of fact, it was the last thing I had laid eyes on before departing.

"You're a bad boy, Emmet," Daddy had said.

I had expected the entire town to turn out to bear witness to my leavetaking. They didn't. It was, I'm afraid, a damp squib of an event.

I just pulled the door after me, and who comes flying right off the fanlight but his holiness—the Infant of Prague.

For the benefit of English people who never go to Mass, the Infant of Prague is a holy young boy who stands guard over doors with a gleaming golden crown and a sceptre in his hand. Sadly, on this occasion, his head had got broken. Which upset Mammy because she loved him so.

"Don't come back!" I heard her shouting.

Then I saw Daddy glaring from the shadows.

"Don't worry," I told him. "You'll be able to give her a proper kicking now."

He had always been very fond of football—especially whenever the ball was Mammy.

He always liked a game at the weekend. And maybe, if he'd the money, after the pub on Mondays, Wednesdays, Thursdays, Fridays—and Tuesdays.

* * *

I went into the great big neon-lit shop. A rubber girl, Rita, who'll never say no. A woman in a mask belting the lard out of a crawling-around city gent clad in a bowler.

"I'll teach you some manners," she says, and she means it.

"Oh no," he says, "please don't do it, but do it."

That would keep me warm, I thought, a good skelp like that, as I retired to my chambers along the banks of the Thames.

I thought of them all the way back there at home—all my turf-molded fellow country-compatriots. By now they would have realized my featherbed had not been slept in. And great consternation would take hold in the midlands.

Little would those gormless fools know just what the true nature of my visit to London was to be. I shivered gleefully as I thought: *The London Assignment. A British cabinet minister is gunned down by an IRA assassin. It's a race against the clock and one false move will be enough to leave him dead before he reaches his target.*

I lovingly stroked the butt of my Smith & Wesson .686— four inches, with Hogue grips—which lay nestled deep in the pocket of my jacket. My shiny jacket of soft black leather— standard-issue terrorist fare, perhaps, but comfortable and stylish nonetheless. What the well-dressed volunteer is wearing this autumn in the mid-1970s.

"Get out of the car," I heard myself say, "I'm requisitioning this vehicle on behalf of the Irish Republican Army. *One-Shot Emmet,* they call me, friend—for one shot is all it takes."

There was a big fat moon swelling above the gasworks, looking like the loveliest floaty balloon. The old man knew a song about that moon. I remembered it well. It went: *When the harvest moon is shining, Molly dear.*

Once I had heard him singing it to the old lady. One night in the kitchen not long after Christmas. Long ago. Or at least I thought I had. Then I fell asleep with my hotshot volunteer's jacket pulled good and tight around me.

So off I went—puff-puff on the train. All the way to Epsom in Surrey. What a spot that turned out to be—a hotel, a kind of club for dilapidated colonels. How many Jimmy Edwards moustaches would you say there were there to be seen?

At least, I would estimate, seventeen examples.

Big potted plants and women like vampires, Epsom Association Dawn of the Dead.

Sitting there yakking about gout and begonias.

"You're not very fond of work, are you?" says the boss. He had apprehended me sleeping under boxes.

I took in everything in the office. The barometer on the wall reading *mild*, the bird creature on the mantelpiece dipping its beak in a jar. Lovely shiny polished-leather furniture—with buttons.

"It seems quite extraordinary but you don't appear ashamed in any way."

I was going to tell him nothing. Mahoney—my officer-in-command—had always said if arrested to focus your attention on a spot on the wall.

He fired me. "Get out," he says. Well, fuck that for a game of cowboys.

By the time I got back to London I was edgy and tired.

Outside a Wimpy, I saw a woman with blood streaming down her face being led away by a man in a raincoat. For no reason at all I stood there for a minute looking in the window of a telly rental shop, and there on the screen is this fellow saying: "I was just coming out of my office when I heard the most frightful bang." The policemen were still shouting: "Will you please clear the area!" All of the pubs were closing their doors. I heard someone running past, shouting: "Murdering bastards!" I hid my face and found a hostel. *The London Assignment* was the name of my book. The book I'd invented to get me to sleep. I was on the cover in a parka— looking dark and mean. Behind me, a mystical pair of old-country hills. The old-timer next to me said: "What time is it now?"

It's the time of Gog and Magog, my friend, when the cloud covers the sun and the moon no longer gives forth any light.

I'd read that in a Gideon's Bible some other old tramp had left on my locker. He must have been unhappy for I could hear him crying.

I don't know why his whimperings should have done it but they got me thinking about Ma and Da. I got up to try and stop their faces coming. Then I saw the two of them— him just standing there with his hand held in hers.

"Ma," I gasped, "Da."

They were dressed in the clothes of all the old-time photographs. There was a picture on the hostel wall of a dance-hall in London and somehow it all got mixed up with that. It wasn't a modern dancehall—one from the '40s or perhaps the early '50s. It was called THE PALAIS—with its string of lights waltzing above the heads of the fresh-faced queue. You'd think to see them that they'd all won the pools. I've never seen people look as happy as that. I could see the inside in my mind—palm trees painted over a tropical ocean and the two of them waltzing. Him with his hair oiled and her with a great big brooch pinned onto her lapel.

"I love you," I heard her say.

It was in those couple of years just before I was born. In the time of the famous detective Lustgarten, when all the cars were fat and black and nobody said *fuck* or visited dirty neon-lit shops. When everyone was happy because at last the war was over. We hadn't been in the war. Eamon de Valera kept us out of it. The old man revered de Valera. Talked about him all the time. He was probably talking about him now—to her. But she wouldn't want to hear about history. She'd simply want to be kissed by him. The history of that kiss would do her just fine. She needed no more than that to look back on.

The doors of the dancehall were swinging open now and assorted couples were drifting out into the night in the loveliest of white dresses and old-style gray suits with big lapels.

Ma was lying back on the bonnet of a car. She put her arms around him and said she wasn't worried about a single thing in the whole world. Her laughter sailed away and I heard her saying that history was a cod, that the only thing that mattered was two people loving one another. He asked her would she love an Englishman, and she said yes she would just so long as it was him. Which was the greatest laugh of the whole of all time—the idea of her husband, Tom Spicer, being an Englishman.

"London," she whispered then, and whatever way she said it, it made the whole place just spread out before me like some truly fabulous palace of stars. Songs that I had only half-remembered seemed to fill themselves out now and take on an entirely new life as they threaded themselves in and out of the most magnificent white buildings of solid Portland stone.

A nightingale, I thought, sang in Berkeley Square and it

made me feel good for I knew that Da had liked it once upon a time. No, still did.

"Don't I?" he said as he tilted her pale chin upwards.

"*Stardust*," she smiled, and I knew she meant Nat King Cole.

With the shimmering sky over London reflected in her eyes.

When I looked again, they were standing in some anonymous part of the city and it wasn't pleasant—there was this aura of threat or unease hanging around them. I wanted it to go away but it wouldn't. Ma was more surprised than anyone when he drew back his cuff and punched her in the face.

A spot of blood went sailing across the Thames. Faraway I saw *CINZANO*, just winking away there, on and off. On and off. On and off. On and—

I heard a scream. I woke up.

I didn't manage to get back to sleep.

Noon, I went into Joe's Café. There was only one thing and it prevailed in my mind. That was the dancehall whose name was THE PALAIS, with its colored lights strung above the door. That was my *London Assignment*. To, once and for all, locate that building. I swore I'd do it—or die in the process.

I smiled as I thought of Mahoney and his reaction. He was standing by the window back at HQ, with both arms folded as he unflinchingly gazed out into the street.

"You were sent over there for one express purpose!" he snapped. "And it's got nothing to do with fucking dancehalls!"

I took out my revolver and placed it on the table.

"So be it," I said. "Then I'm out."

"You're out when I say you're out," replied Mahoney.

I could see a nerve throbbing in his neck. Mahoney had been over the previous summer with an active service unit that had caused mayhem. He was a legend in the movement. His London exploits had passed into history. He would have had no problem coming over himself and filling me in. Taping my confession and leaving me there in some dingy Kilburn flat, with a black plastic bag pulled down over my head.

"The organization is bigger than any one man," he said. "Or any," he sneered "fucking dancehall."

I finished my tea and got up from my chair, swinging from Joe's out into the street.

Not this one, Mahoney. Not this one.

I sat down for a bit in Soho Square Gardens. There was a paper lying beside me on the bench. Looking out from the front page was a photofit picture of an IRA bomber in long hair and sideburns.

I shook the paper and sighed, kind of tired. You could hear the Pandas blaring nearby. I slid into a cinema and tried not to hear what I was hearing. Almost inevitably, there was Edgar—smiling down at me from the screen. How could he possibly have known I was in the city? I thought ruefully. Could my cover possibly have been blown?

It couldn't be, I concluded. Not even the great *Scales of Justice* detective could have managed to pull off a coup like that. I began to relax as I watched him bestride the screen. I dwelt on all his famous cases: *The Mystery of the Burnt-Out Candle; Investigation at Honeydew Farm; The Willow Tree Murders.*

"I know all about the dancehall," he said. "That's my job—I'm here to help."

I was grateful to him for saying that, for I knew if anyone was able to help it was Edgar Lustgarten—having lived through the days when the streets of the great city had been the same as they were in the photograph, shiny and wet and full of gray overcoats, with great big double-deckers bombing around and Big Ben regally resounding across the world.

"Would you like to know what was playing that night?" he asked me. "It was 'Who Do You Know in Heaven?' by the Ink Spots."

"'Who do you know in Heaven?'" I repeated, as the colored lights flickered above the door of THE PALAIS.

There can be little doubt that *The London Assignment* will go down in the annals as one of the most magnificent operations ever undertaken by The Organization. Mahoney, I knew, would be especially proud.

I couldn't believe it when I arrived in Rayner's Lane. I couldn't even remember how I got there. There was a dance-hall, but it wasn't the one I was after. It hadn't even been built until 1960. Anyhow, it was boarded up and left to go to rack.

I went into another café and had a cup of tea. My hands were blue and I was shivering.

I didn't want to hear it but they fell from the lips of a man sitting opposite. In my father's voice. The words: "We're rubbish, us Irish, and all our children—they'll be rubbish. We don't even know how to love or kiss or dance. All we can do is dress in rags. If we were in London now, that would be different. We'd deck ourselves in the finest of silks and we'd stroll down Pall Mall with our proud heads held high. Then do you know what we'd do? We'd go off to dinner in some swanky hotel, and after we'd called a toast to ourselves, we'd take a cab off to a dancehall—we wouldn't really care where it was, just so long as the Inkspots were playing—and what we'd do then is we'd foxtrot and waltz until our feet were sore and bruised."

He was leaning over to kiss her when I knocked over the teacup, its contents dribbling onto my feet.

I think one of the most beautiful days I can ever remember was Boxing Day three years ago. It had been snowing constantly and the city looked like something out of a fairy tale—as though it had been evacuated especially for me. On Trafalgar Square, the Landseer lions appeared even more august than usual, with their Mandarin moustaches of dusty white ice.

Starched and blue, Soho did my heart good. In the gutters, hardened wrappers possessed a special kind of poetry. It was like being a child all over again, when I'd walk the roads of the little country town which I haven't, sadly, been back to now for many years now.

I'm looked after here—I've accepted this country as my home. I have a flat the Council gave me—it's not far from Fenchurch Street, in the suburb of Aldgate.

There's a café which I go to, near Leadenhall Market. I sit at the back. The owner is an Italian—he fancies himself an intellectual. He thought I was writing a West End play. "No," I told him, "I'm writing a novel. A little thriller I've titled *The London Assignment*."

He took up my notebook and read—with superiority: *"Once upon a time there was a young boy who lived in a squat. He had to leave it for reasons best left unreported. The city in those days was as though a place under siege. Emmanuelle was playing at The Odeon. A Clockwork Orange was showing somewhere else. On April 26, an old tramp, who happened to be from Ballyfuckways in the Irish county of Mayo, was stumbling good-humoredly through an underpass, throatily declaiming an old ballad, when he was confronted by three youths—each of them sporting a bowler hat and with a single eye mascaraed. They beat him with their walking canes and left him for dead. A bomb blew out the windows of a restaurant that night—on Frith Street, in Soho. Thirteen people were injured. Carroll's Number Six cigarettes cost fifteen pence for ten."*

He handed me back the notebook and smiled—in that unfortunately unappealing, superior way.

"Did you ever hear of Griffith's theory of consistent memory?" he asked me. He then explained it, in even and measured tones, clearly anticipating my difficulties with its complexity.

"It's like this," he continued, "consciousness prompts you to hypothesize that the story you're creating from a given set of memories is a *consistent history*, justified by a consistent narrative voice . . ."

I half-expected Edgar Lustgarten to appear out of the throng outside, airily drift up to the window, and press his gaunt face to the grimy glass. After a minute or two of this unsolicited advice, I no longer heard a word he said.

What must Sinclair Vane—complete stranger, retired physiotherapist and formerly of 7th (Queen's Own) Hussars—and indeed his wife, have thought when he returned to Frognal Walk Hampstead one night in 1973 to find his parlor window broken open and me, right there in his sitting room, talking to myself and clutching what I had decided was a lethal weapon—in reality a wholly amateur attempt at an imitation firearm, fashioned from a branch I'd found outside? I can only surmise he received the shock of his life. My black bomber jacket was draped across my shoulders as I shivered and menacingly narrowed my eyes. I think I might have giggled a little, in what I thought was a sinister fashion.

"I'm the most feared terrorist in Ireland," I said. "You're going to pay for the sins of your country. I'm sorry to have to tell you but that's the way it is. I'm a soldier, you're a soldier. You're going to die, Mr. Vane."

If I wanted to describe him, I would say he was a young version of Edgar Lustgarten—still retaining most of his hair, complete with touches of distinguished gray.

I encountered him once—a number of years after my discharge from Brixton. The snow had passed and the gutters of Soho had been recently rinsed clean by a deluge of rain, twists of steam all about me rising up into the easeful autumn sky.

He was sitting by the window of a new European-style coffee bar, surrounded by chatting white-T-shirted youths and looking so out of place. It was hard for me to do it but I was glad afterwards that I had made the effort. At first he didn't recognize me when I said his name: *Sinclair Vane.*

As might have been expected, he formally stood to attention and extended his hand to shake mine.

We didn't talk much about that night. His soul was still saddened by the recent passing of his wife.

"She was an angel, you know. She really was."

I thought of her, his angel, as she'd encountered me that ridiculous night—weeping hysterically in the doorway by the stairs. Before Sinclair had expertly calmed her down. I recalled him in that photo on their mantelpiece—battalion commander S. Vane, in complete battledress, authoritatively squinting in the Egreb sun.

* * *

I don't know why I thought it, but it was as clear as day as I sat in the Sir Richard Steele one still and uneventful afternoon—this image of myself and Sinclair sitting so comfortably in a London black cab, gliding along before coming to a halt just outside a dancehall whose entrance was lit by a string of warm and inviting multicolored lightbulbs.

"It was in Brighton all along," I heard him say, as the door swung open and he reached in his pocket for the fare.

Which I knew, of course, it wasn't—and, all of a sudden, hands of accusation seemed to reach out to grab me as I sat there in the corner of the Sir Richard Steele gloom.

I hadn't been allowed out of Brixton for the funeral of my mother, but after my father went into the home, his papers and effects were all passed to me. You can imagine my reaction when I discovered the old photograph—creased and faded but instantly recognizable. I didn't know what to think when I smoothed it out and, having examined it quite exhaustively, came to accept that the image I was looking at—and had been obsessed by—was that of two complete strangers, the inscription on the back reading: *Dublin 1953.* Neither of my parents had been to Dublin in their lives.

It was hard not to weep as I looked at it again, slowly beginning to accept that it definitely was THE PALAIS, and that the two lovers in it, well, they could have been almost anyone. For in those box-pleated suits and stiff-collared shirts, not to mention those fearful faces and averted eyes which seemed so grateful for even the tiniest morsel of hope, they could have been any pair of thrown-together souls, adrift in the black and washed-out gray of the lightless, shrinking sad Irish '50s.

* * *

The London Assignment had been an extremely effective operation—from the British establishment's point of view, not from mine. Or from Sinclair's, I hasten to add. I don't think he wanted me charged at all. My demise and subsequent incarceration hastened due to the fact that the day before the trial had been due to begin, three cleaning ladies, a hotel porter, and two foreign tourists had been blown to pieces in a restaurant in Piccadilly.

In these, the latter days of the '90s, I largely subsist by means of the dole and a couple of hours a night gathering glasses in a pub. I suppose you could say I'm well-known around Aldgate. No one is aware of my murky past. I live in a tower block, not far from the station, which gets lonely sometimes and sees me perhaps in The Hoop & Grapes, nursing a tepid lager, or back in Trinity Square Gardens again, feeding the pigeons and surrounded by clamorous, insatiable, supremacist youth. Whose faith in the future I need to be near. Walkman stereos were just coming in '74. I was bundled into a van, not to see the light of day until mid-'95. I still derive a childish innocence from wearing mine, fancying myself a lone knight of the streets, immersed in shaky '30s-style strings and mellow muted jazz trumpets as I drift, a shadow figure, along the golden streets of Soho.

Among the personal effects forwarded to me after my father's death was a letter to her, written in 1949. I know it so well I can quote it verbatim.

> *Dear Maggie,*
>
> *I hope this finds you as well as it leaves me. Well, since we last met things have not been so bad as you can imag-*

ine things are busy here on the farm. I hope to be back up your way in about three or four months time. DV and I was wondering would you make an appointment with me I would be very grateful. My mother is a bit under the weather these times but Daddy is good thank God for that. I am doing a lot of reading at nighttime mostly because it is so busy. I like the Reader's Digest you will find a lot of articles about London in there it looks like a beautiful city although we shouldn't say it maybe but I would dearly love maybe to go there one day even if just for a little while. Anyhow Maggie I will sign off now and as I say I hope you are in the best of health since I seen you.

Yours truly, your fond friend,
Tommy Spicer, Annakilly

One of the chapters in my forthcoming book is called *The Hampstead Conclusion*. With a walk-on part by Edgar Lustgarten.

I'd wrecked the house that night, of course. And made a speech for the benefit of the Vanes. So that they might clearly comprehend my motivation—the reasons which led to *The London Assignment.*

"Then and only then let my epitaph be written!"—a segment from my Republican firebrand namesake Robert Emmet's famous courtroom speech—I remember bawling as I tipped a small glass table over. "Do you hear me, Vane, you imperious, self-regarding, cold-blooded Englishman?" I'd snapped, before delivering a lengthy soliloquy regarding the inadvisability of antagonizing a "nation who were educating Europe when others were painting themselves with woad," along with any number of references to a certain "Mahoney" whose

underground army was by now primed and about to launch a full-scale assault on "Her Majesty's government of despots and butchers, as well as . . ."

As well as nothing, as a matter of fact, for before I knew it, Sinclair Vane had somehow pinned my two arms behind my back and knocked me out with a well-aimed blow, something which I would have anticipated had I examined the mantelpiece a little bit more comprehensively—there were at least four photos of him attired in military fatigues—or applied myself with more diligence to my researches, particularly those pertaining to ex-servicemen who had distinguished themselves repeatedly in the field of combat, unarmed and otherwise. Particularly, it appeared, with the 7th Armoured Division with Monty at El Alamein.

The notice of his death I happened to come upon in the *Times*. I don't know why I went there—to the funeral in Willesden Cemetery—some unformed notion, a vague desire for closure, maybe. All I remember is shaking his sister, Miss Vane's, hand. She was so distressed I don't think she even saw me.

When I got home I explained to Vonya—or tried to. But in the end gave up about halfway through. I could see it wasn't making any sense. She was a lovely girl, whom I happened to meet quite by chance one day on my bench in Trinity Square Gardens.

She stayed with me but we didn't have sex. As I poured out the coffee, a young Muslim man was arguing with two policemen, employing body language I knew so well.

"But I lie to you," she said, a little choked.

Her mother was long dead, she'd told me. Her father had habitually abused her since childhood. That was the reason she had come to London, the very minute, practically, that she'd come of age. Except that none of it, it turned out, was true.

It was the morning the IRA bombed the Baltic Exchange. I heard the explosion—it's not that far away from my flat—and wondered had Mickey Feane, my old friend, been involved. But then I remembered—Mickey Feane was long dead, sprayed in an ambush on a back road in Tyrone.

I turned to say something and saw she wasn't there.

That was the last I saw of Vonya Prapotnik.

I'd sit there in the gardens opposite the Lutyens monument commemorating the Merchant Navy dead, and think of Mr. Lustgarten arriving—the fat black Panda pulling up outside the building as a burly officer opened the door, clearing a path for the internationally renowned sleuth as he made his way up bare concrete stairs, pushing the door open to reveal the dank interior. Where he'd find me lying prostrate on the bed. I don't know what title might occur to him as he observed me—rigor mortis having already set in, most likely— *An Unfortunate Case,* perhaps, or *Felo-De-Se: A Volunteer's Farewell,* or, perhaps, best of all, *The Aldgate Assignment.*

Yes, I think I like the sound of that.

I made the tape last night and it's good, I think—by which I mean that it's clear and unequivocal. Precise as any good confession ought to be, with or without a black plastic hood. I left it on the table where anyone will be able to see it—you won't need the skills of Edgar Lustgarten. I bought a jiffy bag and a packet of stickers, and in neat felt marker printed on the front: *Who Do You Know in Heaven?*

What I couldn't believe most of all was how wonderfully

bright it was. THE PALAIS in red and yellow strung-up lights. When I went in, the band were already in the middle of their set, performing their dance steps in front of their music stands, with all their silver instruments gleaming. They were wearing little white jackets and neatly pressed graystripe trousers. The Ink Spots, in black, was printed on a drum.

When I heard her call out to me, initially I couldn't make out who it was. Then, to my astonishment, I heard my mother say: "Emmet, will you do something for me? Will you make sure the Infant of Prague is in his proper place on the fanlight and has his little face turned toward the church? We're getting married tomorrow morning at 10, son, you see."

I wasn't sure quite what to say—her taffeta dress looked so nice—and had to think for a minute to decide on an answer. But before I got the chance, the band had started up again, and as he placed his arm around her waist I saw her lean in toward him and smile.

But that was the last I saw of them because in the one or two seconds I'd turned to give my attention to the band, as effortlessly as though they'd grown wings, they'd sailed like moths out far beyond the stars, in search of the heaven they'd been dreaming of for so long.

BETAMAX

BY KEN HOLLINGS

Canary Wharf

1.

I t starts with an accelerating whine that becomes a roaring through darkness and space. You'll find yourself hurtling into emptiness. Lights travel past your eyes at ever increasing speed. The flooring moves beneath your feet. You'll feel the rush, pulling you forward. The roaring continues. Everything lies straight ahead. The expressions around you seem dazed, eyes unfocused and distant.

The sound slows to a stop. A woman's voice speaks to you from out of nowhere. *This station is Canary Wharf. Change here for the Docklands Light Railway.*

Then another woman's voice: *This train terminates at Stratford.*

Everyone around you looks stunned. Lost.

A gun is a dream that fits into your hand.

"So I get out here?"

They used to sleep below ground in places like this. While bombs fell from up above. The steel and glass barrier will slide apart, separating you from nothing. A vast space of columns and moving stairways, designed for handling thousands of people in transit, opens up around you, but it will be almost empty at this hour of the day. On the platform, a young skateboarder drums with his bare hands on a metal guardrail. A little Muslim girl in a glistening pink dress crouches at the edge of the concourse, sniffing at an open pack of Juicy Fruit chewing gum. She holds it up to her face, avidly inhaling the smell. Her father wears black combat boots, the toecaps carefully polished. Behind them, the empty silent track.

You watch the barrier as it closes again, a yellow and black stripe running the length of it at waist height. Two sets of three isosceles triangles pointing away from each other move slowly together until they are almost touching once more.

Standing on the escalator, coming up toward the third level on the concourse, just beneath the surface of the world, you get your first glimpse of towers and tall buildings. Shining high-rise blocks of steel and reflective glass, housing a working population of over 65,000. You only have to kill one of them. But anything over that will also be acceptable.

A scratchy subtitle flickers before your eyes: *It is the acts of men who survive the centuries that gradually and logically destroy them.*

Buildings are machines: electrical systems that listen and see and respond. People are just a planet's biomass redistributing itself in time and space.

"You have a room reserved for me? Under the name Betamax?"

The girl at the reception desk will look up at you and smile brightly. "Yes, we do. Thanks for asking."

You'll be vaguely aware of the color scheme in the hotel lobby: a deep rose pink with polished wood surfaces. Beyond them an empty concrete plaza and a fountain swept by the wind.

You're just product, denied a place in this world. Something played out on an old system, dated and worn. Set aside.

Step out of the elevator when it reaches the twenty-third floor.

"Room 2307?" you'll say. "It's along here?"

The maid will turn from her cleaning cart and smile brightly. "Fifth door to your right, thanks for asking."

Anything over that will also be acceptable.

Your name will appear on the TV screen in your room, incorporated into a message of greeting. You ignore it. You remember a blind operative you once knew who stayed at Holiday Inns all the time because the rooms were always laid out in exactly the same way. It made finding his way around a lot easier.

You will incapacitate your first attacker by crushing his windpipe. The second you will see reflected in the white tiles of the bathroom. That will give you enough time to turn and shoot him in the chest. Twice.

He will fall toward you, fingers trailing blood across the walls and floor.

You will call down to room service to have someone come and clean out the human grease.

"This better not show up on my bill," you'll say on your way out.

"I'll be sure to note that," the girl at the reception desk will reply and smile brightly. "Thanks for asking."

Things dazzle here, but they don't shine. Everything has a hard reflective surface to it. The dominant color is a stormy green. You walk to the end of the block. There must be people in these buildings, but the interiors seem empty and devoid of life, despite the glass and the open structures. The sight of clouds in a vast blue sky moving across the straight edge of a building will give you a slow sense of falling.

You pause for a moment. Motorway. Distant sirens beyond the towers, the strange silence of cars passing, cold ragged wind generated by the close proximity of tall structures to each other, planes passing overhead.

Some of the buildings have names. *HSBC*, *Citigroup*, *Bank of America*.

Have your pass ready for inspection.

You feel like you're in transit.

A woman appears around the windswept corner of an office building. Long black hair, a swing to her hips. She must be an office worker: trim black skirt, black sweater, black patent-leather high heels. You wonder how she can walk in shoes like those. She carries a file of documents. The stiff breeze disturbs the hem of her skirt as she walks.

She will stop and nod toward the ambulance pulled up at the back entrance to your hotel. Two bodies strapped to gurneys are being wheeled out, their faces covered.

"What happened over there?" she will ask.

"Got in the way," you'll reply.

She watches the paramedics load up the ambulance, her file of documents held up to shade the side of her face.

"Wrong place at the wrong time?" she will ask.

"Not really," you will reply, then after a long pause: "Some people don't know it's over till they see the inside of a mortuary drawer."

"You sound like a trailer for a movie no one wants to see," she will say.

"I'm told I have that effect."

"And would it kill you to smile?"

"Why don't we find out?"

The faintest of smiles will appear on her face instead. "Okay," she'll say.

2.

Once you get outside the neat arrangement of precincts around Canada Square, things come apart very quickly. You can see how thin, how artificial and transparent, this shining cluster of buildings really is. You sit at a café table and think about ordering something. Someone has written *Public Enemy No One* on a nearby wall in spray paint. Beyond that is the river: rusting cranes, empty sheds, and disused landings. Worn concrete, green with age.

You will look across at her long black hair and wonder why she came with you so readily. Even so, you made it look like she didn't have any choice. CCTV cameras are everywhere, turning the entire area into a series of flickering electromagnetic shadows.

"They never tell me who I have to kill," you'll remark. "Usually I'm left to figure it out for myself."

"Is that what you meant by those people getting in the way?" she'll ask.

You slide a blurred black-and-white photograph across the table: a snapshot of a man with graying hair, smiling enigmatically, eyes black and closely focused.

"Look at the picture," you'll say. "He had a different name then."

* * *

A waitress in a green coverall will then come over. She'll be wearing a white plastic badge with her name on it and the message, *I'm going to help you,* printed underneath. She will look more like the kind of woman who'd have her first name spelled out in ancient Egyptian hieroglyphs on a gold charm around her neck. You order coffee.

"How do you take it?" the waitress will ask.

"Straight out the jug," you'll reply. "Like my mother's milk."

A silent pause accompanied by a blank stare. Last time you saw a face like that, the word *before* was printed below it.

"Black, no sugar," you'll reply. "Thanks for asking."

She will later hand you a cardboard cup covered with a plastic lid. You stare at it. A newspaper lies on the next table. You notice the headlines out the corner of your eye. *Mars Robot Goes Insane. Weapons of Mass Destruction Found in New York.*

"You're not from around here, are you?" she'll observe as the waitress walks slowly away.

"Is anybody?"

The blurred black-and-white photograph still lies on the table between you.

"It's not what you've done that poses the biggest threat these days," you'll say. "It's what you owe. We want to extract our money before war breaks out in the ghost galaxies."

"And for that you have to find this guy, this . . . ?" She'll pause, waiting for a name.

"John Frederson."

She'll frown.

"I don't think I know him," she'll say. "Where's he from?"

"Standard Oil New York," you reply. "The Ryberg

Electronics Corporation of Los Angeles, Phoenix-Durango, Islam Incorporated, the Russian petroleum industry . . ."

"He gets around."

"Beijing, Moscow, Tokyo, London . . . It's amazing how much damage the system can take while still sending out signals."

"So it's up to you to track him down and . . ."

"Make him see reason."

"All you're missing is a raincoat and a gun," she'll say, a smile playing on her lips. Then she'll take another look at you.

"Well, maybe just the raincoat," she'll add.

"Is that a problem?" you ask before peeling the tight-fitting plastic lid off your cardboard cup and taking a sip.

"I don't like guns," she'll reply. "Guns kill people."

"Isn't that what they're supposed to do?" you'll say, pulling a face. The coffee tastes like weed-killer. "Come on," you'll say. "Let's get out of here."

Total Information Awareness and the Policy Analysis Market focus upon high-level aggregate behavior in order to predict political assassinations or possible terrorist attacks.

"Where are we going now?" she'll ask, taking a pack of cigarettes from her black patent-leather purse.

"Do you have to?" you'll ask. "Cigarettes kill people."

Another scratchy subtitle appears before your eyes: *Ordinary men are unworthy of the position they occupy in this world. An analysis of their past draws you automatically to this conclusion. Therefore they must be destroyed, which is to say, transformed.*

"Isn't that what they're supposed to do?" she'll reply.

* * *

Welcome to the Royal Lounge of the Baghdad Hilton, the sign says. *No caps, no hoods, or tracksuits after 7 p.m.*

You stand together inside the entrance of a cheap hotel, watching tired-looking girls appear and disappear behind a threadbare red-velvet curtain. Their movements are subdued and discreet: all shadows and cellulite.

A door in a dark side passage will open briefly onto a scene of Al Qaeda suspects kneeling manacled in their own private darkness, eyes, ears, and mouths covered, held captive behind a chain-link fence that runs down the center of the "Gitmo Room."

Prostitute phone cards in reception show high-contrast pictures of female GIs in camouflage fatigues leading naked men around on leather leashes. Each one of them reads: *Call Lynndie for discipline and correction. All services. Open late. Thanks for asking.*

"Well, you certainly know how to show a girl a good time," she'll remark.

"Keep quiet and follow me," you'll say.

You push your way through the velvet curtain, but a man in a dark suit puts an arm out to stop you.

"Hey, you can't do that," the man will say.

"I just did," you'll reply. "Get used to it."

Then you snap his forearm just below the elbow joint, breaking both bones instantly. You watch the blood leaking out from his sleeve.

On the second floor you stop outside one of the rooms.

"What are you doing?" she'll hiss at you. "*Trying* to start trouble?"

"Another operative was sent here a few months ago," you'll reply, tapping gently on the door. "He was supposed to contact me when I first arrived. He didn't show."

"Maybe he forgot."

"Impossible."

"Maybe you forgot."

"I know when I can't remember something." You sound dismissive. Impatient. Almost brutal.

"Okay. I have two things to tell you," she'll say after a pause.

"Yes?"

"One: I don't really appreciate you talking to me in that tone of voice, especially if you're still expecting me to help you."

"And two?"

"And two: There's some guy behind you pointing a gun at the back of your head."

You always know what you're doing.

You'll turn around and grab him by the throat. There will be a blind spasming of the flesh, and in another second there will be just you and the girl in the corridor again.

"See if he's got a pass key on him," you'll say.

"As dumps go," she'll remark, looking around at the room, "this is a dump. Who do you suppose did the decorating? The Three Stooges?"

But you're already staring at the body on the bed.

"Is that your contact?" she'll say.

You'll nod.

"What happened?"

"Electrocuted."

"You can tell just by looking?"

The closets and drawers are filled with the worn smell of clothes long unworn. There's dried shaving cream on the bathroom mirror.

"It stinks in here," she'll say, a flat statement delivered in a flat tone. "Should I open a window?"

It can be a small event: like a window opening in a nearby apartment block or blood sluicing onto the dock from a rusty outlet in a harbor wall.

"No, leave it."

She'll pick up a plastic entry pass from off the floor, its chain swinging gently from her long slim fingers. She'll point at the photograph on it.

"Looks like John Frederson's got a new face and name," you'll say, staring closely at the man in the picture.

She'll turn the entry pass over, examining it carefully on both sides. "This will get you into his private suite of offices at One Canada Square," she'll say. "I can take you there, if you want."

Outside the contact's hotel you'll be approached by a young Thai kid wearing a T-shirt with *Listen to Dr. Hook* printed on it. He's selling DVDs out of a black Samsonite case. *Homo Abduction: Series Red, Teenage Revolutionary Martyrs. Handcuff Party. Necktie Strangler Meets the Teenage Crushers. Baby Cream Pimp IV.*

No one's around: just the late afternoon glare.

"Anything I can't get anywhere else?" you'll ask.

The kid opens a back compartment in the case. These DVDs show people doing things that seem meaningless to you.

"Interested?" the kid will ask hopefully.

But you will just walk away.

3.

The tower at One Canada Square is not open to the general

public. It has 3,960 windows and 4,388 steps, divided into four fire stairways linking all fifty floors. It is 800 feet high. Seen through glass, the sun leaves long white streaks across the sky.

You wander through crowds of people in the underground mall directly beneath Canary Wharf, checking entrances and exits, noting the location of cameras, sensors, and security points. Cities have scenes of their own destruction programmed into them. The world is in hock to itself.

You hear voices all around you, children playing, the rattling of cups on saucers, heels on tiled walkways. You notice frosted glass tables outside cafés, bars, and restaurants. Curved metal and plastic chairs. Music playing. Laughter. Everyone has a sleepy tranquilized look. As if they've been caught too far from daylight. The only things that seem familiar to you down here are the names on the brightly lit storefronts: *Starbucks, Krispy Kreme, The Gap, Mont Blanc.*

People have become slaves to probability. You'll assume you've been on CCTV since you first arrived. A woman takes your photograph with her cell phone. She will have blond highlights in her feather-cut hair and wear a gold plastic leather jacket, bleach-washed blue jeans, and black Cuban heel boots. You will have come to expect this kind of thing by now.

Chemical tests indicate that Prozac is now seeping into the main water supply.

The woman leans forward unobtrusively to get another shot, revealing a portion of flesh so suntanned that it looks almost gray when exposed to the strip lighting in the mall's main concourse.

You'll also notice that she has a tattoo at the base of her

spine. They all have tattoos at the base of their spine. Or on their ankles. It's a form of protection.

"Against what?" you'll ask.

At one minute past 7 on the evening of Friday, February 9, 1996, a bomb concealed inside a flatbed truck wrecked an office complex at Canary Warf, killing two and injuring over a hundred. The device was detonated in an underground garage near Canada Square. It tore the front off the building next door, damaging the roof and shattering the glass atrium. Windows were sucked out of buildings a quarter-mile away. Bystanders were thrown to the floor and showered with flying glass. Things just kept on falling.

You search up and down the concourse again, checking the benches, the artificial displays of greenery, the rest areas and waste bins. You look at faces, gestures: arrangements of groups and individuals. Families are a bland nightmare when seen out in public: a series of aimless and incessant demands. The entire underground mall is designed to keep them moving. They look well fed and cared for and pink from the sun. As if they are all brand new.

You will think you can stay and rest for a moment, but you can't. You remain on the outside of everything that's happening down here, watching and waiting. But that's never really been a problem for you, has it?

You see people with laptops, people with wires trailing from their ears.

You wonder where she's got to: what can be keeping her.

Suddenly she's there again. Walking toward you from across the mall. You recognize the long black hair, the swing of her hips, the clicking of her high heels on the tile floor. At first she doesn't appear to be with anyone, but you quickly realize that she is not alone. Two security guards in dark suits will be following at a discreet distance. They're almost invisible, but they never move too far from her side.

A third subtitle flickers before your eyes: *It would not be logical to prevent superior beings from attacking the other parts of the galaxies.*

The tower at One Canada Square consists of nearly 16,000 pieces of steel that provide both the structural frame and the exterior cladding. It is designed to sway thirteen inches in the strongest winds, which are estimated to occur once every hundred years.

She will now be standing before you, the security guards taking up position on either side of her.

"Search him," she'll say. "He's got a gun." She'll smile as they pat you down. "I told you I didn't like them," she'll say.

You call her a name. She won't like that either.

The guards step in a little closer. "Another word out of you and we'll slice your heart in half."

They find the gun. You'll let them take it away from you.

"You're coming with us," one of them will say.

Crowds of shoppers move past you in a dream.

"Or what?"

"Or a bullet's going right through your head, so which will it be?"

They won't try anything here: you're fairly certain of that. All the same, you will go along with them.

Fujitsu high-definition screens read out Bloomberg averages

on the ground floor at One Canada Square. A market ana-
lyst sits back and talks on camera against a weightless array
of numbers. "The shares as you can see here are just digest-
ing reactions to that conference call, although their profits
next year, he said, are set to grow by as much as fifteen . . ."

The lobby contains over 90,000 square feet of Italian and
Guatemalan marble. It's the color of spilled blood and gray
veins.

Percentages flash by on-screen: *Omni Consumer Products,
LuthorCorp, Heartland Play Systems, Wayland Yutani.* Nothing
arouses pity and terror in us like an unsuccessful franchise.
It's the same as watching the commercials in the middle of a
murder documentary on television: showing you things that
the dead can never see and will never know about.

You keep walking, trying to look casual, feeling the gun
that's been pushed into the small of your back ever since you
were first escorted up the stairs and into the lobby.

The tower at One Canada Square has thirty-two elevators
divided into four banks, each serving a different section of
the building. They form a central column just beyond the
main reception area. A heavy security cordon is in operation
around them at all times. Access to any of the upper floors is
impossible without a valid entry pass.

You're in a world made up of names and numbers now.
Reception, thirty-first floor: Bank of New York, Tyrell
Corporation; reception, forty-ninth floor: Cyberdyne Systems
Corporation, Computech, Stevenson Biochemical,
Instantron.

A nearby sign reads: *For your safety and security, twenty-
four-hour CCTV surveillance is in operation.*

Outside the wide lobby windows, a deep red sunset

shines through empty buildings and sheets of mirror glass, high-rise floors glowing scarlet in the far distance.

You will go where they take you in the sure and certain knowledge that you aren't the first and you certainly won't be the last. There will be a brief shadowy movement behind you just before the elevator doors open. Then the gun will come down hard on the back of your neck, catching you unawares.

"Okay, you're done," you'll hear one of the guards remark as you fall heavily toward the elevator floor. "Thanks for asking."

4.

Except, of course, you never get there.

You're already spinning round before the elevator doors have even closed properly. By the twenty-third floor, both security guards are down.

By the thirtieth floor, you will have stamped on one guard's head until his nose, mouth, and ears are bleeding.

By the fortieth floor, you will have your own gun back and the other guard will be kneeling before you, begging for his life.

He will tell you he's afraid. That he doesn't want this. You shoot him once. Right through the left eye.

It's only then that you will notice there's Muzak playing in the elevator.

"Was that absolutely necessary?" she will ask, looking down at the bodies on the elevator floor and frowning. "The only reason I agreed to help you get up here in the first place was to avoid anything like this."

"Made me feel better," you'll reply with a shrug.

* * *

The building's floors have a compact-steel core surrounded by an outer perimeter constructed from closely spaced columns. It is capped by a pyramid 130 feet high and weighing eleven tons.

The exterior is clad in approximately 370,000 square feet of Patten Hyclad Cambric finish stainless steel.

She will throw her arms around you just as the elevator reaches the fiftieth floor. You embrace. Your hungry mouths will find each other.

An aircraft warning light at the apex of the pyramid flashes forty times a minute, 57,600 times a day.

"Coming with me?" you'll ask.

"No."

"Don't you want to see this through, now that we're both here?"

"I got you to his office," she'll reply. "That's what you want, isn't it?"

"That's what I want."

You exchange one last look. One last kiss.

"The pass we found in the hotel will get you through to his office," she'll say. "But you'd better get rid of the gun. It'll trip the metal detectors."

"Fine," you'll say. "I don't need it anymore."

You toss the gun into a nearby waste bin.

"You're sure he'll be there?" you'll ask.

"He never leaves," she'll reply.

You are now entering the main reception area at Virex International, an uninflected machine voice will announce as soon as the main office doors slide open. *Thank you for not stopping.*

All the rooms but the last one will be empty.

You'll find him sitting at his desk, a wadded-up piece of human gum, drained and useless, gazing out at the sunset.

"John Frederson?"

His head moves slowly, painfully, away from the deep crimson light still spreading over London.

"No one's called me that in years," he'll say.

"Then you'll know who sent me."

And still he'll sit before you, empty and staring soberly at the sun: a baffling configuration of success and failure that has confounded history.

"A little far from home, aren't you?" he'll finally remark.

"We've had some . . . local difficulties."

John Frederson will nod.

"And the ghost galaxies hired you?" he'll reply. "I'm almost insulted. I'd have thought I rated better than a mere . . ." He'll pause, peer at you. "Do you even have a name?" he'll ask, looking like the man who just patented cancer.

You know why you're here and why we sent you. You're clean, filed down, all biometrics erased so they can no longer be read. The best false identity is no identity at all.

"Betamax," you reply.

John Frederson will nod again. You notice a moth skeleton still clinging to one of the net curtains over his office windows.

She'll be taking the maintenance elevator up to the pyramid by now. She'll remove her cell phone from the side pocket of her black patent-leather handbag and carefully slide off the back. Then she'll start removing the SIM card. The machinery around her moves with a smooth patience.

"You owe billions to the wrong people," you'll say.

John Frederson will shake his head and smile.

"No," he'll say. "They entrusted billions to the wrong person . . . They made an unwise investment."

"You overdrew your credit."

"Credit is a matter of confidence, of one party having trust in another," he'll say. "We can get that back in a second."

"You no longer have the time."

"Fifteen years ago there was nothing here but rusting sheds, dirty water, and oil slicks," he'll say, and then wave a stiffening arm toward his office windows. "Everything you see out there took less than a decade and a half to accomplish. In ancient Egypt they couldn't even get a pharaoh buried in that time."

You can't argue with history, especially when it hasn't been written yet.

You stare at the moth skeleton instead.

Your name is Betamax, and you know what you're doing.

Banks of fluorescent lights flicker into life somewhere high above you, while the clicking of her high heels on the polished metal flooring continues to reverberate around the inside of the stainless steel pyramid.

She works as she walks, quickly and efficiently taking apart her cell phone, sliding a new card into the back.

You always know what you're doing.

You grip your left wrist in your right hand and twist. A liquid splintering sound comes from deep within your arm as bone, cartilage, and gristle slide over each other. You'll watch the hand retract, your fingers folding themselves back into the hard geometry of a gun barrel.

* * *

John Frederson is still talking, but you're not listening anymore.

"It's no longer a matter of generating money but of determining how it's used, creating behavior patterns, displacing populations, altering demographics, shifting perceptions . . ."

The gun starts to assemble itself from inside your flesh, pieces snapping into place by their own intelligence. Their movement trips a switch inside your throat. You swallow hard. There's a brief gagging sensation, followed by a mild electrical popping. You reach in and pull out the firing pin.

A pale sliver of movement flashes across a security monitor. She has finished replacing the chip in her cell phone and is preparing it to operate as a weapon. She will enter a numerical code using the phone's keypad. The device will automatically arm itself.

"Immortality . . . free-market commodities like reality and fame," John Frederson continues. "We're just the universe returning to itself. Humanity is simply another system, a wave of development that expands and dissipates, reaching out who knows how far into space."

You hold your breath and aim for the head.

He catches a glimpse of her on the monitor, standing at the center of the steel pyramid, clutching the cell phone in a tight white fist.

He'll point at the monitor. "Who's she?" he'll ask.

One last scratchy subtitle appears before your eyes: *Those who are not born . . . do not weep . . . and do not regret . . . Thus it is logical to condemn you to death.*

"I thought she worked for you," is all you'll say.

* * *

Last-minute shifts on the international money markets indicate that an all-out strike against the London business sector is due to take place.

John Frederson will shake his head for the last time.

The framework of One Canada Square contains 500,000 bolts. Lifts travel from the fiftieth floor to the lobby in just forty seconds.

All over the planet, people will be switching on their television sets to watch the dust cloud rising darkly over London.

End transmission.

ACKNOWLEDGMENTS

Daniel Bennett would like to thank Catty May.

Joolz Denby would like to thank Justin Sullivan & New Model Army, Michael Davis & New York Alcoholic Anxiety Attack, Dr. Christine Alvin, Nina Baptiste, Spotti-Alexander & Miss Dragon Pearl, and Kate Gordon.

Cathi Unsworth would like to thank everyone who wrote a piece for this book. Also for help, support, and inspiration: Michael Meekin, Caroline Montgomery, Ann Scanlon, Lynn Taylor, Mr. & Mrs. Murphy, Paul Duane, and Michael Dillon.

ABOUT THE CONTRIBUTORS:

BARRY ADAMSON (www.barryadamson.com) was born and bred in Moss Side, Manchester, before heading for the West Side of London, where he has written and produced six or so of his own musical albums, including the Mercury Music Prize–nominated *Soul Murder*. Adamson has also scored several movies, TV shows, and commercials, and he now writes stories and screenplays.

DESMOND BARRY is a rootless vagabond and the author of three novels, *The Chivalry of Crime, A Bloody Good Friday,* and *Cressida's Bed*. He's been published in the *New Yorker* and *Granta*. He grew up in Merthyr Tydfil and moved to London, where he lived from 1972–82. He currently teaches creative writing at the University of Glamorgan.

DAN BENNETT was born in Shropshire in 1974, and has lived and worked around London for the past eight years. He recently finished his first novel.

KEN BRUEN is the the author of many novels, including *The Guards,* winner of the 2004 Shamus Award. His books have been published in many languages around the world. He is the editor of *Dublin Noir* and currently lives in Galway, Ireland.

MAX DÉCHARNÉ is the author of *Hardboiled Hollywood, Straight from the Fridge, Dad,* and three collections of short stories. His latest book is called *King's Road*. A regular contributor to *MOJO*, he was the drummer in Gallon Drunk and since 1994 has been the singer with The Flaming Stars.

JOOLZ DENBY was born in 1955. She has been an outlaw biker, a punk rocker, a Goth queen, and is an academic in the field of body modification. She is an internationally respected poet, spoken word artist, illustrator, and author of the novels *Stone Baby, Corazon,* and *Billie Morgan* (nominated for the 2005 Orange Prize). Check out www.joolz.net.

Eugenie Dolberg

KEN HOLLINGS is a writer living in London. His work has appeared in a wide range of journals and publications, including the anthologies *Digital Delirium, The Last Sex,* and *Undercurrents,* as well as on BBC Radio Three, Radio Four, NPS in Holland, ABC in Australia, and London's Resonance FM. His mind-bending novel *Destroy All Monsters* is available from Marion Boyars Publishers.

Marc Atkins

STEWART HOME was born in South London in 1962 and currently lives in East London. He is the author of twenty-one books, including the novels *Slow Death, Blow Job, Come Before Christ & Murder Love,* and *Down & Out in Shoredtich and Hoxton,* all of which might be considered twisted love letters to his home town of London.

PATRICK MCCABE was born in 1955. His novels include *Carn, The Butcher Boy, The Dead School,* and *Breakfast on Pluto.* He has written for stage and screen and has just finished a new novel, *Winterwood.* He lives in Sligo, Ireland.

Simon Crubellier

JOE MCNALLY is a journalist and photographer who has lived in London for ten years. He has worked on publications as diverse as *Fortean Times* and *Take a Break.* This is his first published fiction.

Alyssa Joye

MARK PILKINGTON edits and publishes *Strange Attractor Journal* and has written for the *Guardian, Fortean Times, Plan B, Arthur,* and others. He is currently working on a feature documentary film and performs with experimental musical outfits including Raagnagrok, Stella Maris Drone Orchestra, and Disinformation. More info at www.strangeattractor.co.uk.

Neil Adams

SYLVIE SIMMONS, one the best-known names in rock writing, was born and raised in North London. She is the author of *Serge Gainsbourg: A Fistful of Gitanes,* the book J.G. Ballard declared his favorite of 2001. These days she writes for *MOJO* and the *Guardian.* Her latest book is the short story collection *Too Weird for Ziggy,* and her latest address is San Francisco.

Grant Wilkinson

JERRY SYKES has twice won the Crime Writers' Association's Short Story Dagger. His stories have appeared in various publications on both sides of the Atlantic, as well as in Italy and Japan. He was born and raised in Yorkshire, but has lived in London for over twenty years. His first novel will be published in Fall 2006.

Joe McNally

CATHI UNSWORTH moved to Ladbroke Grove in 1987 and has stayed there ever since. She began a career in rock writing with *Sounds* and *Melody Maker,* before coediting the arts journal *Purr* and then *Bizarre* magazine. Her first novel, *The Not Knowing,* was published by Serpent's Tail in August 2005.

MARTYN WAITES was born and brought up in Newcastle Upon Tyne in the northeast of England, but once he was able to make his own mind up about where he lived, moved to London. He now lives in East London, and his latest book is *The Mercy Seat.*

MICHAEL WARD was born in Vancouver in 1967 and grew up in Toronto before moving to Hull, East Yorkshire when he was eleven. He briefly studied philosophy at Leicester University and moved to London in 1987, where he soon gave up a promising career sorting mail for the British Council to play in a band. A chance meeting in a pub led him into journalism, a field in which he has worked as a freelancer since 1997. He lives in Notting Hill.

JOHN WILLIAMS was born in Cardiff in 1961. He wrote a punk fanzine and played in bands before moving to London and becoming a journalist, writing for everyone from the *Face* to the *Financial Times*. He published his first book, *Into the Badlands*, in 1991, and his next, *Bloody Valentine*, in 1994. Following a subsequent libel action from the police, he turned to fiction and has now written five novels, including the London-set *Faithless*.

Also available from the Akashic Books Noir Series

D.C. NOIR
edited by George Pelecanos
304 pages, a trade paperback original, $14.95

Brand new stories by: George Pelecanos, Laura Lippman, James Grady, Kenji Jasper, Jim Beane, Ruben Castaneda, Robert Wisdom, James Patton, Norman Kelley, Jennifer Howard, Jim Fusilli, Richard Currey, Lester Irby, Quintin Peterson, Robert Andrews, and David Slater.

GEORGE PELECANOS is a screenwriter, independent-film producer, award-winning journalist, and the author of the bestselling series of Derek Strange novels set in and around Washington, D.C., where he lives with his wife and children.

BROOKLYN NOIR
edited by Tim McLoughlin
350 pages, a trade paperback original, $15.95
*Winner of SHAMUS AWARD, ANTHONY AWARD, ROBERT L. FISH MEMORIAL AWARD; Finalist for EDGAR AWARD, PUSHCART PRIZE

Twenty brand new crime stories from New York's punchiest borough. Contributors include: Pete Hamill, Arthur Nersesian, Maggie Estep, Nelson George, Neal Pollack, Sidney Offit, Ken Bruen, and others.

"*Brooklyn Noir* is such a stunningly perfect combination that you can't believe you haven't read an anthology like this before. But trust me—you haven't. Story after story is a revelation, filled with the requisite sense of place, but also the perfect twists that crime stories demand. The writing is flat-out superb, filled with lines that will sing in your head for a long time to come."
—Laura Lippman, winner of the Edgar, Agatha, and Shamus awards

DUBLIN NOIR: The Celtic Tiger vs. The Ugly American
edited by Ken Bruen
228 pages, trade paperback, $14.95

Brand new stories by: Ken Bruen, Eoin Colfer, Jason Starr, Laura Lippman, Olen Steinhauer, Peter Spiegelman, Kevin Wignall, Jim Fusilli, John Rickards, Patrick J. Lambe, Charlie Stella, Ray Banks, James O. Born, Sarah Weinman, Pat Mullan, Reed Farrel Coleman, Gary Phillips, Duane Swierczynski, and Craig McDonald.

MANHATTAN NOIR
edited by Lawrence Block
257 pages, a trade paperback original, $14.95

Brand new stories by: Jeffery Deaver, Lawrence Block, Charles Ardai, Carol Lea Benjamin, Thomas H. Cook, Jim Fusilli, Robert Knightly, John Lutz, Liz Martínez, Maan Meyers, Martin Meyers, S.J. Rozan, Justin Scott, C.J. Sullivan, and Xu Xi.

LAWRENCE BLOCK has won most of the major mystery awards, and has been called the quintessential New York writer, although he insists the city's far too big to have a quintessential writer. His series characters—Matthew Scudder, Bernie Rhodenbarr, Evan Tanner, Chip Harrison, and Keller—all live in Manhattan; like their creator, they wouldn't really be happy anywhere else.

SAN FRANCISCO NOIR
edited by Peter Maravelis
292 pages, a trade paperback original, $14.95

Brand new stories by: Domenic Stansberry, Barry Gifford, Eddie Muller, Robert Mailer Anderson, Michelle Tea, Peter Plate, Kate Braverman, David Corbett, Alejandro Murguía, Sin Soracco, Alvin Lu, Jon Longhi, Will Christopher Baer, Jim Nesbit, and David Henry Sterry.

BALTIMORE NOIR
edited by Laura Lippman
298 pages, a trade paperback original, $14.95

Brand new stories by: David Simon, Laura Lippman, Tim Cockey, Rob Hiaasen, Robert Ward, Sujata Massey, Jack Bludis, Rafael Alvarez, Marcia Talley, Joseph Wallace, Lisa Respers France, Charlie Stella, Sarah Weinman, Dan Fesperman, Jim Fusilli, and Ben Neihart.